WASH

⌐
└ ⌐

2

A YEAR OF SCANDAL

A gentleman for every season

At the mercy of a ghostly matchmaker, four gentlemen must perform a shocking task. But claiming their inheritance might just lead them to the women who will steal their hearts!

Don't miss this wonderful new quartet by Mills & Boon® Historical Romance author

Elizabeth Beacon!

First out:
THE VISCOUNT'S FROZEN HEART
Available August 2014

AUTHOR NOTE

Welcome to THE VISCOUNT'S FROZEN HEART, the first book in my new quartet of novels *A Year of Scandal*. Each book is set during a different season of the year. THE VISCOUNT'S FROZEN HEART starts the series off in January, with a new beginning for dark and brooding Luke and the most unlikely housekeeper he has ever met.

Each book should stand alone, but I would love you to meet the rest of my heroes and heroines as *A Year of Scandal* unfolds. Thank you for being my tolerant, loyal readers. This book is dedicated to all of you. I really hope you enjoy it.

THE VISCOUNT'S FROZEN HEART

Elizabeth Beacon

First published in Great Britain 2014
by Mills & Boon, an imprint of Harlequin (UK) Limited,
Large Print edition 2014
Harlequin (UK) Limited, Eton House, 18-24 Paradise Road,
Richmond, Surrey TW9 1SR

ISBN: 978-0-263-24001-6

Harlequin (UK) Limited's policy is to use papers that are natural, renewable and recyclable products and made from wood grown in sustainable forests. The logging and manufacturing processes conform to the legal environmental regulations of the country of origin.

Printed and bound in Great Britain
by CPI Antony Rowe, Chippenham, Wiltshire

Elizabeth Beacon lives in the beautiful English West Country, and is finally putting her insatiable curiosity about the past to good use. Over the years Elizabeth has worked in her family's horticultural business, become a mature student, qualified as an English teacher, worked as a secretary and, briefly, tried to be a civil servant. She is now happily ensconced behind her computer, when not trying to exhaust her bouncy rescue dog with as many walks as the Inexhaustible Lurcher can finagle. Elizabeth can't bring herself to call researching the wonderfully diverse, scandalous Regency period and creating charismatic heroes and feisty heroines *work*, and she is waiting for someone to find out how much fun she is having and tell her to stop it.

Previous novels by the same author:

AN INNOCENT COURTESAN
HOUSEMAID HEIRESS
A LESS THAN PERFECT LADY
CAPTAIN LANGTHORNE'S PROPOSAL
REBELLIOUS RAKE, INNOCENT GOVERNESS
THE RAKE OF HOLLOWHURST CASTLE
ONE FINAL SEASON
    (part of *Courtship & Candlelight*)
A MOST UNLADYLIKE ADVENTURE
GOVERNESS UNDER THE MISTLETOE
    (part of *Candlelit Christmas Kisses*)
THE DUCHESS HUNT
THE SCARRED EARL
THE BLACK SHEEP'S RETURN

Chapter One

Luke Winterley, Viscount Farenze, turned to help his daughter down from the carriage and watched Eve eye the fine house nestled into the rolling Wiltshire hillside like a jewel bedded on winter-pale green velvet.

'If only I had remembered Farenze Lodge was this beautiful I'd have teased you to bring me here a long time ago, Papa. I do recall Aunt Virginia giving me a sugarplum after I fell down the steps and cut my knee as a little tot, but that's about all,' she said and he had to smother a pang of guilt as he handed Eve's small but formidable maid from the carriage before answering, since he had kept Eve away so he wouldn't have to spend any more time here than necessary.

'No wonder that event stuck in your memory, but, yes, it *is* a very fine house,' Luke said with the second look the Palladian villa's neat elegance always deserved.

He had to brace himself for the empty feel of it without the last Viscountess Farenze here to make it a home, though. It was his duty to see Eve didn't feel the loss of her great-great-aunt even more acutely here, despite his own sorrow and frustration, and the less anyone knew about that second, rough-edged emotion and how hard it always bit him under this roof, the better.

'It doesn't seem anywhere near as vast to me now as it did back then,' Eve said, as determined to be cheerful for him as he was for her.

'No, it was built as a home, for all its grace and classical proportions,' he replied rather absently. It was currently home to a full complement of grieving staff and one very inconvenient housekeeper.

The mere thought of Mrs Chloe Wheaton waiting inside this serenely lovely house made him want to groan out loud, but somehow he kept silent and smothered another pang of guilt that he was about to make her homeless. He couldn't live under the same roof as Chloe Wheaton, yet still he felt this urgent need to see her again, if only to find out if she was as bitterly overwound by ten years of avoiding each other as he was.

'Virginia and Virgil liked their comfort, although I'm sure she would have done her best to love Darkmere if he really wanted to live there. Luckily he was always far happier in the home they made together here,' he told his daughter.

Somehow he must distract himself from Mrs Chloe Wheaton's presence here one more time, or he would end up wanting her almost beyond reason again. She was a widow with a young daughter. He had no right to long for her with this nagging, nonsensical ache whenever they were in the same county, let alone the same house.

'I don't remember your Uncle Virgil, Papa, but he looks far too rakish and cynical in that portrait of him in the gallery at home to fall deep in love with anyone, however lovely Aunt Virginia must have been sixty years ago.'

'Ah, but that was painted before they met and Virginia was a woman of character as well as an exotic beauty if <i>her</i> portraits are to be believed. I thought them the most deeply devoted couple I ever encountered and I'm far more of a cynic than Virgil ever was,' he said with a smile that went awry as he missed them both for the first time now Virginia had joined her beloved the other side of eternity.

'I'm not so sure you're as hard-headed as you think, Papa, but this is a fine house and it certainly *feels* as if it's been done with love.'

'I know what you mean,' Luke said with a brooding glance at the lovely place.

Unlike his predecessor, he loved Darkmere Castle and the stark beauty of its airy, windswept setting, but could see the attraction of having a smaller, more modern dwelling to retreat to on an ice-cold January afternoon like this one. He would need to spend part of the year here if he was to make sure it remained the gracious and elegant home Virgil and Virginia had always intended it to be. He cast a brooding glance at the lush parkland and rolling hills around him and decided most men would think him a fool or a liar if he said it was a mixed blessing. Yes, Mrs Chloe Wheaton would have to leave if he was to live here for very long, for both their sakes.

Even as he reaffirmed the rightness of his decision he saw a slender feminine figure come to stand below one of the half-lowered blinds at the long window of Virginia's bedchamber to see who had arrived. Luke felt his heart jar, then race on at the double when the youthful housekeeper of Farenze Lodge visibly flinched under his fierce scrutiny. She met it with a proud lift of her chin and an icy composure he could only envy.

He couldn't swear under his breath with Eve standing so close she could hear every syllable, yet a clutch of unwanted need tightened its hot claw in his gut while he gazed back with furious hunger. It seemed my Lord Farenze wanted the dratted woman as hotly as ever and he still couldn't have her.

He's here, whispered the siren voice of unreason as Chloe glared at her bugbear and did her best to ignore it. *He's come back to you at last*, it whispered yearningly and she wished she could silence it for ever. It sprang back to life like some annoying spectre, refusing to be banished to outer darkness whenever she tried to pretend Lord Farenze was a gruff and disagreeable gentleman she could forget when she left for good. Since Virginia became so ill they lost hope of her survival, the thought of the viscount's arrival to mourn his beloved great-aunt only added to her desolation.

Yet she still felt a charge crackle in the air when he set foot on the straw-muffled gravel. Chloe knew who the latest arrival at Farenze Lodge was by some misplaced instinct, so why was she standing here staring at him like an idiot? Lord Farenze quirked a haughty eyebrow as if to ask why she had the right to stare? He was master of Farenze Lodge and so much more and she was only the housekeeper. Her inner fool was so hungry it kept her gazing at him even after she'd made it clear she wasn't going to shrink and tremble at the sight of him.

'Imbecile,' she muttered to herself.

He looked dominant, vigorous and cross-grained as ever. She could see that his crow-black hair was untouched by silver and too long for fashion when he mockingly swept off his hat and gave her an almost bow; dark brows drawn sharply above eyes she knew were nothing like the simple grey they looked from here. Close up they were complex as he was; silver grey and would-be icy, but with hints of well-hidden poetry and passion in the rays of gold and green at the centre of his clear irises.

She wondered if such feelings would die if a man refused to admit he had them long enough.

Recalling a time when he'd almost swept them both to disaster on a raging tide of wanting and needing, she did her best to pretend her shiver was for the cold day and this dark time in both their lives, not the memory of a Luke Winterley nobody else at Farenze Lodge would recognise in the chilly lord on the gravel sweep below. The besotted, angry girl of a decade ago longed for him like a lost puppy, but mature Mrs Wheaton shuddered at the idea of succumbing to the fire and false promise of a younger, more vulnerable Lord Farenze and knew she had been right to say no to him.

'Who is it, my dear?' Culdrose, her late mistress's elderly dresser, asked from her seat by the vast and luxurious bed.

'Lord Farenze, Cully,' Chloe said with an unwary sigh and almost felt the older woman's gaze focusing on her back.

'And very good time he's made then, but why call him "imbecile" when he got here as fast as he could?'

'You have sharp ears, Cully. I wasn't talking

about Lord Farenze,' Chloe said and promised herself she'd break free of his compelling gaze any moment now.

'I may have white hair, but my wits haven't gone a-begging. His lordship is a fine man, as any woman with two good eyes in her head can see. You'll only be a fool if you lose your wits over him.'

'I shall not,' Chloe murmured and turned away with a dignified nod she hoped told him: *I have seen you, my lord. I will avoid you like the plague from now on, so kindly return the compliment.*

What was so special about the woman his toes tingled and his innards burned at even the sight of her from afar? Luke told himself to be relieved when she broke that long gaze into each other's eyes across yards of icy January air. He didn't want more reminders of how close to disaster he once walked with her. Feeling ruffled and torn by feelings he didn't want to think about right now, he did his best to let the frigid breeze cool his inner beast and shivered at the idea of how cold it would be to ruin a good woman's reputation and mire her little girl's prospects with scandal.

He was six and thirty, not a green boy with every second thought of the female sex and an incessant urge to mate. If she could turn away with such cool disdain, he would get through this without begging for her glorious body in his bed. She was an upper servant; he recalled the fate of such women whose lovers wanted them so badly that they married beneath them out of desperation and shuddered. He might not like her much just now, but he couldn't wish such a fate on a woman he respected for her strength of character, even if it got confoundedly in the way of the pleasure they could have had in each other if she wasn't so sternly armoured against it.

'I wonder how it feels to love someone as deeply as Virginia did,' Eve mused and jarred Luke back to here and now. His heartbeat leapt into a panicky race at the idea his daughter had inherited her mother's ridiculous romantic notions.

'Painful and dangerous, I should imagine,' he replied brusquely.

'Now I think it could be wondrous and exhilarating to love the right person and have them love you back, Papa.'

'Your mother would have agreed with you, time after time,' he cautioned and shuddered at the memory of his wife falling in 'love' again and again as soon as she decided her young husband wasn't her ideal after all.

Sometimes traces of Pamela's pettish outbursts shook him if Eve pouted mulishly, or flounced out of the room in a headlong temper, but his Eve was too kind-hearted to treat a man as if he had no more feelings than a block of wood. He often wondered how such a loving child came from such an ill-starred marriage.

'Please choose someone worthy of you when you marry, Eve,' he cautioned. 'Don't accept the first beau to say he loves you one day and someone else the next.'

'I'm not an idiot, Papa, and you'll end up a lonely old cynic when I do find a fine man to spend my life with if you're not careful.'

'I want you settled before I find a suitable wife.'

Eve grimaced and rolled her eyes. 'Suitable?' she echoed dubiously. 'Aunt Virginia would hate to hear you speak so. It sounds as if you're expecting to choose a wife from an emporium and have her delivered to the church on an appropriate day for a wedding, complete with her bridal attire and a suite of attendants.'

'Although you're an impertinent young miss, I have to admit Virginia wasn't happy with the idea,' Luke said, his last conversation with his great-aunt by marriage running through his mind a little too vividly for comfort.

'You only married That Fool because your father and stepmother threw her at your head and it seemed a good idea at the time,' Virginia raged when he unwarily set out his plan to remarry as soon as Eve was settled. 'If you wed a "suitable" young lady, at least have the decency to fall in love with a mistress.'

Virginia had given a weary sigh when he smiled cynically at the very idea of loving a female he must marry to beget an heir.

'No,' she argued with herself. 'Don't. No woman deserves to marry the cold fish you think you are, then watch you love a hussy instead. You're a passionate man under all the starch and to-hell-with-you manner and another marriage like the last one will break you. Please don't imagine you'll be lucky enough to breed a sweet child on a ninny twice in one lifetime— no man deserves to be that fortunate.'

'I'm not a lovable man,' Luke said gruffly. His

mistress's enthusiasm told him he was a good enough lover, but lust wasn't love.

'Then your Eve and I secretly hate you, do we?' Virginia argued. 'And your staff and tenants loathe you behind your back as well, I suppose? Obviously they only put up with you brooding and barking at them because you pay well enough and don't burn their cottages down for fun, or prey on their womenfolk when you feel the urge to rut. You married an empty-headed flirt who dedicated her life to falling in love with any rogue she took a fancy to when she had a good and handsome husband, but it wasn't your fault, Luke. Your father knew he was dying and persuaded you to marry far too young, and how lucky for that harridan he wed after your mother died that Pamela birthed a daughter, then ran off with the first rogue who would have her.'

'Lucky for me as well. I love Eve dearly,' he had said stiffly.

'Yes, yes I know, and James will be your heir if needs be. But he needs to be his own man instead and your second trip up the aisle will be a bigger disaster than the first if you only intend to wed a "suitable" wife,' she warned a little too seriously for comfort.

'If I thought James would manage the Winter-ley interests with half the dedication he puts into carousing, curricle racing and gambling, he could have it all with my blessing. If I were leaving my downtrodden tenants in safe hands when I meet my maker, there would be no need for me to remarry.'

'Safer than either of you think, but James can't spend his life waiting to step into your shoes; he deserves better.'

'Does he indeed?' Luke had replied harshly, wondering if even Virginia had any idea how deep the rift between them ran.

'Papa?' Eve prompted now and he wondered how Chloe Wheaton stepping into that window shot his concentration into the ether.

'I should have made you stay home, Eve. For all Virginia wanted nobody to mourn her, her house-hold loved her too much to carry on as if nothing has happened.'

'This is real life, not a pretty fairy story, Papa,' his daughter chided as if she were an adult and he the sixteen-year-old.

'Then I suppose we'd better get on with facing this place without Virginia to welcome us, since you would come.'

'Yes, I would. I loved her too.'

'And she adored you from the day she laid eyes on the squalling brat you were back then, my Eve. It was beyond the rest of us at the time why she should, since you were screaming like a banshee about some new teeth we were all having trouble with at the time. Virginia spent three months at Darkmere every summer until you were old enough for us to meet her in Brighton for sea air and shopping, so you must know she loved you back, considering she couldn't abide the place.'

'I do,' she said and looked so bereft he wanted to hug her, then send her back to Darkmere straight away, but he knew she was right—his daughter was almost an adult. He must let her make her own decisions, even if they went against his instincts to guard her from anything that might hurt her. 'Why didn't we come here instead when I was young, Papa?' she asked. 'You never stay at Farenze Lodge for more than a few days, yet you seem to love it almost as much as Darkmere.'

'It's easier not to,' Luke replied carefully.

Easier for him, since it was either that or stay here and make Chloe Wheaton his mistress by stoking this fire between them until she gave in instead of dousing it as best he could by avoiding her. The lady had had some very pithy things to say when he was driven to suggest it years ago and it would have been a long siege, but something told him it would have succeeded in the end.

So how *would* it feel to love and be loved? Impossible; intolerable even and he didn't love the woman and she certainly didn't love him. He would wait a year or two and find his suitable wife once Eve had decided her own future. A pretty and biddable young widow or some sweet-natured, overlooked spinster lady he could marry for an heir would suit him very well. Even as he reaffirmed that sensible plan with his rational mind the image of a very different Mrs Chloe Winterley from the sad-eyed female he'd just seen drifted into his head and made him bite back a virulent curse.

The first summer day she strolled into his life she looked warm and open as well as ridiculously young and stunningly beautiful. That version of Chloe Wheaton jarred something into life inside him he'd thought he was far too cynical and weary to feel by the time he was six and twenty. Luke frowned now as he had then, because people who felt that vividly got hurt. He hadn't wanted that lovely, ardent young creature with her red-gold locks escaping the bands she'd tried to confine them to end up narrowed and disappointed as he was, yet the woman he had just seen was nothing like the warm and irresistible girl he thought he'd met that day.

Somehow he had made himself leave her to swing her bonnet by its strings as she walked home to whatever well-to-do family she hailed from with impossible dreams in her heart he'd only wished he could make come true. No, he was too embittered and shop-soiled for such a hopeful young lady, he'd decided regretfully, even as he met her aston-ishing violet eyes and only just prevented himself falling headlong into them as if that was where he belonged. Riding away from her was one of the hardest things he'd ever had to do, but he'd been disillusioned about her even sooner than he had about Pamela.

Only a couple of hours later he found out the girl was Virginia's new companion and supposed housekeeper, on the way back from visiting her baby daughter at nurse. A widow who claimed to be two and twenty and looked a young eighteen. Virginia had reassured him she was as well aware of the tallness of Mrs Chloe Wheaton's story, but she hadn't had so much fun in years. So what could he do about an encroaching so-called widow when Virginia did indeed seem almost as full of life again at last as she had been when her beloved Virgil was still alive?

Her furious rejection of his offer of a *carte blanche* ten years ago still rang in his ears as if she'd denounced him an arrogant and repellent rake only yesterday. If she still felt the same hellish tension that roared through him whenever he set eyes on her, she had learnt to hide it very well. Seeing her drawn and exhausted hadn't helped *him* ignore it so regally though. Instead it laid a line of fellow feeling between them to see her so grief-stricken and he didn't want to share anything with Mrs Chloe Wheaton.

Luke shook his head and thanked heaven he was wearing a long greatcoat to conceal how eagerly his body ignored his stern orders not to want the housekeeper as he turned his gaze away from the now empty windows and silently cursed himself for being such a fool.

Chapter Two

'Who was that, Papa?' Eve asked.

'Whom do you mean?' he asked stiffly, like a schoolboy caught out in a blatant lie, he decided, as he wondered what sort of blundering beast the wretched woman would turn him into next.

'The lady at the window.'

'A maid on the alert for mourners?'

'She looked more like the housekeeper, although if so she looked very young for such a responsible role.'

'She is,' Luke replied grimly. 'She must have been in the schoolroom when she met Wheaton.'

'Who on earth is Wheaton? The January air seems to have addled your brain instead of sharpening it as you claimed it would when you left us to count church spires and grey mares while you rode most of the way here, Papa.'

'I thought you two had enough schemes to hatch out for who was to do what and when after we got here to keep you occupied for a sennight.'

'Slander; we're not at all managing, are we, Bran?' Eve quizzed her diminutive one time-nurse and now ladies' maid.

'Even if we was, we'd be well and truly talked to a standstill by now,' Eve's unlikely personal dragon answered with a sharp look that told Luke she understood his latest battle of wills with Chloe Wheaton even if his innocent daughter didn't.

'Well, now we're here you will have too many people to talk to rather than too few,' he warned as they climbed the shallow steps.

The hatchment over the door was a stark reminder why they were here and Luke felt the wrongness of this place without the lady who had loved and lived here for so long to bid him welcome. He sighed and told himself the next few days would pass and life would go relentlessly on, whatever he had to say about it.

'Miss Winterley is with his lordship,' Chloe remarked as she turned from the window and only wished she dared avoid the master of the house a little longer.

'No doubt she had to plague Master Luke something relentless to make that happen. Very protective he is; a good father and a fine man, whatever that stepmother of his says.'

'I imagine he takes little very notice of her,' Chloe said absently.

Having been on the wrong end of his protective nature herself, ten years of enduring his distrust stung more sharply than it should. He was probably surprised she hadn't run off with Virginia's jewellery or the housekeeping money long ago.

'That woman made the poor lad's life a misery. I can't understand to this day why Mr Oswald married her. Mr Oakham overheard her telling Mr James to do all he could to blacken Mr Luke's name now the family are here to put the "old besom in her grave", as the nasty-minded old crow put it. Lady Virginia wouldn't have her over the threshold if she was alive to say her nay, but Master Luke was always too kind-hearted for his own good and no doubt he'll let her stay.'

'I'm sure Mrs Winterley will behave herself now his lordship is here, whatever she might say to her son. She seems in awe of Lord Farenze and I've heard he controls her purse strings.'

'Then I hope he gives her short shrift one day; she deserves no better.'

'I don't want any more tension and upset, so please don't put something noxious in her soup, Cully. She might never leave if she fancied herself too ill to travel and think how awful it might be if she once got her feet under the table.'

'She'll leave fast enough if I put a purge in her coffee, and good riddance.'

'No, wait out the week and most of the mourners will go home and leave you all in peace,' Chloe urged, trying not to wonder where she would be by then.

'I suppose so,' Culdrose agreed reluctantly, 'but it's hard to stay silent when we loved her ladyship dearly. I won't have her name blackened now she's not here to stand up for herself.'

'Nobody would do so at her funeral. It would be disrespectful and heartless.'

Culdrose sniffed loudly; 'I still caught the woman sneaking about her ladyship's boudoir yesterday. Searching through her letters and personal things she was as if she had every right to do what she liked here. It's as well we locked Lady Virginia's treasures away in the strongroom after Oakham caught that Miss Carbottle taking her ladyship's diamond brooch as a keepsake, or so she said. Keepsake indeed, she's no better than a jackdaw.'

'She does have a habit of taking anything pretty or shiny that's lying about. Her sister always brings it back, but I'm glad you spared her the embarrassment. Now I must go down and greet Miss Winterley as she is the new mistress of the house. Promise you won't make things worse between Mrs Winterley and the staff than they already are though, Cully?'

'You know it's my way to let my feelings out with them I trust to keep their counsel, so I don't say aught I shouldn't in front of the quality. Miss Eve being mistress of this house until his lordship marries again won't go down well with Mrs Winterley though, you mark my words.'

'So noted,' Chloe said and went downstairs to do her duty.

Stupid to feel as if a knife had been stabbed in her heart at mention of Lord Farenze remarrying, as he must to beget an heir. Best not to think where she would go next until the mourners left either. Lord Farenze wouldn't keep her on and she couldn't stay even if he wanted her to, but there *was* a deal of work before she could walk away with her last duty to her late mistress done.

Luke signalled at the waiting footman to close the doors behind them against the icy easterly wind and missed Virginia's imperious command to come on in do, lest she expire in the howling gale he was letting in.

'Thank you, Oakham,' he said, seeing the butler had set chairs near the blazing fire and offered hot toddies to Eve and Bran to stave off the cold. 'I would wish you a good day, but we both know there is no such thing right now.'

'Indeed not, my lord,' the elderly manservant replied with a sad shake of his head that said more than words.

Even over the mild stir of activity Luke caught the sound of Mrs Wheaton's inky skirts and disapproving petticoats as she descended the grand staircase and tried to pretend neither of them were really here. *So, she steeled herself to meet the new master of the house, did she?* Luke admired her courage even as he wished it would fail her and his senses sprang to attention. Even in buttoned-up mourning array she was hauntingly lovely, but close to she looked even more drawn and weary. Feelings that seemed far more dangerous than simple desire kicked him in the gut and he wished her a hundred miles away more fervently than ever.

'Good day, Mrs Wheaton,' he greeted her woodenly. 'Please show my daughter and her maid to their rooms, then see their luggage is sent up.'

'Good afternoon, my lord; Miss Winterley,' she replied with an almost respectful curtsey in his direction.

'Good afternoon, Mrs Wheaton,' Eve said with a smile that seemed to relax the stubborn woman's air of tightly wound tension. 'I've heard so much about you. Great-Aunt Virginia was always full of your daughter's quaint sayings and doings when she was a babe and she sounds a bright and lively girl now she's at school.'

'By "bright and lively" folks usually mean a limb of Satan, into every piece of mischief she can find. If the girl is anything like you were at that age, Miss Eve, Mrs Wheaton has my sympathy. I could fill a book with the things you got up to when you were a child,' Bran said dourly.

Luke concluded Bran liked Mrs Wheaton for some reason and, whatever the facts of Eve's birth, Mrs Brandy Brown was the closest thing to a mother his Eve had. He was grateful to the diminutive dragon for loving his daughter fiercely after losing her husband, then her own babe soon after birth, but he wished Bran would show her usual distrust of any servant likely to look down their noses at such a unique ex-nurse and ladies' maid. The last thing he needed was closer contacts between his family and the Wheatons, but, if she diverted Eve from her grief, he supposed he would have to endure it.

'My Verity is on pins to meet you, Miss Winterley, and Lady Virginia told her lots of exotic tales about the castle you live in and the wild Border Reivers who once fought over it. As my daughter persuaded her teachers I need her to come home, she will be here as soon as a carriage can be spared to fetch her,' Chloe said ruefully.

A smile softened her generous mouth and lit her violet-blue eyes to depths of enchantment that would make a poet quiver with excitement, when she talked of her only child. Even Luke's workaday imagination wanted to go on the rampage when a red-gold curl escaped her black-trimmed house-keeper's lace bonnet and threatened to curl about her heart-shaped face. Given freedom, her rebellious auburn locks would kiss her forehead with escaped fronds of red-gold fire. Or maybe they would lie in loose ringlets down the refined line of her long neck and on to white shoulders revealed by a gown cut to show off her womanly charms… Poetry be damned, the woman was a temptation to pure sin and never mind the romantic sighing of buffle-headed dreamers who ought to wake up to the realities of life.

'She's probably right,' Eve was insisting softly and Luke had to rack his brains to recall who *she* was and what she was right about. 'Papa would have it I should stay in Northumberland and sit out Aunt Virginia's funeral, but that would only make me miss her more. Your daughter has lost a good friend, Mrs Wheaton.'

'And you are a wise young lady, Miss Winterley.'

'Oh, I doubt that, but you must call me Eve, ma'am.'

'I can hardly do that if you insist on calling me so and it would be considered sadly coming in a housekeeper to address you by your given name.'

'Then will you do so when we are private to-gether? And I think we could resort to my rooms and send for tea now, don't you? We must discuss how best to go on over the next few days and I'd rather not be Miss Winterley-ed all the time we're doing it.'

Listening to his remarkable daughter do what he couldn't and coax Chloe Wheaton upstairs to join her for tea and some gentle gossip, Luke sighed and met Oakham's eyes in a manly admission: they didn't understand the restorative power of tea or small talk and probably never would.

'I have refilled the decanters in the library, my lord, or I could bring some of his late lordship's best Canary wine to your room. I believe Mr Sleeford and his father-in-law are currently occu-pying the billiard room.'

Taking the warning in that impassive observa-tion, Luke murmured his thanks and made his way up the nearest branch of the elegant double stair-way. He entered the suite of rooms Virginia had insisted he took over as the one-day master of the house a year after Great-Uncle Virgil died, and was glad Mrs Wheaton had ordered fires lit in all three rooms against his eventual arrival.

He was grateful for the warmth and sanctuary the suite promised him tonight, despite his reluctance to use it at first. With so many people gathering for his great-aunt's funeral he must savour any peace he could get over the next few days.

As they sipped tea and discussed arrangements for the household over the next few days, Chloe wondered why Miss Evelina Winterley hadn't been permitted to stay here during the decade Chloe had lived here. Lord Farenze and his daughter always joined Lady Virginia in Brighton or Ramsgate for several weeks every summer, but his visits to Farenze Lodge were so fleeting he rarely stayed so much as a night, let alone long enough to uproot his daughter and bring her with him. Fury flashed through her as the familiar notion *she* was the reason he had kept Eve away until now fitted neatly into her mind.

It was true that scandalised whispers spread through the neighbourhood when she first came here as Virginia's companion-housekeeper, with a baby daughter and no visible husband all those years ago. If only they knew, she decided bleakly, weariness threatening to overcome her once more.

She fought it off by using her anger with the new master of the house to stiffen her backbone, for she might be about to leave this place, but she intended to do it with dignity intact.

'Lady Virginia told me I would like you if I ever had the chance, Mrs Wheaton, and I feel I know you already,' Eve Winterley said as she refilled a teacup and passed it to her maid without even needing to ask if she would like seconds after their long journey.

Such closeness between mistress and maid should not surprise her, she supposed, but Chloe recalled Lord Farenze's attitude to those he considered beneath him and contrasted it with his daughter's more liberal one. Reluctantly she decided it spoke well of him that he was so relaxed about Mrs Brown's role in his daughter's life, then did her best to forget him for a few blissful moments.

'And I'm very glad to meet you, Miss Winterley, even at this sad time.'

'You will miss Lady Virginia as badly as any of us after being her friend and companion for so long,' Eve said sincerely and for a long moment all three women sat thinking about how odd their lives felt without that vivid presence. 'Although this is a beautiful house, Papa has never coveted it. He always said the Lodge was Aunt Virginia's home and wouldn't hear of her moving out of it when Uncle Virgil died. It's quite lovely, don't you think?' Eve asked with a guileless look Chloe didn't quite trust.

'Exquisite,' she said carefully.

'No wonder Aunt Virginia couldn't bear to leave when Uncle Virgil died, although I believe Papa was very worried about her when rumours went about she had run mad with grief, wasn't he, Bran?'

'Indeed he was, the poor lady.'

'Papa says he wondered if she should still live here for her own sake then, but she couldn't abide Darkmere and refused to set foot in our house in Kent. Papa could hardly evict Mrs Winterley from the Dower House there, so he let the subject drop when Virginia bought the house in Hill Street and we all went on very much as we were, or so I'm told, since I was but a babe in arms at the time and don't remember.'

'Her ladyship thought the Kentish house old and dreary and she said most of the chimneys smoked, so I doubt she would have wanted to live there, even if the Dower House was vacant,' Chloe said, hoping her dislike of Mrs Oswald Winterley didn't show.

She wouldn't want to live within a day's drive of the lady herself, given the choice, and, as Mrs Winterley reluctantly resided in the Haslett Hall dower house, instead of the fashionable London town house she thought Luke Winterley owed her, for some reason nobody else could fathom, Virginia had avoided Haslett Hall like the plague.

'Papa had several chimney stacks rebuilt when he took over the Farenze estates, so I doubt any smoke now. He won't have climbing boys used in any of our houses and if the sweep says they're too small or crooked to use brushes on, he has the stacks rebuilt until they can be done that way without sending those poor little boys up into the dark to choke or get stuck.'

'My little brother was put up chimneys when hardly old enough to walk and he didn't live to see his tenth birthday. His lordship's a good man,' Mrs Brandy Brown insisted and Eve Winterley agreed then watched Chloe with expectant eyes.

'To oppose such a practice he must be,' she said as tactfully as she could and tried to pretend he meant no more to her than any good man would.

Liar, a more truthful inner Chloe prodded her uncomfortably, but somehow she would make it true. Ten years ago she had longed for gruff and embittered Luke, Lord Farenze, with every fibre of her being. At seventeen she'd been little more than a wilful, embittered child though; it took her daughter's dependence on her to force her to grow up and realise she couldn't have what she wanted and keep her self-respect.

Chloe sighed at the familiar tug of hot warmth she'd felt at first sight of the viscount in possession even today. No, it didn't matter. Whatever she felt changed nothing. She only had to keep out of his way and stamp on any wayward desires left over from that heady time for a few more days then she would be free of him.

Yet this infernal tiredness was dragging at her like a pall and threatened to spin her back into dreams of forbidden things if she let her control slip. First there would be the old fantasy of the Chloe she should be—if life was fair. A charming, alluring lady who could win, and hold, the passionate devotion of gruff Lord Farenze as they danced off into a rosy future. An image of him; his expression impossibly tender as he made it clear how desperately he longed for her with every fibre of his cynical being, shimmered like a mirage.

Horrified, she snapped her nodding head upright and righted her empty teacup before it slipped from her slack grip and shattered. *Oh, heavens, had she muttered any of that out loud?* She met compassion instead of horror when she plucked up the courage to meet her new friend's eyes, so perhaps not.

'I hope you don't mind me saying so, Mrs Wheaton, but you need a nap,' Mrs Brandy Brown told her.

Chloe shivered at the thought of nightmare-haunted snatches of sleep she'd had since her beloved mistress died. 'You must know how long a woman can go without sleep from your experience when Miss Evelina was a baby, Mrs Brown,' she forced herself to say instead of admitting the turmoil had awoken old memories that haunted her dreams until she avoided her bed as if it was stuffed with thistles.

'Aye, some nights the poor little mite cried as if her heart was broken and it was all I could do not to join her,' the tiny, forceful little woman agreed with a rueful, loving look for the girl who seemed so equable nowadays it seemed hard to believe.

'I know exactly what you mean,' Chloe said with a picture of her own struggles to calm a restless and furious baby when Verity was teething, or ill, or just plain fretful and she felt about as useful as a tailor's dummy, making her very glad those times were over for both their sakes.

'His lordship used to put his little miss into a pack on his shoulders and carry her for miles over the moors until she slept at long last. I'd stay behind, telling myself they were quite safe and he could see like a cat in the dark and knows the paths across his land like the back of his hand until I fell asleep too, whether I wanted to or not. You had to cope with all that on your own and run this great house at the same time. It sounds as if you got through it stoutly enough all these years, but we're here now, so at least you can have a rest when you need one,' Bran told her with an earnest nod that disarmed Chloe and made her wonder if it might be bliss to lay her burdens down and do as she was bid after all.

'Indeed you must, Mrs Wheaton,' Eve told her with some of her father's authority sitting quaintly on her slender shoulders. 'Sleep is the last thing on *my* mind after hours shut up in that stuffy carriage dozing because there was nothing else to do—how about you, Bran?'

She gave the comfortable bed in the slip of a room the other side of the dressing room, reserved for a maid if her mistress wanted one close, a significant look and her maid nodded her approval of the unspoken idea. It looked just right for an afternoon nap if Chloe did happen to be as bone weary as she obviously looked.

'I had a nice doze on the way to Bath this morning, as you know very well, Miss Eve, since you've been twitting me about it ever since.'

'How disrespectful of me, but I think we should wrap ourselves up in cloaks and shawls to walk in that pretty Winter Garden I saw from the window on the half-landing. I'd like to stretch my legs and it would do us good to air our wits before it gets dark. Nobody will disturb you if I order them to leave our unpacking until we return, Mrs Wheaton, and Bran and I will soon have everything arranged when we get back. I can be very finicky about the disposal of my things when occasion demands and nobody will interfere.'

'She can indeed, Mrs Wheaton,' Bran agreed

smugly and Chloe felt weariness weigh down as she wondered if she dare risk her dreams for once.

'You would wake me the moment you came back in?' she asked and heard her own words slur with tiredness, as if she'd been fighting it so long it now had to win.

Lord Farenze was here to shoulder the responsibility of the estate and the ageing staff and she would rather sleep than think about him.

'If you can sleep through madam here ordering me about, you're a better woman than I am,' Bran said, then followed her young mistress from the room.

Chloe barely managed to slip off her shoes, unhook her gown and slip out of it before falling fast asleep the moment her head hit the pillow.

'Lasted as best she could until help came, if you ask me,' Bran observed softly as soon as she and her young mistress were finally clear of the house unseen and able to speak freely.

'Poor lady,' Eve replied carefully.

'Aye, she seems like one to me as well,' Bran mused and met Eve's speculative gaze with a thoughtful frown.

Bran did not believe a fairytale lay behind whatever made a lady become a housekeeper. Even if a story started out with garlands of roses and fairy dust, it rarely ended so in the stark light of day in Brandy Brown's experience.

Chapter Three

Luke waited until his valet accompanied a footman upstairs, his luggage borne along as carefully as the crown jewels, before quitting his private sitting room with an exasperated sigh. He wondered why he'd employed such an exacting valet; he was old enough to dress himself and could tie a necktie that wouldn't scare the horses. In a year or so he'd have to present a neat appearance for Eve's début and his wife-hunting campaign, though, and it had seemed a sensible enough idea at the time. Right now he'd welcome a tramp across the countryside, or a long ride on a swift horse to banish his blue devils, but wealth, power and a title came at a cost so he ignored the urge to escape.

Hearing his stepmother's sharp voice in the drawing room and the rumble of male ones from the billiard room, Luke tried to find some peace in the library. Virginia's godson, the Marquis of Mantaigne, was ensconced in a comfortable chair by the fire, but Luke gave a sigh of relief. The air of world-weary cynicism Tom wore like a suit of armour drove women wild with desire for some odd reason, but he was good company and a loyal friend.

'Tom, you rascal,' he said, managing a genuine smile and a sincere manly handshake even on this sad day. 'When did you get here?'

'This morning—you must have travelled in my dust.'

'You only had to come from Derbyshire and there was more mud than dust.'

'How unobservant of me,' Tom drawled.

'Don't try to hoodwink me that you're too idle to take an interest in what's about you, Tom. I know you too well to be taken in by the air of cynicism you use to keep the world at bay. Just tell me who has come here to gladden our heavy hearts and your estimate of how long I'll be forced to house them for, there's a good fellow.'

'Whoever told you I'm a good fellow clearly needs disillusioning.'

'I don't pay much heed to the opinions of others

when it comes to my real friends, my lord Marquis,' Luke said and accepted the glass of fine burgundy his friend poured out of the decanter at his side with an almost smile.

Feeling more relaxed after the mellowing effect of the very finest wine and a shrewd and succinct summary of his assembled guests from Tom Banburgh, Luke left him to his solitude and the burgundy and avoided the groups in the billiard room and drawing room to go up and reassure himself Eve and Bran were settling in after the trials and discomfort of their long journey.

Chloe felt weighed down by sleep when she managed to blink her heavy eyes open and tried to gauge how long she'd been lost to the world. For a moment she had no idea where she was and had to force her eyes open to stop herself sinking under the weight of sleep beckoning her back like a siren. Virginia would probably be the first to order her to get up and face the world, so she blinked several times and did her best to banish the huge waves of sleep trying to drag her under again.

Even an upper servant could enjoy the luxury of a long stretch, so she yawned and extended her legs fully against the fine cotton sheets of Brandy Brown's narrow bed, then reached her hands high above her head so her arms could feel the pull and strength of youth in them. She shook her head so the auburn locks tumbled down in a tangle it would take far too long to tease out when she'd already wasted goodness knew how long asleep when she should be up and doing.

'Bran?' a deep masculine voice questioned from the other side of the slightly open door and Chloe felt her heartbeat speed up like a greyhound after a rabbit. 'You can't be asleep because I saw you in the garden not five minutes ago. Where's Eve and why is her luggage still cluttering up her bedroom?'

If she wasn't in her shift with her hair falling down her back, she could call out a brusque answer and he would go away. Would that serve anyway? If she sounded assured and awake enough, he might go away rather than risk being discovered here with a female servant in the middle of a winter afternoon?

'Mrs Brown is taking the air with your daughter, Lord Farenze,' she managed to call out as if she was busy and didn't have time for answering questions.

A stiff moment of shocked silence and she could almost feel him flinch at the sound of her voice a room and a half away. Unfortunately, she didn't hear him walking away though. *Yet did she really want him to?* As usual her inner Chloe chose the worst moment to stage a revolution. She told her to be quiet and get back in her cage and stop there. She *did* want him to leave and sat up in the neat little tent bed, holding every muscle and sinew tense and still in the hope he would go. Something about the silence on the other side of the door told her he was still there, but a woman could always hope.

'Why the devil are you unpacking Eve's things when one of the maids could do it if Bran is busy?'

'I…' She ground to a halt and told herself if she hadn't slept so deeply and so stupidly in the middle of a working day she might be able to find an answer that would satisfy him somewhere in her befuddled brain.

'Cat got your tongue?' he growled and was that really a thread of laughter in his deep voice?

Impossible—Lord Farenze and Mrs Wheaton had nothing to laugh about. There was no level of intimacy to put a hint of smoky amusement in his voice. She'd imagined it and now her inner Chloe was busy imagining more than she ought to all over again. Such as how it might feel to wake up in his bed with her mind misted with sleep and loving, then share the closeness of lovers with him as he teased her back to full awareness of where she was, and who she was with, in his own unique fashion.

'No, it's still in perfect working order,' she managed to reply as if she was merely too busy to argue with him.

'Then come out here and talk to me face to face; I refuse to hold a conversation through inches of fine mahogany.'

'I can't, I'm far too busy today, my lord,' she managed and heard the note of panic in her voice as she sensed him stepping closer to the door in question and about to discover her sitting here in a state of scandalous disarray.

'No doubt but, since I'm master here now, you must deal with me sooner or later. Far better to get the plans we must make for the next few days out of the way as soon as possible and rub along as best we can, rather than skirt round the subject

all week and send the staff spinning about in opposite directions between us.'

He sounded as reluctant to have that discussion
as she was, so why couldn't he put it off until he
was rested from his journey and she was back
in her buttoned-up gown with her wretched hair
wound safely under a neat cap and hidden away
with feral Chloe, who so badly wanted to respond
to him in every way a woman could?

'Very well, my lord, I will meet you downstairs
as soon as I have finished here,' she said and heard
the waver of uncertainty in her own voice.

Her reluctance to confront him with the memory
of sitting here half-naked and all he could have
been to her, if everything was different, wobbled
in her too breathy voice. She didn't dare stir in case
he heard the rustle of crisply laundered sheets and
realised she was in bed. Sitting frozen and speechless, she gasped in horror when he finally lost patience and thrust the door open.

Time seemed to stretch and waver as he strode
into the little room then stopped dead, as if a
wicked witch's spell had frozen him in his tracks.
He stood staring hungrily back at her and how

could she fool herself everything that could have been between them was dead now?

He should turn and walk away of course; leave her to blush and squirm and be furious with herself for giving in to exhaustion and his daughter's urgings to rest. He didn't, though, and it was there in his eyes, the might be. Not a never, but a might be; a dangerous chance of more between master and servant than there ought to be.

A detached part of her seemed to be looking down on them; speculating how two rational human beings could look so much like codfish and still stare rapt into each other's eyes as if they'd longed for the sight of the other all unguarded for the years they'd been apart. The rest couldn't even find the presence of mind to squirm down in her bed and hide her disarray.

Now he looked like all the robber barons who founded his mighty dynasty rolled into one as he stood stock still, so vividly present he seemed to suck the air out of the room along with her common sense. *Like a very well-dressed statue of a warrior prince*, that annoying wanton Chloe remarked, *would he was a little less still and a lot less well dressed.* 'Be quiet!' she whispered, then covered her mouth. She couldn't believe she was arguing with her wicked inner self with *him* in the room. Perhaps she really was going mad?

A wistful hope she might wake up and find she'd dreamt him made the tension drain out of her muscles for all of half a minute. Nobody could dream muscular, powerful, intimidating Lord Farenze when he was all too present. He was a living, breathing human being, staring at her as if being torn by a raging tumult of contrary emotions as well. There just wasn't enough dreaming in the world to conjure up a man like him, here, locked in this particular moment with her.

'I didn't say a word,' he managed in a rusty voice that sounded forced out.

'Not you.'

'You have a lover hidden under the bed?' he barked as if he thought her everything a woman shouldn't be if she wanted to retain her self-respect.

His hot eyes dwelt on her wildly flushed cheeks, shocked and hazy eyes and the tumble of hot gold curls she knew were in nearly as big a tangle as her tongue.

'No room,' he mused more softly and let his gaze

explore the little room as if he'd never seen one like it before and saw the exposed space under the high little bed with what looked suspiciously like satisfaction, 'nor a second door for a coward to escape through if he was in danger of being found and the closet's not big enough.'

'I don't have a lover.'

Now she sounded like an outraged stage heroine and Chloe thought it as well he couldn't see her toes curling under the bedclothes. His black brows rose and a smile of cynical appreciation she assured herself she would like to slap off his face kicked up his mouth and made him look nigh irresistible for a breathless moment.

'Any man who saw you thus would be your slave as soon as he could persuade you into his eager arms. Say the word and we'll adjourn to my own lonely and echoing suite along the hallway,' he offered half-seriously.

'Never, never, never,' she shot back at him, spine rigid and chin high.

He couldn't know she burned for his touch. Even the tips of her toes seared her with a need to be kissed and seduced that made a lie of her conviction there could never be anything between them, after she'd angrily informed him she would rather die than become his mistress ten years ago.

And he just stood there; let his complex grey gaze play over her as if she had been arranged here especially for his pleasure. He wanted her, the need in his complicated eyes was as real as the hot rush of heat between her legs. She clamped them together under the sheets then instantly regretted it as the movement drew his attention to the fact her breasts had rounded and peaked under the inadequate fine lawn chemise.

'Oh, come now, ma'am,' he gritted, as if her denial made him angry as finding her half-naked in Bran's bed when she should be working had not. 'We have a decade worth of wanting on the slate between us. Sooner or later we'll have an accounting.'

'No, there isn't and, no, we won't,' she informed him as furiously as she could when sitting here nearly naked.

She could hardly thrust the bedclothes aside and run away when her legs would refuse to carry her and where would she run to without scandalising half the household and any guests who happened to be standing about with their mouths open?

'I may be a fool, Mrs Wheaton, but not such a one I'm prepared to pretend to you that passion couldn't break us, if we let it. It might do us both less harm if we admit its existence,' he said sombrely and their eyes met.

Chloe almost said the words in her head—*Why not try it and see?* There it was again, her wicked inner self, whispering sinfully in her ears and offering lures she thought she'd cut off in their heady prime a decade ago. She squirmed and made herself be glad even the sleep still clouding her brain hadn't let her speak that impossible invitation aloud.

Wasn't it exactly the sort of rash remark that landed her and her twin sister Daphne in the suds in their younger days? Chloe clamped cold fetters on her wilder self at the reminder how it came about she was sitting here glaring at her new employer like a hungry she-wolf. If she was careful enough, they could go back to stiffly avoiding each other until she left.

'It might not do that much harm to *you*,' she muttered crossly and folded her bare arms across her chest; because she couldn't endure him standing there knowing how much she wanted him.

'I shouldn't be too sure about that,' he rasped as his hot gaze now dwelt on the exposed upper slopes of her breasts, Chloe looked down to see she'd only made them look fuller and even more rounded by seeking to hide her tight, need-peaked nipples from his fascinated gaze. 'I've always known you could be my ruin,' he murmured, looking ready to resign himself to it if he could climb into this narrow bed and make use of every tight inch of space it would leave him to seduce her until she screamed for him with a sombre house party of guests a mere misplaced call away.

'No, never!' she croaked and almost gave in to the urge to scissor her legs together to deny the hot need and frustration grinding at the heart of her.

He was here; not some fevered fantasy she had woken up with, as she so often had in the first days, weeks and years after he left Farenze Lodge as if the devil himself was riding on his shoulders. Until today she thought she'd banished that folly to outer darkness along with him and now she knew better.

'If things were different, I could make you eat those words with one kiss and you know it,' he said grimly.

'They're not though, are they?' she whispered and almost sobbed at the years of regret she'd betrayed with those stark words. 'Please leave me be, my lord. I should never have slept when there is so much to do and it won't happen again, I assure you.'

'Nonsense,' he said gruffly. 'When I first laid eyes on you today I thought you looked as if you might break if you didn't bend soon. You're too thin and look as if you haven't slept or eaten properly in weeks.'

'I can't sleep and food seems to choke me at times,' she admitted reluctantly.

'Go on like this and you'll make yourself ill. Do that to yourself if you must, but how can you risk shocking your daughter with your wan appearance when she sees you? She must be struggling to come to terms with losing Virginia, close as I know they had become to each other while she was growing up.'

'Yes, she was heartbroken,' Chloe said heavily, remembering how it felt to hold her sobbing daughter whilst she cried as if her poor heart might break the day Chloe had Lady Virginia's coachman drive her to Bath so she could tell Verity Lady Virginia was dead.

'So eat something,' he demanded.

'I have, at regular intervals.'

'Then eat more and go to bed and sleep properly tonight, instead of pacing the corridors like a ghost and making the night watchman think he's being haunted.'

His voice was brusque, but there was what looked like genuine concern in his eyes as he inspected her face. His well-hidden kindness touched her as she couldn't let herself be touched by her employer. She rubbed her eyes self-consciously, pushed an annoying curl behind her ear and tried not to gaze back at him as if she might adore him, if things were different.

'I must look like something the cat brought in,' she muttered unwarily.

The wretched man stared at her with a glint of humour and something they'd both declared forbidden in the depths of those grey-, gold- and green-rayed eyes of his. She wanted to fall into them and never land on solid ground again for a long moment.

'You must know you're beautiful,' he said wryly,

almost as if talking to himself and being overheard by the wide-eyed sceptic in front of him.

She shook her head in hasty denial and tried not to love the fact he thought so.

'But you're still too thin,' he insisted, 'and you have shadows under your eyes a Gothic heroine would envy.'

'Well, she'd be welcome to them,' she said unwarily and the quirk of humour kicking up his fascinating mouth became a true smile.

There was all the warmth and hope and unwary fellow feeling in them that had nearly carried them over the precipice a decade ago. Chloe felt them both balance on the edge of the inevitable again. It felt terrible and utterly desirable, as if even their thoughts were cursed to curl up together and purr with delight at being reunited.

He reached out a long finger, as if he wanted to physically brush the shadows away from her eyes. She felt the whisper of his almost touch on her skin and gasped with hope and fear at how much she wanted it. She slicked parched lips with her tongue and watched him hesitate, had the sense of a strong man fighting what he knew was wrong, yet he was still drawn on by what felt so strong between them it could overrule everything, if they let it. There was curiosity and impatience in his eyes, before he blanked them and my Lord Farenze was himself again; remote, self-assured and cynical and as distant from the housekeeper of Farenze Lodge as ever.

'Eve and Bran are coming,' he warned her huskily.

Chloe strained her senses to catch a hint of whatever sound or instinct told him they were about to be rescued from folly, whether they wanted to be or not.

'Pretend I never came in here. Act as if you woke up the moment they asked what I'm doing here,' he whispered.

Chapter Four

Lost for words again, Chloe nodded, then burrowed her face into the pillows and drew the bedclothes over her chilled shoulders. At least pretending to be fuzzy with sleep would give her time to pull wanton Chloe into line and forget he'd been here as best she could. If she proved as obedient to the curb as his rampant side, she had nothing to worry about.

'Bah!' she muttered crossly into the pillow, 'just bah, my Lord Farenze!'

No danger he might hear her. He was back through the door and nearly closing it again before she could slide down the bed and cover her now-shivering body. Nobody else would ever know he'd found her here, heavy-eyed with sleep and wanton desire.

She heard Miss Winterley express surprise at her

father's presence in an over-loud voice meant to warn Chloe not to start awake and betray herself and felt a hard flush of shame burn her cheeks at the thought she knew of Luke Winterley's presence all too well. She felt it in every fibre of her being and the man was Miss Winterley's father, for goodness' sake.

'You took my book,' he replied and if his excuse sounded lame and defensive, it might explain what he was doing here better than a smoother lie, designed to cover something clandestine and shocking.

'And there are none downstairs in the famously well-stocked library Aunt Virginia and Uncle Virgil amassed between them?' Eve asked, as if she knew very well her father had really stumbled on the housekeeper enjoying a nap in the wrong place at entirely the wrong time, but how could she?

'Not the one I was reading before you stole it,' he said grumpily.

'And now *I* am reading it, so you would be stealing it from me. I can't believe you to need distraction so badly, especially in the midst of a house party you must play host to, that you need to barge into my bedchamber when I am not there and try to repossess part of your library, Papa. I'm not even going to think about the list of tasks awaiting you here that you reeled off as an excuse for not being able to spend much time greeting neighbours who call to express their condolences.'

'I didn't know then how much distraction I'd need,' he muttered darkly.

Chloe's eyes stung at the sound of him so gruffly sheepish it opened up a host of new temptations inside her. She didn't want to love him and screwed her eyes shut in denial of any tears tempted to come further.

'Don't be such a cross old bear, Papa,' Eve told him and Chloe could hear the rustle of her skirts as she marched up and hugged her father.

Wrong to envy Eve such ease with her father, that ability to breach the chilly touch-me-not air he normally carried about with him like a shield.

'I'll try not to be, my she-cub, but there will be reasons aplenty for me to growl over the next few days.'

'Aye,' Brandy Brown added from what sounded like a position just inside the room, 'you'll need the patience of a saint before the vultures fly off at last.'

'They're not all vultures, Bran,' Eve chided.

'We don't know them well enough to judge what they are yet, my lamb,' her maid said cynically and Chloe decided there was no need to worry about Eve Winterley with such a formidable protector at her side, as well as a father who would clearly walk through fire to keep his beloved daughter safe.

'I know Lord Mantaigne and Great-Uncle Giles perfectly well and even Uncle James isn't as savage and sarcastic as he used to be. Aunt Virginia was always trying to persuade him to live a steadier life, so perhaps he will turn over a new leaf in her honour.'

'And I'm a Dutchman,' Chloe thought she heard Lord Farenze mutter darkly and wondered what divided the half-brothers so deeply, so alike in colouring and stature as they were, yet as sharply distant with each other as two siblings could be without openly declaring war.

'No, what you are is a curmudgeon, Papa, so I can't imagine why you're worrying about reading a book you seem very familiar with when you have your brother nearby to argue with once more. I dare say if you start now you could have Uncle James simmering nicely by dinner and ready to call you out the moment Aunt Virginia's funeral is over.'

'Thank you, minx, the gossips have plenty to say already, without a brotherly feud or a family riot breaking out. I'm not sure I should have let you read *Tom Jones* after all, it seems to have given you some odd ideas.'

'There's a copy in the study, if you truly want to take up where you left off,' Eve called after the sound of her father's retreating footsteps and surely it was wrong of Chloe to wish he wouldn't go at the same time as she longed to be up and away and pretend he hardly impinged on her thoughts, let alone her wildest dreams? 'Virginia told me where all her warm novels were in the event of my ever having to be bored here in her absence. It's all right, Papa, she told me anything she and Uncle Virgil locked away was far too warm for a young lady to read and I really can't think why the tabbies make such a fuss about Mr Fielding's splendid book.'

'Don't get caught with it, then, and it's probably best if you don't admit to reading it in polite company. I won't have you labelled fast before you're even out.'

'Of course not and stop being such a worrywart, I'll be so painfully good over the next few weeks you will hardly recognise me.'

The only reply Chloe heard was a distant masculine humph then Eve ordered her maid to shut the outer door before hastily pushing open the one to the bedroom where Chloe was sitting up in bed, feeling flustered and confused.

'That was close,' Eve confided with an impish smile.

'We should have locked the door,' Bran told them. 'Imagine if his lordship had opened it and found you lying here asleep, Mrs Wheaton.'

'Yes, only imagine,' Chloe echoed hollowly and used her artistic shudder as an excuse to spring out of bed and start setting herself to rights.

'I'll help,' Bran said as Chloe then tried to struggle into her gown and wrestle with her rebellious curls at the same time. 'Button yourself up and I'll comb out your hair and dress it for you, although it seems a crying shame to screw it into a knot and hide it under that thing when it's so beautiful. There's many a fine lady as would give her eye teeth for hair half as thick and full of life.'

'It's wild and unruly and people get entirely the

wrong impression of me if I allow it to show. Anyway, I'm nearly thirty years of age and a respectable widow, not a dewy-eyed débutante.'

'You don't look much older than one right now,' Bran observed as her eyes met Chloe's in the square of mirror above the diminutive washstand.

'I can't afford dreams,' Chloe murmured.

'Neither of us can, but it don't stop us 'avin' 'em, do it?'

'What do you dream of, Mrs Brown?'

'A fine man for my girl; one who'll love her as she is and not try to make her into a society missus without a good word to say to anyone but a lord.'

'I can't see him doing that, whoever he might be.'

'Can't you, ma'am? Then you've been a lucky woman up to now.'

'Maybe I have at that,' Chloe admitted and suppressed a shudder at the thought of all the ways in which a man might mould his wife.

'His lordship now, he's a man as would let a woman be herself and love her all the more for it, if you know what I mean?' Bran said as she finished pinning Chloe's wild mane back in place, then eyed the cap with disfavour before fitting it over her handiwork with a sigh.

'He doesn't strike me as a man on the lookout for love,' Chloe argued.

'Ah, well, there's what a man *says* he wants then there's what he really does want. They don't always meet in the middle, until the right woman comes along and changes his mind.'

'If I understood all that I might argue, but since I don't and dinner will be served in a little over an hour, neither of us has enough time for riddles,' Chloe said with a last glance in the mirror to make sure she was correct and subdued again.

'Just as well, since we'll never agree about his lordship.'

'Maybe not,' Chloe said distractedly and, picking up her keys, clipped them back on her belt and with a word of breathless thanks fled the room.

Luke stumped back downstairs to the study and cursed as rampant need roiled inside him. This wasn't some unique enchantment; he was tired and it was too long since he'd visited his mistress. Forcing the pace on a long journey had left him weary and less in control of himself and his masculine appetites than usual. Combine tiredness and grief with Mrs Wheaton's exhaustion and Eve's kind heart and trouble looked inevitable with hindsight, but at least it hadn't led to catastrophe.

He bit out another fearsome curse at his painful arousal over the mere thought of Chloe Wheaton sitting up in that neat little bed, looking at him as if every fantasy he'd ever had of her as his lover was about to come true, before she awoke fully and recalled who they were. Of course he'd wanted her since she was painfully young and hauntingly beautiful, with a tiny dependent child. He felt the familiar dragging heat of frustrated desire, as if his senses were soaked in need of the woman and refused to give her up, however hard he told them they must.

On some level he'd known she was there even when he saw the inner door slightly ajar and Eve's baggage piled on the Aubusson carpet, as if the footmen had been told to leave it there and depart in order not to disturb Chloe Wheaton while Bran and Eve took a stroll about the Winter Garden. He wished they hadn't done what he couldn't and ordered the woman to bed for an hour or so.

Eve had a heart big enough to sacrifice her comfort for a woman she barely knew, because the housekeeper looked so breakable. How could he be anything but proud of such a daughter, even if he wished she'd left well alone? Eve had done the right thing, but now he wanted to run upstairs and throw the pig-headed Mrs Wheaton over his shoulders and tell the world to go hang and do the wrong one.

If he was not to avoid Farenze Lodge as if he hated it for another decade she had to leave, but he must find a place where her skills were valued and her fine figure and spellbinding violet eyes ignored. Did convents have housekeepers? Luke forced his hands to unclench at the idea of her being leered at by her employer's husband, or some gangling oaf of a son, and decided to keep a stern eye on Mrs Wheaton's next household from afar.

Yes, he should have trusted his instincts, but curiosity, or something even more dangerous, led him to open that door. Once he had, he could no more bow coolly and leave than stop breathing. Even now the scent of her seemed to linger in the air. It was only the lavender in the big bowls Virginia always insisted on having about to sweeten the air in winter-closed rooms.

He suspected Chloe had lavender water used on the last rinse of her linen and that was why he couldn't seem to get her out of his head. The rest of that exotic scent he associated with her was probably lingering aroma of a spicy moth bag or two, deployed to stop the industrious creatures chewing through her mourning attire. So it was a mix of simple strewing herbs, cinnamon, orris and perhaps cloves, but the memory fogged his senses, reminding him how tempted he'd been to kiss the fine creamy skin at the base of her elegant throat and find out if she tasted as exotically artless as she smelt.

Confound it, he hadn't kissed her and could still savour the taste of her on his tongue. He ran it over his lips and the memory of her doing the same took fire and wrenched a tortured groan from him. After a decade of avoidance and abstinence he *still* wanted her, wanted her more than at first sight and now they were both mature adults and better designed for mischief.

The waif was a woman and he'd been wrong about the figure under that deplorable gown— Chloe the woman was nothing like the skinny girl she'd once been. She was slender, yes, probably too much so after forgetting to eat for grief and worry. What there was of her was sweetly curved, though, and her skin looked so silken and perfect he could imagine the feel of those full high breasts of hers against his palms. He held up his hands as if convicting them of a heinous crime for flexing on thin air as if they knew what they wanted better than the rest of him did. His other senses were betraying him, so why shouldn't touch join the turncoat army?

Because somehow he had to resist what he and Chloe Wheaton might be to each other, he supposed with a heavy sigh. For a decade he'd done his best to stay away; he'd seen the desperation in her eyes; the hunger for the love Virginia had to offer a pair of homeless waifs. So he'd taken her rebuff to heart.

Easy enough to make a holiday of visits to Brighton so Virginia and Eve could enjoy one another's company. He had even endured a few weeks in London each spring so they could eat ices at Gunter's and visit Astley's Amphitheatre and there was no more noble fatherly sacrifice when Darkmere was the finest place to be in the spring.

He suspected Virginia knew why he avoided the Lodge, but she didn't say a word because she knew as well as he did that it was as impossible for Lord

Farenze to do aught but ruin a housekeeper. The polite world would laugh at him and sneer at her if he tried to make anything of Chloe Wheaton *but* his mistress.

'There you are,' Tom Banburgh remarked from the doorway and he welcomed the interruption, didn't he?

'There's no fooling you, is there?'

'I can go away again until you're in a better humour if you like, but I thought misery might like some company.'

'Devil take it, I'm not miserable.'

'Face like thunder.'

Luke stopped himself pacing up and down like a general before a crucial battle and took the filled glass Tom was holding out to him for the second time today. He took a sip of the finest cognac Virginia always kept for a favoured few and felt a little better after all.

'I miss her so much, Tom,' he finally admitted the lesser of two evils.

'How could you not? I expect Virginia saved you from the tender mercies of your family when she could. She certainly rescued me from my unloving guardian when I was a scrubby boy nobody else cared enough to worry about.'

'True, and she was always taking in waifs and strays. Seems a shame she couldn't give Virgil children when she was born to be a mother.'

'And this remark is coming from a man who would be a mere mister today if she had? You're either a saint or a liar, my friend.'

'I'm neither and you know as well as I do a title can't change the beat of a man's heart or make him any happier.'

'I really wouldn't know,' Tom said indifferently and Luke reminded himself his friend had been a marquis since he was five years old.

'Well, I do,' he argued, 'and mine hasn't bought me any great joy.'

'That's because you hadn't much left in you when you acquired it, Luke,' Tom said sagely.

Luke wondered if anyone else would get away with saying some of the things Mantaigne came out with so blithely without being called out. 'And you have no memory of being without one, so are necessarily full of fun and laughter, I suppose?'

'Going a bit far, but I never saw the point in being gloomy. I'll go on trying to laugh at the world even now, because Virginia wouldn't want long faces and a grand carry on over her departure from this vale of tears.'

'True, and we both know she missed my great-uncle as if someone had lopped off an arm or a leg after Virgil died.'

'Aye, and if there *is* a heaven at least they're in it together again.'

'Since it clearly wouldn't be so for one without the other, you must be right.'

'Makes you wonder though, don't it?' Tom said.

'No, love is still a myth for the rest of us.'

Luke gave his friend a long hard look before deciding he was the one obsessed with love and lovers and in danger of tripping over his own tongue. Not that he felt anything like love for Chloe Wheaton.

'Thing about myths is a lot of people believe them,' Tom said with a long look at Luke that left him puzzled and fidgety.

Was he being warned not to lightly charm the object of his desires? He could imagine nobody *less* likely to fall in love with him than aloof and sceptical Mrs Chloe Wheaton. Then he recalled the sight of her disarmed by sleep and a hundred times more vulnerable and wondered all over again.

'I don't,' he muttered half to himself.

'You could have been cut straight out of the pages of a Gothic tale and pasted into a young girl's scrapbook of fantasies you look so close to the little darlings' ideal of a heroic villain.'

'What nonsense have you been feeding yourself this afternoon, man—a three-decker novel from the yellow press, perhaps? Or are you already three parts cast away?' Luke asked incredulously.

'Neither, but you don't have the faintest idea, do you?'

'Faintest idea of what?'

'That your long and dusky locks, brooding frowns and touch-me-not air are sure to drive the débutantes insane with longing at their first sight of you across a crowded ballroom. The moment you stand among a London rout glaring at any boy brave enough to dance with your Eve, the little darlings will start swooning by rote for the lack of space to do it all at once in comfort.'

Luke felt himself pale at the very idea, so no wonder Tom laughed. 'Why?' he asked hollowly. 'I'll be old enough to be their father.'

'As are all those dark and brooding villains out of the Gothic novels they devour by the yard, I suppose. Who knows what flights of the imagination such silly chits are capable of dreaming up between them, but you'll be a prime target for them and their ambitious mamas if you set foot in London without a viscountess at your side.'

'I wasn't going to worry about one of those until Eve is safely wed.'

'Leave Eve to find her husband when she's ready, man; you owe her that for enduring life with a hermit like you all these years.'

Luke shook his head, but was Mantaigne right? He couldn't see much attraction in a beetle-browed countenance and raven's wing black hair he only kept overlong because he had no patience with constant visits from a barber or his new valet's fussing and primping. When it came to his features, he'd just been relieved Eve had escaped the Winterley Roman nose and put down the occasional appreciative feminine stare as a penchant for his acres and title. Marriage to Pamela Verdoyne had cured him of vanity and he wondered if she'd done him such a great favour if he was about to blunder into the ballrooms of the *ton* unprepared.

'I won't have Eve endure a stepmother like mine,' he said with a shudder.

'That's in your hands,' Tom said with a shrug.

'What is this, some sort of conspiracy to marry me off?'

'That takes more than one person, my lord, and I'm not a matchmaker.'

'So Virginia, you and my own dear, sweet scheming Eve don't make a set?'

'Not through prior agreement, but all three of us can't be wrong.'

'Yes, you can—by Heaven you're more wrong in triplicate than alone.'

Tom merely raised his eyebrows and looked sceptical before calmly helping himself to another glass of cognac.

'Did Virginia put you up to this?' Luke asked suspiciously.

'Don't you think I've a mind of my own and the sense to see what you won't yourself? If she wasn't dead, I could strangle that spoilt witch you wed so hastily, Luke; she married you for your expectations, then rejected you for so-called love, as if it was your fault she was born vain, empty-headed and contrary.'

'I should never have agreed to marry her,' Luke said with a shrug, recalling the long and bitter rows of his marriage with a shudder that sent him back to the brandy decanter for a second glass before he'd quite taken in the fact he'd drunk the first.

'Your father and wicked stepmother should take the blame for pushing such a paltry marriage on an infatuated lad. You're not a boy now, though, and you badly need a wife, my friend, at least you do if you're to avoid being ruthlessly pursued through every ballroom in London by a pack of ninnies when Eve makes her début.'

'Shouldn't you be more concerned with securing your own succession, since you're the last of the Banburghs and I have a younger brother?'

'The Banburghs can go hang as far as I'm concerned, but it's not good for James to be in limbo, never sure if he's to be your heir or only the "what if tragedy struck?" spare Winterley male. He's bored and restless and probably lonely and who knows what he gets up to when our backs are turned?'

'You know very well he'd never confide in me,' Luke said and let himself feel how much it hurt that his brother hated him, even if he had cause to hate him back.

'Left to himself, he would have followed you about like a stray puppy when you were younger.'

Luke gave a snort of derision at the idea of elegant and sophisticated James Winterley following anyone slavishly, let alone his despised elder brother. 'That particular apple never fell far from the tree,' he said darkly, even as the laziness of the cliché made him wonder if he wasn't guilty of prejudice himself.

'And you think his lot so much better than your own?' Tom persisted impatiently.

'Whatever I think, let's postpone feeling sorry for James because his mother loved him and hated me for another day, shall we?'

'Don't leave it too late to remedy,' Tom warned with a steady look that made Luke wonder if he didn't know more about James's dark and tangled affairs than he was letting on. 'I'm going off to bother my valet and idle away an hour until dinner. Who knows, maybe we'll have a pleasant and peaceful evening against all the odds,' his friend said before he sauntered from the room.

'Slim enough chance of anything of the kind under this roof,' Luke muttered grumpily and finished his brandy before going upstairs.

Chapter Five

The January twilight was already all but over when Luke stumped up the elegant staircase. He rang for the bath he needed as soon as he reached his bedchamber and heard hot water carried in within minutes, so there was no excuse to sack the housekeeper on the spot and end this torture. As he relaxed into the tub images of the dratted woman slid slyly into his head.

Why her? Why was it Chloe Wheaton he seemed doomed to want every time he set eyes on her? She was a fine-looking woman, despite the deplorable gowns and concealing cap, but he'd met other fine-looking women and some of them diamonds of the first water. No other woman on this fair earth could get him in a stew of frustrated yearning with one distrustful glance and how he wished it otherwise.

If only it was merely the thought of a fine female body in his bed that made him want her so badly. He ached with the frustration of not having her as his lover. There was something unique about her that even ten years of trying couldn't expunge from his senses. He recalled a fateful day that summer when they first met; he'd come upon her playing with her little girl in the woods above the house and just stood and watched where neither could see him.

At last the heat of the day drained the child's energy and Chloe had sung softly to calm her, then rocked little Verity to sleep in her arms. Luke recalled envy eating at him like acid as he wanted such love and tenderness for the babes they could bring into the world together, if only everything was different.

Instead it had been Wheaton who recklessly married a schoolgirl and got a baby on her, or so she had once told him. Luke felt his fists tighten at the thought of Wheaton exposing the woman he was supposed to love to such a hard, narrow life as she'd had to lead since.

He had been about to turn away when the June sunlight picked out the trail of tears on Chloe's face as she gazed down at her sleeping babe. Even now he felt the jar of it as his heart thudded at the memory. Back then he had had to clamp down on the need to stride over to her and take her in his arms so hard he discovered afterwards he'd clenched his fists until the blood flowed.

He left the next day, all his wild schemes for somehow making it easier for her to be his mistress by getting her to act the quietly respectable wife, whose reclusive husband sailed the seven seas, then wanted no company but hers whenever he was home, shattered. He couldn't do that to her, or little Verity or any other babies they might make between them. It was a half-life and he couldn't offer her so little.

Curse it; he wouldn't let passion waft him along as if he had no free will now either. Yet when he conjured a picture of his late wife ranting at him that he was a stern, unlovable stick to correct his obsession, the fantasy of his great-aunt's housekeeper naked and eager in the great bed next door blotted her out. Luke felt heat roar through him at the very idea and the physical evidence of his arousal with nothing between him and civilisation made him a fool.

Chloe only had to be in the same county for him to want her and from the moment he saw her at Virginia's window today he'd barely been able to conceal his ridiculous state from the world. Idiot body! Hadn't marriage taught it anything at all?

His response to Pamela's challenge to his manhood when she refused to let him bed her again after they returned from their bride trip slotted into his memory and reminded him how easy it was to need a woman without liking her. He relived his distaste at himself and his wife when she enjoyed his furious promise to seduce her into taking him until she screamed for more as she never had during his gentle lovemaking. The fulfilment of that vow excited her and left him at odds with himself.

Their marriage limped on for six months, Pamela blowing hot and cold as Luke grew sick of her and himself. How typical that she announced her pregnancy the day she finally left him. Her letter from her sister's London address saying she'd been brought to bed of a daughter and he'd better come and get her arrived on his twentieth birthday. To this day Luke couldn't recall the journey and it took Eve to blast through his rage as the real innocent in the whole wretched business.

'You're welcome to the squalling brat,' his wife had shouted when he dodged past her to reach the attic where, the butler informed him, his daughter had been banished for crying a little too loudly. Pamela scurried after him; 'Pushing it out nigh killed me and I never want to see it again.'

'Don't you feel the need to raise a heroine in your own tawdry image?'

'Not one of your get, not that I'm sure she *is* yours. You're not the only Winterley ready to rut like a hog,' she said smugly.

His bellow of fury woke the baby and made her furious nurse run out of the bare attic bedroom he wouldn't wish on a foundling to upbraid them.

'If you two 'ave a mite of pity in your black hearts, you'll be quiet,' she barked in a hoarse voice that sounded as if its skinny owner spent most of her years on this earth bellowing to be heard and had worn it out in the process.

A smile replaced Luke's frown as he recalled his shock at being addressed so sharply by a tiny female who looked as if she'd dashed in off the street to feed his child out of the kindness of her weary heart. She hardly reached his elbow and her face had the wizened yet somehow ageless look of one used to hardship since birth.

'Whose get is she then?' he'd asked his wife more quietly, as the furious girl-woman was still barring his way like a flea-bitten terrier confronting an angry bear.

'Oh, she's a Winterley all right; which is probably why I can't endure to have her near me.'

'Then she's mine.'

'There are other vultures crouched in the branches of your family tree, hoping their seed will carry off the family honours under your long nose, Luke Winterley.'

It wasn't the unlikely idea of his already ailing father laying hands on his wife that made Luke feel as if the finest Toledo blade had sliced into his heart. A terrible possibility dawned as he stood there and mentally crossed all his male relatives off the list but one. His stepmother resented the fact he was heir to the Farenze titles and always had done her best to make the half-brothers hate each other. Luke thought a gruff affection bound him and James even so, until that moment.

Would even Pamela stoop to seduce a seventeen-year-old boy? Yes, he'd decided with bitter sickness threatening to choke him. To take a twisted revenge on Luke for marrying her without adoring her slavishly she would, and enjoy every moment of her betrayal. Young enough to hurt to his very soul, he felt as if sharing a city with her a moment longer would surely suffocate him.

'Bring the child, we're leaving,' he'd snapped at the street urchin wet-nurse.

'Not 'til I'm sure she's better off with you than the ragman,' she said, appearing at the nursery door with Eve wrapped in a worn shawl that had to be her own since Pamela wouldn't even give it to her maid.

'Why didn't I think of that?' Pamela said spitefully.

'How can you say such terrible things, dearest?' her sister, Alexandra, Lady Derneley, protested faintly from behind her. 'She's your own dear baby.'

'I'd prefer to house a ferret or a weasel than that squalling brat. Has James visited me once while I was fat and lumbering like a cow because of a *girl* they got on me between them? You know he hasn't, Lexie; he promised undying devotion when he seduced me behind his brother's back and look how long it lasted. I'd hate her for ruining my figure, then chasing dear Blasedon away with her wailing and whining, even if she wasn't a Winterley. I'll be happy never to set eyes on the whelp again as long as I live, she can go to hell along with him and the sooner the better.'

Lady Derneley turned chalk white as her little sister's true nature hit home and fainted to avoid it.

'To hell with *you*, you unnatural bitch,' Luke roared.

'To 'ell with both of you,' the street urchin's voice somehow rose above the uproar. 'This poor babe ain't 'ad time to do wrong, whatever the rest of you 'ave been up to and you be quiet,' she ordered Pamela, who gaped at her open-mouthed. 'If you've a spot of pity, use it on an 'elpless mite who din't ask to come into this world instead of yourself for once. Mister, you can take us both away from 'ere afore the poor little thing dies of cold and 'unger, or missus 'ere murders 'er while I'm asleep, never mind if you're 'er pa or no.'

It was then Luke made the life-transforming error of looking at the tiny little being in the girl's bony arms and realised she was right. Almost as frightened by the quiet as by the shouting, the baby screwed her tiny face up to wail her woes to the world. He put out a finger, more by instinct than in hope his touch would soothe her. Eve paused, opened her eyes wide and seemed to focus on him as if she'd been waiting for him to come since the day she was born. She made him her father, whatever the facts, by latching on to his finger and refusing to let go.

Somehow he managed to hide that fact while convincing Pamela he would stop her allowance and sue for divorce, instead of legal separation, if word got out Eve might not be his. The journey to Darkmere with Eve and Brandy Brown in tow was a nightmare he shuddered to think of now, but they all survived it somehow and Eve grew up free of a mother who hated her for being a Winterley.

Luke made himself ignore news of Pamela cavorting round any bits of the Continent free of revolutionary wars with a succession of lovers. He didn't care if the generous allowance he paid her kept her and her latest love in luxury and when news of his wife's death reached Darkmere three years later he hadn't enough hypocrisy left to mourn.

Now Lord Farenze might seem harsh and indifferent as the moors in sight of his castle towards the wider world, but he truly loved his daughter. A sneaky voice whispered it was safe to love Eve. If remembering his wife kept Chloe Wheaton and the danger of feeling more than he ought to for her at arm's length, then he would dwell on the last time he let a woman walk into his life and rearrange it for however long it took to put him off the idea.

Resolved to do so often over the next few days, he was dressed before he found out dinner had been put back an hour. Eve *had* been informed, however, and was discussing which black gown was better suited to the occasion with Chloe and Bran. He could see little difference and left the room as if the devil was on his tail as soon as he saw the housekeeper lurking in the darkest corner of the room. Feeling thoroughly out of sorts with the world, Luke went downstairs like a guest arriving too early for a party.

Chloe was consulting Cook about the number of entrées Mrs Winterley thought fashionable to serve at dinner and agreeing this wasn't the time for excess, even if they could find half-a-dozen more dishes at the drop of a hat, when the sound of a

late arrival surprised them all. The terse announcement she was needed outside made her scurry in
the head groom's wake to the stable yard.

'Verity, oh, my love!' she cried as she saw her
daughter blink against the flare of the stable lads'
lanterns when she stepped down from the coach.

'Oh, Mama, I'm so glad to see you,' Verity said
with a wobbly smile that made Chloe want to cry;
instead she hugged her as if they'd been parted
for months.

'But how did this come about?' Chloe asked as
Lord Farenze's coachman nodded tersely at her
and she could only marvel at his endurance.

'His lordship ordered it soon as he heard little
miss here was waiting to come home,' Birtkin said
as if he drove all the way to Bath and back after
enduring the long drive here from Northumberland at least once a week.

'I'm very grateful to you,' she replied with a
warm smile of gratitude.

'Not my doing, ma'am, you should thank his
lordship,' Birtkin mumbled as if trying to reclaim
his dour reputation.

'You and your men were the ones who drove

through twilight, then darkness, on Verity's behalf, so I'm grateful to you, whether you like it or not.'

'We was doing our duty, ma'am.'

'I will stop saying thank you, since it seems to trouble you, but I'll ask Cook to send plenty of the food left from feeding his lordship's guests to the servants' hall for dinner. You and your men need good food and some cheer on such a night.'

'My thanks, ma'am, we'll settle the beasts and see we're clean and tidy before we comes in.'

'See that you do,' Chloe said and led Verity into the house.

She could afford time away from her duties; Oakham would supervise the dining room while Cook organised the footmen behind the scenes with dire threats of retribution if they dropped even a teaspoon of her food.

'I should scold you for telling your teachers I need you here when I wanted to spare you this, my love, but I'm far too pleased to see you for that,' she said as she urged Verity upstairs, guessing she'd slept very little since the day Chloe made that sad trip to Bath to tell her daughter Lady Virginia was dead. 'But now you are here you must go straight to bed,'

'Oh, Mama, why? I'm not in the least bit tired.'

'I can see that, but I suppose you will just have to humour me, now you have got your way in everything else,' Chloe said with a wry smile.

How hard it was not to spoil this wilful, clever little conundrum of hers and how right Virginia had been to insist Verity went to Miss Thibett's very good school. Her daughter needed to learn the self-discipline and all the other disciplines that Miss Thibett considered made up a well-rounded human being who happened to have been born female. Chloe and her sister had never had a governess, let alone gone to school, and look where that lack of any learning but what they happened to light on in their maternal grandfather's long-neglected library landed them.

Verity's room was in the nursery wing the late Lord and Lady Farenze had built in hope of a family of their own, then used for other people's children, such as Verity and Lord Mantaigne and the current master of the house and his half-brother when they were boys. Chloe had been sleeping within call of Lady Virginia's room and she didn't want to move back and risk Verity hearing the terrifying nightmares that were plaguing her again.

When Verity was a baby, her night terrors had returned again and again, and Chloe had been glad to be up here where nobody else could hear. Her daughter would no longer sleep through any screams and shouts Chloe let out though, and she wished there was a way of stopping them. She suppressed a weary sigh at the very thought of trying to relax and pretend all was well on the eve of Virginia's funeral with Viscount Farenze sleeping under the same roof.

'I'm still in the Triangle room; you will remember where I am if you wake up and want me, won't you, love?' she asked as she helped Verity undress.

'Very well, Mama, but I won't,' her child said as she held up her arms to accept her nightgown being slipped over her head as if she was much younger than the self-sufficient young lady she was now. 'I'm so glad to be home I know I shall sleep well tonight. Can I really eat supper in bed?'

'I'll be hurt if you don't, I had to coax the cook to make it for you and she is very busy,' Chloe said.

She undid the plaits constraining Verity's unruly golden hair and brushed it as gently as she could while her daughter tried to do justice to the chicken soup, dainty sandwich and apple flummery brought up by the shy little scullery maid.

'There, I think that's all the knots out at last,' Chloe murmured as she began to re-plait it into a thick tail in a ritual that reminded her poignantly of doing so for her sister at Verity's age.

'I do love you, Mama,' Verity assured her with sleepy seriousness. 'I shall always miss Lady Virginia, but you're my mother and I won't let you leave me,' she said so seriously Chloe knew she was feeling the loss of her best and oldest friend in this world even more deeply than a mother had to hope she would.

'I can't imagine anything nicer than being with you as long as you need me and becoming a sad charge on you when I am old and grey and a little bit disgraceful, love,' she said with a deliberately comical grimace. 'For now it's time you went to sleep and I made sure all is ready when the family and guests retire as well.'

'Goodnight then, Mama,' Verity murmured sleepily as Chloe pulled the covers up and checked the nightlight was safe.

'Goodnight, my darling,' Chloe said softly and

Verity fell fast asleep as soon as her head hit the pillow.

Taking the tray and her own candle, Chloe allowed herself a long look at her sleeping child before returning to her duties. This was what her life was truly about. Verity's arrival was a timely reminder why she was housekeeper at Farenze Lodge and would be one somewhere else for as long as Verity needed her to be. She refused to consider the day her daughter left school to a world where a young lady with a mother who worked for a living might find her a liability. By then she might be able to afford the cottage by the sea she'd promised herself when even housekeepers with daughters to raise alone needed dreams to distract them from harsh reality.

'I wished to thank you, Lord Farenze,' the cool voice he'd been doing his best not to hear in his head all evening informed Luke when he sought a few moments' peace and quiet in the library after dinner.

'Did you? I doubt it,' he replied dourly.

'You believe me so ill mannered I wouldn't say a simple "thank you" that you ordered my daughter to be fetched from school tonight?' Chloe Wheaton asked and surely that wasn't hurt in her necessarily soft tones as they murmured in the corridor where anyone might overhear them?

'I wasn't casting aspersions on your manners, but on your pride, madam,' he said shortly, secretly shocked he was being so disagreeable yet not quite able to stop himself being so somehow.

'You believe housekeepers are not entitled to that commodity, my lord?'

'I believe *you* have a superfluity of it, entitled or not.'

'How revolutionary of me,' she said blandly and turned to go, presumably before she said something she regretted.

'Stop, I'm sorry. That was ill-mannered of me and now I owe you another apology,' he said and grasped her hand to stop her leaving then felt as if he'd been struck down by lightning from the mere feel of her bare wrist under his hand.

'You owe me nothing,' she said stiffly and glared at him before wrenching her hand away then stalking off as if she could imagine nothing more repulsive.

He entered the study he still considered the

domain of his predecessor and glared moodily into the fire. Just when he had been feeling calmer and altogether more able to resist the charms of women who clearly didn't like him, she loomed out of the semi-darkness to throw him into turmoil. It wasn't as if it cost *him* anything to order Virginia's coachman to fetch the housekeeper's daughter. Her manners were better than his today and he only just muffled an impatient groan when someone else loomed out of the shadows to disturb his evening.

'What is it, man?' he demanded as he met his own coachman's sharp gaze.

'Just thought you ought to know, m'lord,' the man said stoically.

'Know what?'

'I drove the carriage to Bath and back.'

Luke cursed as he would never dream of doing in front of a lady and felt no better. 'What the devil for? I ordered Binns out, as you drove here from Northumberland.'

'He don't see well in the dark,' Josiah admitted uncomfortably and Luke wondered if the old coachman could see much at all. Josiah wasn't a man to betray any man's secrets lightly, though, and Luke sensed there was more to come.

'It's high time I pensioned him off, he must be nigh seventy,' he said anyway.

'Likely a bit more if you ask me, but that ain't what I came to tell you.'

'What was it then? That you're a disobedient ruffian who should be abed rather than dashing about the countryside? The head groom could have gone, man, he's no top sawyer, but even he could keep Lady Virginia's ancient team up to their bridles.'

'I knew it would be black dark long before they could stumble home, so I ordered the bays harnessed instead. I couldn't have Miss Verity careering about the country with a whipster holding the reins.'

Luke struggled to be fair. Chloe would hate him if her precious child was involved in a carriage accident because he had an urge to please her and he deserved censure for not thinking his impulsive scheme out better, not Josiah.

'You did the right thing,' he conceded reluctantly. 'I should have told you to wait until morning for all the difference it will make.'

'The little wench was that happy to know she wasn't forgotten I'd go twice as far in the dark to see her face light up when she realised I was there to fetch her home.'

Since he was about to evict her from that home, Luke felt the goad of his own weakness bite. 'Then what *did* you want to say?' he asked brusquely.

'That we was followed back,' Josiah told him with a straight look that told his master there was no point saying he might have imagined it.

'Who by and why the devil would anyone trail *you* home?'

'Don't know, m'lord, all I cared about was if he had a gun and if we was about to be held up.'

'Why didn't you inform the authorities in Bath?'

'Because he wasn't nowhere in sight when I got there. Nearly caught us up about a mile this side of Bath, then stayed on our tail all the way back.'

'Why didn't you challenge him then?'

'Because he never got close enough to answer me, nor take a clean shot. I drove as fast as I dared and Miss Verity thought it was a great lark to go like the devil was on our tail.'

'She's well plucked?'

'Game for any lark going if you ask me,' Josiah agreed with a grin that told Luke to be glad Eve was five or six years older than Verity Wheaton, or they might set the countryside by the ears with misdeeds.

'Do your best to keep an eye on her over the next few days for me then, Josh. I don't like the idea of anyone wasting time in such a fashion and he's more likely to have a grudge against me than a child from a Bath seminary, but it won't hurt to make sure the girl's kept safe. We've trouble enough without the girl tumbling into more.'

'You think she's like Miss Eve was at her age, m'lord?'

'Very like from the sound of things. You know as well as I do what mischief a reckless girl can find if left to her own devices too often.'

'Aye, well, girls will be girls,' the coachman said with a reminiscent grin. 'I'll keep an eye on her when she's out, or get young Seth to if I'm busy. When she's in the house you're far better placed to keep watch over her than me, my lord.'

Josiah's tone was so bland Luke wondered if the old villain knew how much he needed to avoid the girl's mother over the next few days. He truly hoped not.

'Oakham will tell me if anyone breathes on her

the wrong way,' Luke informed his childhood ally in the hope he'd stop making bricks without straw.

'Then we don't need to worry ourselves, do we?'

'I'd still like to know who our curious stranger is, though,' Luke mused and at least it gave him a problem to consider for the rest of the evening, instead of wondering how he'd get through the next days and weeks without disaster befalling himself and Mrs Chloe Wheaton.

Chapter Six

When the household was settled at last, Chloe made her weary way to Lady Farenze's bedchamber ready to take over the night vigil from Culdrose. She braced herself to try to appear as awake and cheerful as any of them could be tonight. She couldn't let the elderly maid know she felt tired to the bone, even after her ill-advised nap this afternoon.

Especially not after that; she shuddered at the very idea of what she might have given away in those unguarded moments while she gazed into Lord Farenze's hot grey eyes like a besotted schoolgirl. At the time a strange sort of exhilaration had buoyed her up, as if a wicked part of her was whispering she should stop fighting and give in to fiery attraction. Except he was a lord and she an upper servant and in a few weeks they would part, never to meet again.

The notion of such heady freedom stretching ahead of her made it an effort to set one foot in front of the other. The notion of all those empty years to come without even the occasional sight of him pressed down on her like a ton weight. She stopped outside the door to put on a suitably serene expression before she met Cully's shrewd gaze, then walked in.

'Oh, there you are, my dear. There's no need for you to stay with her ladyship tonight,' the elderly maid said with a nod to the other side of the bed where the new master of the house sat. 'Master Luke won't hear of anyone else keeping vigil.'

'No, I won't,' he said in a flatly emotionless voice that told her there was no point arguing.

'Quite right too,' Cully said with an approving nod. 'You need a good night's sleep and no argument, Mrs Wheaton. If you spend one more day trying to fit a month's worth of work into twenty-four hours, you'll collapse. Your little miss is home now and we don't want her more upset than she is already.'

'Aye, go to bed,' Lord Farenze barked from the most heavily shadowed corner of the room.

'Very well,' she said, knowing she couldn't argue in front of Culdrose and turned to go before the temptation to do it anyway overtook her.

'See she drinks one of your noxious potions and really does sleep, Cully,' she heard Lord Farenze say when she'd almost shut the door behind her. 'I wouldn't put it past the confounded woman to steal in here if I fall asleep to take your place, so she can boast she sat by her employer day and night when she applies for her next post.'

As if she would be so mercenary. Arrogant, un-feeling wretch—he would never believe she had loved wonderful, complicated Lady Virginia Win-terley very deeply. He was always on the lookout for a base motive, a different sin to visit on her, as if she might have sprouted horns and a tail when he wasn't looking.

'Now then, Master Luke, you're being unjust. That girl loved her ladyship and would have done almost anything for her.'

'Except go away,' he raised his voice just enough to grumble so she couldn't fail to hear him.

Chloe flinched and wondered how he knew she

couldn't bring herself to leave when Lady Virginia breathed her last, before he got here. Bracing herself against the fact he wanted her gone, she made herself walk away noisily enough to let him know he could say whatever he liked and she didn't care.

Back in her room, she wished it as many rooms as possible from where Lord Farenze was taking the last vigil at his great-aunt's side. To be within call if her mistress needed her, Chloe was using an odd little bedchamber over the grand gallery that only unimportant guests were ever given, because the high ceiling of the room below meant the floor of this one was raised on a minor staircase with three other cramped chambers. It had been convenient to stay close to Lady Virginia's lofty suite, until now. So why hadn't she moved back to her modest room a floor up and at the back of the house as soon as Lord Farenze had set foot in Farenze Lodge? She hadn't known Verity would be home then and marvelled at herself for being so foolish as to stay within shouting distance of the state rooms now.

It was too late to change even if Verity hadn't arrived so much in need of a good night's sleep, so she yawned and hoped for a dreamless sleep against the odds. She had more to disturb her than ever, but after a soft tap came on the door, Cully opened it a half-inch on her invitation to enter.

'Are you decent, dear?' she whispered.

'Aye,' Chloe admitted with a half-smile at herself in the dimly visible mirror that said it was as well nobody could see into her head. 'Come in, Cully.'

'His lordship says you're to drink this down and I'm to stay until you do,' her old friend told her sternly.

Chloe sniffed the fumes coming from the steaming mug she held out and caught a hint of camomile, a waft of cinnamon and some honey to sweeten it all and decided there was nothing in it to worry her, even if such a mild concoction was unlikely to make her sleep soundly tonight.

'Very well,' she said with a resigned shrug. She knew that resolute expression of Cully's of old and didn't feel like a battle to resist her at the moment.

'I'll sit here until you're finished then go to bed myself. My lady is in safe hands and would be the first to tell us to get to bed and show some sense.'

'I know, but you're the last person I need to tell how hard it is to be sensible at a time like this,' Chloe said with a sigh as she paused her drinking and earned a frown. 'If I drink any faster, I'll choke,' she excused herself.

'I suppose so, but his lordship is right. You look as if a strong gust of wind could blow you into next week.'

'Kind of him,' Chloe retorted ruefully.

'He *is* a kind man, child, if only you would see it. You two bring out the worst in each another, but Master Luke was a good-hearted, gallant lad before that silly girl nagged and flouted him until he hardly knew which way was up any more.'

'He's hardly a lad now, or very gallant.'

'No, he's a man nowadays and a fine-looking one at that.'

Chloe distrusted the sly glance her old friend was shooting her. Cully knew her a little too well, after ten years of service in the same house. So, if the elderly ladies' maid knew she was deeply attracted to her gallant lad, who else might have their suspicions she wouldn't leave Farenze Lodge as heart-whole as a sober and respectable house-keeper should?

Chloe shook her head and carefully ignored that truth as she swallowed the last of Cully's brew. She felt as if she was back in the nursery herself when

Cully unpinned her tightly bound locks and gently combed them out, but the deft touch soothed her as the potion hadn't yet managed to.

'There, is that better?' Cully asked as she brushed Chloe's heavy locks into a burnished red-gold mass.

'Aye,' Chloe admitted with a long sigh. 'You're very good at your job, Cully,' she murmured when she felt the silken thickness gathered into the elderly maid's hand and separated into three as Cully began a loose plait.

'And you have beautiful hair, Mrs Chloe,' the maid told her with a hint of sternness in her voice. 'A good many ladies would give their eye-teeth for such a colour and it's so fine and thick they would be green with envy if they ever saw it. You shouldn't screw it into such a tight knot. It's not good for it and small wonder if you have the head-ache after going about with all those pins skewered into it all day.'

'If I don't, it keeps trying to escape.'

'And a very good thing if it succeeded, if you ask me,' she thought she heard Cully mumble under her breath, but looking up she found the older woman was looking back at her in the mirror with such a look of bland innocence she told herself she must have been mistaken. 'There you are, you're all ready for bed and make sure you stay there till you're rested in the morning. Martha Lange's quite capable of getting breakfast cooked without you there to tell her how to coddle an egg and that head housemaid you set such store by can set the maids to work for once.'

'Yes, Miss Culdrose, ma'am,' Chloe said with a mock salute and was brusquely told not to be impudent before Cully wished her a dignified goodnight and went off to spend a full night in her own bed for the first time in weeks as well.

At first it was the most wonderful dream. Chloe shifted under the smooth linen sheets to murmur approval in her sleep. Luke was here, kissing her and doing all the things she had longed for him to do all these years. She had sent him away and told him she could imagine nothing more humiliating than being his mistress all those years ago, but she'd lied. In her unchecked fantasy he was indeed Luke and not Lord Farenze and he kissed her as if the next beat of his heart depended on her kissing him back.

She writhed against her hot pillow and keened a protest as a dash of reality beat in and she knew the hands running over her excited curves in the heat of the night were her own and not the firm, male touch her body truly longed for, as if it had found its ideal long ago and had no intention of letting the idea of him go, ever.

She wanted him, wanted him here and now and in her bed, in her. Even in her deepest sleep, her cheeks flushed with even more heat at the very thought of such emphatic possession as she knew his would be. Then the part of her that longed for him all the time she was trying to forget took over and wrenched that spectre lover back into her bed. He followed her impatient hands with kisses, tracked merciless trails of slick heat over her sensitised skin, pressed questing fingertips into the places she most wanted them to explore and she gasped in pleasure, at last.

In her dreams he was hers as surely as she was his, so why wake up to cold reality? Her unconscious self conspired with her inner wanton to revel in their heat and closeness and her body tingled and writhed and strove for something more against the heavy bedclothes and the depths of the long night. *He's here!* The words seemed to have been whispered, as if he truly was with her in every way there was between lovers. Doubt invaded even her imaginary idyll as soon as she felt they were not alone in this dream of fulfilment she had given herself, though.

Even as her phantom lover reared over her to feast his hungry mouth on her waiting lips and sink his mighty, roused body blissfully into her longing depths to complete them as lovers, she heard a voice from beyond the grave whisper, 'No, no, don't let him love you like that. Never love a man, Chloe. Look where love got me. Push him out of your heart, keep him out of your body and never, *ever* let yourself love him,' it ended on a wail, as pain took a deeper hold and the pale ghost sliced a dead and icy hand down on dream Luke's warm neck and he vanished like smoke on the wind.

Chloe's dreams landed her back into a cold, windswept wreck of a house high on the moors where nobody went unless they had to and even then they came away crossing themselves as if they'd met the devil at the back door. She writhed against the cooling sheets in terrified protest as images flashed through her sleep like the torn black of mourning weeds, weathered to faded shreds of their midnight prime.

There was blood, so much blood, and Chloe began to whimper in her sleep. The unending awfulness of the time and tragedy of that forsaken place bit into her. However hard she tried to clean the gore up she couldn't wash it away and into her terrifying dream flashed images of a fragile young woman laid out pale and cold on the narrow, mean bed as love leeched out of that wretched house and grief rolled in to replace it like the dense cloud hanging over the wintry moor.

Then she was back to the following December day, winds beating savage and remorseless on the tiny windows until even the stout shutters shivered and shifted against the threat of it as if they might break open. The younger Chloe wept and over the roar of the wind came the relentless slash of rain, beating on the narrow windows as if it wanted to drown every last breath of life in this place where only wind and rain should rule and people didn't belong.

Now she desperately needed Luke and he wasn't there. He faded and forsook her when she drifted back to a time when there was no Luke to tempt and tantalise her, only a howling and an empty stretch of pain inside that seemed to go on for ever. Then the storm softened and grew less with every breath and instead of tempest outside there was one within determined to give her no peace. A howl rose high and demanding as the child she'd done her best to forget refused to be comforted, or to sleep when there was no solace to be had here. The baby's enraged cries beat louder and louder on her poor ears until they filled her whole world. Young Chloe wanted it to die, too, if that would make it stop. The woman she became wanted to shake the girl so she forgot her selfish woe and got on with the life that came out of all that pain.

'No, don't take her with you!' she woke screaming and shot upright in the bed, trembling and sobbing. The coils of that terrible dream still wrapped round her, she began to rock as she tried to fight her way back to now and tell herself it wasn't true.

'Whatever is it? Who frightened you?' a gruff demand came out of the night as the door creaked open and she hadn't breath enough to reassure anyone she was perfectly all right, let alone him. 'What the devil is it?' Lord Farenze barked.

He pushed the door to behind himself and set

his candle in the nightstick to peer more closely at the tousled wreckage of her once neat bed and the shivering wild woman staring back at him with all the terrors of the night in her eyes.

Some detached part of her knew she was behaving like a ninny, but she couldn't wave away the terror that still made her heartbeat race and her breath gasp between parched lips as if she had just finished running a mile in her dreams.

Luke was glad he had sense left to listen for the sound of anyone else stirring, not sure if he was glad or sorry when he didn't hear it. His daughter and Bran were too weary from their journey to wake easily and nobody else was within earshot.

'A dream,' she finally managed to gasp as if even that cost her dear.

'I never heard one like it then, even in Eve's wildest nightmares,' he said and did what he'd wanted the moment she looked up at him with terror in her eyes; took her in his arms and dared the devil to do his worst.

'Cry it out,' he encouraged, feeling helpless against the fear still ruling her.

Eve was about six years old when some fool told

her the truth about her mother's death, dashed to oblivion at the bottom of a mountain road after a wild race to some would-be poet's latest party only a fool would embark on in winter. He spared a moment from the feel of Chloe shivering in his arms to be glad Eve was over her night horrors and now slept soundly of a night.

For a long moment Chloe felt stiff and resistant in his arms then, with a great heartfelt sigh, she squirmed closer with a ragged sob she tried to stifle against his shoulder, as if she wasn't allowed the luxury of tears. No storm of feminine hysterics could disarm him more. He could feel the shudders that still racked her body and the hand he rubbed across her slender back was meant to comfort. She stilled as if remembering who he was, then seemed unable to fight the security of another being close enough to push away her nightmares. Giving in to her need for human contact for once, she moulded herself against him so intimately her head rested on his shoulder and he felt the impact of her closeness through several layers of fine tailoring.

Feminine heat cindered all the distance he'd tried to put between them. The scent of warm, frightened woman teased his nose along with stray wisps of fiery gold hair that escaped the heavy plait down her back. She shivered and he reassembled the sense to recall it was January. Wrapping her in the bedcover, he murmured a promise not to leave her as he crossed to the fireplace and set his candle to the fire laid there. He must have words with her in the morning about why, when every other chamber on this floor had a fire to warm it, hers was as cold as charity.

Once flames were licking about the pine cones and sea coal, he went to the bed and picked her up, bedcover and all. It said much for her emotional state that she let him and still seemed to be staring sightlessly into some dire fate with horror in her wide eyes. He carried her to an old-fashioned chair banished from a more important bedchamber. *You might as well sleep in a lumber room,* Luke silently chided the shivering woman, then sat down with her in his arms, covering and all.

Despite a half-hearted shake of her head she clearly didn't want him to go. She tucked a slender foot into his side to warm it when the bedcover slipped and it felt more intimate than a week of passionate lovemaking in another woman's bed. *Steady,* he ordered his inner fool; *she doesn't see*

you as a rampant male, but a source of comfort.
You could be anyone.

'If you refuse to cry it out, at least tell me what frightened you,' he urged and felt her squirm in protest at the thought of giving so much of her inner life away. He fought his predictable male response to the slide of supple feminine curves against his over-eager body and hoped she was too deep in shock to notice. 'No? Then I'll puzzle it out for myself, shall I?' he suggested softly against the ear she hadn't snuggled into his shoulder and felt her flinch.

She shook her head a fraction in denial and he heard her breath hitch, as if she wanted to scold him for bad-mannered prying into her private life, but couldn't quite manage it, so she wriggled even closer instead.

'I presume my arrival roused a fine nest of vipers in your clever, contrary head to upset you so deeply,' he murmured into that tempting ear and thought she managed a muffled 'no' to deny it. 'I don't think I'm unduly vain to suspect I'm the reason you dreamt so vividly,' he persisted.

'No,' she protested more distinctly, so he knew he was right.

Although they had sworn never to kiss or long for each other again on a night of almost love they had shared a decade ago, this unwanted, ill-starred connection between them refused to die.

'Yes, madam, you did,' he persisted, 'you very likely cause yourself to dream even more vividly by denying this feeling between us so fervently when you're awake. So that explains why you dreamt, but not what. Not even the way we don't want to feel about each other explains *why* you scream out in your sleep, then look as if all the devils of hell are on your heels the moment you wake.'

Chapter Seven

That was it then; the frustrated desire of ten years finally said and in the open. Luke waited for Chloe's reply, resigned to the fact she mattered to him more than either of them wanted to admit—except he just had.

'I've had nightmares night after night since Virginia died,' she admitted as if living with them was better than feeling something unique for him.

'Why?'

The story behind her arrival must be even more painful than he'd thought. Luke willed his hands not to fist when he thought of the rogue who got a child on her, then left her to cope alone. Back then he'd told himself it was best not to know her story when he felt so damned guilty she was trying to build a respectable life and he wanted to ruin her more thoroughly than the rake who found her first.

'Do you think you're the only one to see love as a disaster?' she demanded, but he knew a diversionary tactic when he heard one.

'I thought you adored your reckless, headlong husband and regretted every minute of your life you must live without him? That's what you told me when you whistled my dishonourable proposals down the wind.'

'And you *believed* me?'

'You were very convincing.'

'Of course I was; it was a dishonourable proposal.'

'Surely you didn't expect me to offer marriage?' he demanded unwarily.

She stiffened as if about to jump up and glare at him with her usual armed disapproval. 'No,' she admitted with a sigh instead. She must be too comfortable or too much in need of human comfort to push him away, but she sat up in his arms and stared into the fire instead. 'I learnt not to expect much of anyone the day Verity was born. There was nobody left to care what became of us.'

'Then she was truly a posthumous child?' he asked gently, wanting to know about the man who left her with child, but feeling he was intruding on girlish dreams that might feel very private even if they'd rapidly turned into nightmares.

'Yes, Verity only had me.'

The admission was bleak and he bit back his frustration at having to prise information out of her like a miner hewing coal. 'Could neither family help you?'

'No,' she denied as if it hurt even now.

Luke felt she had a storm of emotions behind the calm she was forcing herself to hold as if her life depended on it. They seemed so much nearer the surface now he wanted to take the heavy weight off her shoulders, then put her world right. He wanted to protect her so badly, yet she insisted on shutting him out. This contrary, complicated woman was making him a stranger to himself.

'Did you ask them?'

'Not then,' she bit out and somehow he managed to stifle a curse that she still wouldn't let him into her true past or trust him with her real self.

'Had they refused earlier?'

'It was a runaway match,' she said so blankly he suspected she was telling him a well-rehearsed version of what might be the truth, but didn't feel like it.

'They might be glad to meet their grandchild now.'

'I'd walk barefoot across Britain or beg in the streets before I let them near her.'

It sounded as if unforgivable things had been said or done when she was so painfully young, alone and vulnerable. Fury burnt in his gut that anyone could treat a young girl so harshly that she never wanted to see them again. Conscience whispered he'd treated her pretty appallingly himself by offering *carte blanche* to such a youthful widow with a tiny child to consider.

Shame joined fury then; it wasn't Chloe's fault his wife smashed a young man's dreams to powder, or that he was too wrapped up in not hurting to risk having any more. The revelation that he truly cared for this woman as he never had for Pamela, even before they married and hurt each other so much, overtook him with the force of a natural disaster. It felt as if the real Luke Winterley had woken from hibernation. He flexed powerful muscles against an almost physical ache and wished he'd go back to sleep.

'I'm not saying you should,' he managed to say as he gathered up the threads of their not-quite conversation and reminded himself he was rated a very fine whip by the sporting set and ought to be able to do this a lot better.

'I wouldn't do it if you did,' she said scornfully.

'And I couldn't ask you to do something that went so strongly against the grain. We mean too much to each other for that; like it or not.'

'I'm sure you underestimate our will-power, Lord Farenze,' she said icily, as if not ready to make a similar leap into the dark.

'Maybe I do. I still intend to find out why you were driven to take this job to keep yourself and your daughter out of the poor house.'

'Then how dared you use me as entertainment for an idle moment?'

Luke felt oddly wounded she thought so little of him, but he couldn't leave her to lie sleepless or tumble back into night terrors.

'I would not dream of it and we're talking about you and your daughter, not my many and varied shortcomings.'

'No, we're not. Please go to bed and leave me to watch by Virginia one last time, my lord. You must sleep if you're going to be chief mourner at your great-aunt's funeral. I have had my fill of sleeping for now and really don't want to experience that nightmare again tonight.'

Luke opened his mouth to deny he felt the least need to rest, but a huge yawn stopped him. 'I'm not a nodding infant,' he insisted brusquely afterwards.

'No, you're a stubborn man who rode here as fast as coach and horses could go in order to be in time for your great-aunt's funeral. What good you will be for that if you're nodding over your duties is beyond me, but I'm only the housekeeper, so who am I to tell you not to be a fool?'

'It never stopped you in the past,' he muttered crossly.

'Oh, just go to bed, my lord. As a mere woman, I'm not required to put in an appearance until after you return from church tomorrow, so I can sleep in the morning. You owe it to Lady Virginia to be properly awake and aware for her last rites.'

Luke saw the logic of her words, but couldn't let go his duty to care for all those who lived under one of his roofs. His housekeeper would be heavy eyed and weary tomorrow if he did as she suggested. The idea of her keeping watch when he should be the one to hold his loved ones safe also made him feel as if he was less of a man, foolish though that might be.

Still, it seemed as if she preferred waking to sleeping and didn't that betray how haunted and disturbing her nightmares truly were? He longed to offer her simple comfort and scout her demons, so she might sleep sweetly and wake without the shadows under her remarkable eyes. Folly to find it touching that she appeared to care he was tired, despite the dagger-look she shot him, as if he'd made her another dishonourable offer.

'How can I let you take on a duty rightly belonging to me?' he said clumsily.

'Mere servant as I am?' she bit out furiously.

Luke wondered if he'd imagined her burrowing so desperately into his arms when he came to this room to find out why she was shouting in her sleep and why his tongue always tied itself in knots when he was with her.

'No, because you have done more for my greataunt than anyone had a right to ask you; not that I'm suggesting you can't withstand every tempest life throws at you, so don't bite my nose off,' he argued and wondered why his temper wasn't rising to her barbed comments this time.

He was weary to his very bones, but he knew she was trying to get him out of here before heat and awareness flared back to life. In some ways he knew her so well it hurt, in others she felt as much of a mystery to him as she was the first day he laid eyes on his great-aunt's new companion–housekeeper and felt his world tilt on its axis for a terrifying moment.

'If you watch for an hour or so, I will lie on the bed in the Lord's Chamber with the connecting door open. It's been locked since Virgil died and nobody will recall it's there at a time like this. That way you won't be alone and I'll feel more of a man.'

She looked unconvinced, but eventually nodded and seemed prepared to accept a compromise to end this uncomfortable intimacy. 'I loved Lady Virginia too much in life to be frightened now she's with her Virgil again at last. I'll miss her all my days, but she wouldn't want to live without him any longer than she had to. So please take yourself off whilst I dress, my lord.'

'Very well, my lady,' he said with a bow he might give to the equal in rank she suddenly sounded.

'Exasperating man,' she muttered as he left the

room to wait in the cramped little corridor over the nobly proportioned room below.

Out in the dark, Luke fought a battle between physical tiredness and feelings he didn't want to examine. He'd wanted to stay in that neglected room and feel her sleep in his arms. It shocked him to feel so much for the contrary mixture of a woman Chloe had grown into. He'd tried to convince himself for years only his daughter was allowed under his guard and into his heart, but right now it looked like a battle lost.

'What are you doing here?' she demanded in a fierce whisper as she came out of her room and nearly cannoned into him in the gloom.

'Waiting for you,' he managed suavely.

He saw something in the depths of her dark eyes when her candle wavered in her shaking hands that said he wasn't the only one fighting his feelings tonight. He forced himself not to grin like a triumphant boy.

'Well, don't,' she said crossly.

He raised his eyebrows and let some of the passion he felt for her show as their eyes met.

'Verity is ten years old, my lord, and has a right to all I am. I won't accept a lover when my daughter would be harmed by association, so waiting for me to do so will only waste your time and energy you need for the obligations ahead of you.'

'I'm here to escort you to Virginia's bedchamber.'

'Where I don't belong,' she said to herself as much as him.

'Where you will be doing me a favour I should not permit, considering you're so tired yourself,' he corrected.

'I didn't ride all the way from Northumberland in the depths of winter.'

'And I wasn't here to nurse Virginia through her last illness, but if we're not to be caught in a tryst and forced into wedlock, Mrs Wheaton, it's about time we quit this draughty corridor and got on with all that needs doing.'

Chloe sniffed a very expressive sniff of reproach, yet something else lurked behind her coolly composed look. The thought of what Virginia would make of them standing here like a pair of star-crossed lovers unwilling to say goodnight hung unspoken in the air between them and made him flinch.

His beloved but infuriating great-aunt would be

planning their wedding before one more late and reluctant January dawn had passed. Virginia usually opposed misalliances and a viscount and a housekeeper were one of those many times over, but something told him she would have been delighted if they ever found the courage to defy convention and wed. So what did Virginia know about the woman he didn't?

'I am going to sit with my beloved late employer and friend and you are going to sleep, my lord, and that is all,' Chloe said sternly and he let her lead the way while he struggled with puzzlement and weariness and did as he was bid for once in his life.

The next morning was bright and frosty with a sky as clear and delicate a blue as the flower of a mountain harebell. Chloe finished drying her hair by the fire Lord Farenze had ordered to be lit in her room and told herself she hadn't really needed the bath he ordered after she spent half the night nodding in a comfortable chair in the late viscountess's bedchamber. Even so, it felt good to be clean and new vitality sparked through her along with the crackle of electricity in her heavy auburn hair. She really ought to have it cut, but it had been easier and cheaper to let it grow so ridiculously long she could sit on it when it hung down her back.

It seemed wrong she should feel vital and alive, today of all days, and she looked at the frosty scene outside the window and let herself be sad Virginia wasn't here to see the rolling hillsides wrapped in sparkling crystal, or the dark bare branches of the trees in the wood that couldn't quite hide the brave snowdrops flowering in the sheltered hollows. She almost heard the words as if Virginia put them straight in her heart.

Don't mourn me, Chloe; after sixteen years without my love we'll never be apart again.

If she took that last piece of advice she could glory in the morning and forget the future until the funeral was over and the will read. Impatient of the last damp strand of hair, she wound it into the heavy knot she usually confined it to, but left out some of the pins that would have screwed it back from her face and made it possible to wear the all-enveloping housekeeper's bonnet she'd bought herself behind Virginia's back.

Today she'd restricted herself to the frivolous piece of lawn and lace her late mistress had reluctantly allowed became a companion and let herself be the girl who shared Virginia's lonelier years again. She recalled her employer saying she wanted bright faces about her, not a death's head got up to fright babies when Verity took one look at her mama in her first all-enveloping cap and burst into tears.

Mrs Winterley would send her a hard-eyed glare for being a housekeeper got up as a lady today, but Chloe owed Virginia one last glimpse of the light-hearted girl she would have had her be, if she could spoil her and Verity as she wanted. There would be little enough cause to be anyone but her mature and sensible self once she took a post in another household.

She tiptoed down the secondary staircase the architect ordered for less important visitors lodged in her corridor of this grand house and wondered who she was being quiet for. Lord Farenze was up and being his usual lordly self, Miss Eve Winterley was downstairs and Verity had begged to be allowed an early morning ride with the grooms, before anyone else was awake to forbid it on this solemn day.

'Mr Filkin says horses need exercise whatever the day brings and I might as well help with the ponies as lie a-bed fretting,' she reported when she came in to ask if she could go and change into her habit.

'Be sure to come back by the nursery stairs though, love. I doubt his lordship's stepmama would approve of you careering about the countryside today.'

'She's an old misery and his lordship won't listen to her,' Verity claimed confidently and Chloe wondered how Luke Winterley had made such a favourable impression on her daughter in such a short time.

She felt beleaguered; the indoor staff adored him; the stable boys and grooms were always full of tales about his horsemanship and now Verity appeared very ready to admire him as well. He sounded as if he'd been reckless and outrageously lucky to live through most of the incidents she'd heard related and she frowned and wondered what manner of man he'd be now if he hadn't made such a disastrous early marriage. A happy one, she decided gloomily.

She snatched up the old cloak she kept in the flower room and stepped out into the winter sunshine to escape the house and her duties for a few precious moments. How unworthy of her to find the idea of Lord Farenze happily wed and content with his wife depressing, rather than wishing him better luck next time.

'Dratted man,' she muttered under her breath as she marched towards the Winter Garden. 'Why does he have to disturb me so deeply?' she asked the statue of some god among the frost-rimed box and the few brave winter flowers hiding their heads under frozen leaves this morning. 'For years he pretends I don't exist, now he's back and I'm wasting time dreaming about him all over again.'

The statue stared into the parkland as if silently slumbering winter trees made more sense than she did and Chloe suppressed a childish urge to kick him.

'Men!' she informed it, glad nobody could hear her. 'You vex women with your ridiculous arguments, pretend logic and stupid longings, then you swat us aside like annoying insects and walk away. How the devil does the contrary great idiot expect me to carry on as if nothing happened now? Does he think we can act as if he never saw me sitting in that bed staring at him like a besotted schoolgirl or came to rescue me from my nightmares? Oh, I'm sorry, you're a man, aren't you? Or at least you would be if you were real. Then you'd huff and puff like the rest of them and drive us all mad before you stamped off to roam about the country shooting innocent animals or riding your poor horses into the ground until you felt better.'

'He might do, if he wasn't made of stone,' Luke Winterley's deep voice said from far too close for comfort and Chloe refused to turn round and blush at being caught talking to a piece of stone. 'Otherwise you would probably be quite right, of course.'

'You should still be asleep,' she told him crossly.

'Lucky I'm not then, for this would be the oddest dream I've ever had,' he told her with a lazy grin.

She wanted to walk into his arms and kiss him good morning so badly she had to swing away and march down the nearest path away from him to stop herself doing exactly that.

'What are you doing?' he asked, following and putting out a hand to prevent her walking straight into a sacking-shrouded potted plant the gardeners had wrapped up for winter.

'I'm counting to a hundred,' she told him between clenched teeth.

'Isn't it supposed to be ten?'

'With you ten is never enough.'

'Oh dear, that bad, am I?'

'Worse,' she bit out.

She would *not* turn round at the warm rumble of his laughter; refused to feel warmed and soothed into good humour because she'd amused him at this saddest of times. Half of her might want to be in his arms so badly she could almost feel his warmth and strength wrapping her up again; more than half if she was honest, but dishonesty was safer.

'Leave me be, my lord.'

'No, you spend far too much time alone already,' he said impatiently, as if it was her fault her role in his household demanded a certain aloofness of her.

'And you shut yourself up in that northern fortress of yours years ago and did your best to pretend the rest of the world doesn't exist, so you have no room to talk.'

'We're lone souls with much in common then, but I didn't walk away from the danger we posed each other then in order to take advantage of you today.'

'I'm sure you're a man of infinite honour, my lord.'

'No, but I fight my demons as best I can; something you should consider before you provoke me again, madam.'

'*I* provoke *you*?'

'Yes, you should have the sense to realise you're always in acute danger when I'm about, Mrs Wheaton, yet you seem determined to court it.'

'You're the one with a large house, acres of garden and an entire estate to avoid *me* in. I don't see how you can berate me for taking a brief walk within hailing distance of the house? In your shoes I could use my freedom to simply walk away.'

'Marching about in front of the windows of a room you know I always work in when I'm at Farenze Lodge is *not* disturbing me then? Did I not give you fair warning this could happen if you teased me instead of avoiding me like the plague?,' he rasped and tugged her into his arms as if she'd driven him to it.

'Let me go, you barbarian,' she snapped, but he lowered his head and met her eyes with a storm of fury and need in his that mirrored the argument raging between her heart and head and making her feel recklessly susceptible to his nearness.

'Stop me,' he demanded gruffly, so close she felt a warm whisper on her skin.

Chapter Eight

Chloe knew Lord Farenze would leave her alone if she breathed *no* or flinched away. Yet she couldn't say it, or take that step back. His mouth on hers was gentle as a plea and she waited for him to remember he was kissing the housekeeper and retreat in horror. She had to breathe at last and he followed the winter air into her mouth as if he was starving for her. Heat flooded every inch of her body and mind as his lips and tongue explored her mouth in sensual wonder.

Needs she had fought for so long clamoured and fidgeted to let a decade of frustration and loneliness go. She swayed into his arms and opened her mouth even as sensible Chloe whispered she was a fool. Somehow the slight shake in his touch freed some last curb on her conscience and she felt him test her narrow waist, banding her closer to the difference and heat of him, narrow flanked and broad shouldered as he was against her curves and unable to conceal how badly he wanted, no, needed her.

Intrigued by such wild heat, despite the frigid January air and this saddest of days, she felt every pore and whisper come uniquely alive to him. Senses sharpened as if they'd slept since that last kiss so long ago. She wanted to strip off her tight tan gloves and feel this exceptional man under her naked touch. Doing her best to add the soft covering to her senses instead, she brushed a finger along his high cheekbone and wherever he felt the butterfly touch of fine leather on taut skin a flush of hard colour tracked her fingers. Shocked by her own boldness, she rose on tiptoe and rested her hands on his broad shoulders so she could watch him more closely, more intimately. For these few seconds outside time he was hers and she was his.

His coat was frost chilly where they'd had no contact, yet where their bodies strove to meld no cold could reach them. They had an antidote to winter and who would guess so much heat was pent up between gruff Lord Farenze and his coolly composed housekeeper?

He moved his hands up from her waist to cup a shamefully hot and responsive breast under her layers of winter disguise and the sweet novelty of his long-remembered touch, real again on her eager body, made her heart leap and her stomach fall into that familiar burning longing only he could stir in her. She gave a low moan as need ground at her insides like hot knives and heated her inner core with impossible promises.

Shocked by her own need of him, she pulled back far enough to watch him and hotly unanswerable questions flashed into his grey gaze and echoed her own. He'd focused too much formidable attention on her at last, given too much away to snatch it back and pretend they were nothing to each other, hadn't he? This was the real Luke Winterley, the passionate man behind Lord Farenze's cold exterior and reclusive reputation. She felt too much for that man and she was opening her mouth to ask questions neither of them wanted to know when the return of the riding party sounded on the clear air and let Chloe's real life back in with a sickening thump and a deep breath of icy January air. She tugged free of Lord Farenze's arms and faced him with all she shouldn't feel in her eyes.

'I can't,' she gasped. 'Neither of us can,' she told him sadly, then hurried off towards the stable yard and her beloved daughter before Luke could argue.

'I quite agree, Mrs Wheaton,' Luke muttered to the January air. 'So what the devil have you done to me this time, my conundrum-in-petticoats?'

No point trying to sit and work on the letters of sympathy and solutions to estate matters now. All he'd see out of the window now was an image of himself, tangled so tight in kissing Virginia's protégé he'd forgotten where, when and what they were. He couldn't settle for the ordeal ahead and hardly knew how to live in his own skin without Chloe to remake him every time he set eyes on her.

The very thought of her as she was just now set his pulses jumping and his manhood rigid with need. Yet she was Virginia's housekeeper-cum-companion; a lady already burned by the chilling harshness the world showed those who fell from grace; a woman who'd wed recklessly, then found herself alone with a babe to support when she should have been in the schoolroom herself.

Recalling her list of activities for crass males, Luke wished he *could* ask for a hack to be saddled and ride for hours to avoid longing for more unsuitable meetings with the Farenze Lodge house-keeper. No, there could be no more of those and it was high time he turned his mind to the sad and solemn occasion ahead of him.

If he'd had his way they would celebrate Virginia's long life and the fact she was reunited with her beloved Virgil, instead of mourning the passing she had begun to long for of late. Instead, he was chief mourner at a solemn funeral and must hide his grief as best he could for the sake of those who looked to him as head of the family and master of the house and estate.

His great-uncle's will left his wife only a life-time tenure on the house they had built so lovingly between them with ultimate ownership going to Luke. He'd been too wound up in baby Eve and playing down the chaos Pamela had raised on the Continent when Virgil died to take much notice, but lately he'd tried to discuss the future of Farenze Lodge with Virginia and got nowhere even faster than usual.

'Virgil left you this house and estate to save me having people constantly badgering me to leave it elsewhere,' Virginia told him.

'But why me?' he asked. 'James might change if

he had an estate of his own. You have told me he needs to be his own man.'

'Let me worry about James,' she said mysteriously, 'you're the only man we wanted living here after us, Luke. You love and understand it as we did, so enjoy it as a holiday from that grim barrack you live in most of the year. You can retreat here when the rigours of Darkmere become too great for your wife.'

'I don't have a wife, nor shall I until Eve is wed,' he replied, meeting her level gaze steadily to show her he meant it and there was no point scheming to pair him off with some hopeful young lady she might have handy before then.

'One day you'll have to take that armour off and learn to be happy,' she had replied with a knowing smile he didn't want to question, so he shrugged and accepted their decision, since he could hardly do otherwise now the deed was done.

And now the whole world seemed to be conspiring against his long-held plan to find a convenient wife once Eve was old enough to marry. Virginia, Eve and even Tom Banburgh seemed to think he ought to wed for something warmer than mere convenience and surely they were all wrong?

'There you are, m'lord,' Josiah Birtkin's bass voice rumbled at him from the doorway leading from the gardens to the stableyard and Luke swore at himself for getting distracted from all he had to cope with today.

'So it would seem,' he replied mildly enough.

'Thought you should know,' Josiah went on as if words had a tax on them.

'Know what?'

'Cross said they was followed back from the gallops just now.'

'Why on earth would anyone follow a schoolgirl?' Luke mused.

'Don't know, m'lord.'

'Have you any idea who it was?'

'No, he stayed well back. Cross thought it was his fancy to start with.'

Luke frowned even more darkly at the thought of Chloe's daughter as quarry. 'It makes no sense,' he muttered and Josiah shrugged as if nothing his fellow humans did made much of that. 'Where is he now?' Luke asked, resolving to confront the rogue and demand what he was about.

'Rode off when they got back to the paddocks, and, since he managed to look as if he was on his way somewhere else, nobody thought to challenge him.'

'And you saw him close up, I hope?'

'No, he was some way off by the time Cross mentioned him and had his hat pulled down over his eyes and a scarf over his mouth.'

'It's a cold day and a traveller might cover up against it, I suppose.'

And why trail a schoolgirl back to Farenze Lodge when a few casual questions would reveal her mother was only housekeeper here? And why would Verity Wheaton's location matter to anyone but her mother, after all the years when nobody outside the household took any notice of either of them?

'His beast had some Arab in him though, m'lord, and if the man wasn't dressed like a farmer I'd have to call him a gentleman.'

'Keep a lookout for him and I'll have the watch doubled at night. If Miss Wheaton or my daughter ride out again, please make sure you or Seth stay with them and go armed, Josh, just in case,' Luke ordered with a frown. 'Be discreet about it; the fewer people who know the better since I don't want panic breaking out, or the man scared off before we find out what he's up to.'

'Trust me not to blab,' Josiah said, looking offended anyone might think he could, let alone Luke who'd known him since he was set on his first pony at Darkmere while still in short coats.

'Aye, of course I do,' Luke said with a wry grin and sent him back to the stables with orders to keep an eye on those who came and went on what would be a busy day for them all.

Luke intended to catch the man haunting Verity Wheaton and challenge him, so why was a prickle of apprehension sliding down his spine like ice water? He didn't know the girl, had only set eyes on her a few times since she was a baby. Yet Eve had taken to her instantly and Chloe adored her, so how could he not be furious at any man who might try to harm or bother the child?

He would feel so about any girl, he reassured himself, and it was probably true, given the appalling hazards that could stalk a child as distinctive as Verity Wheaton. She had her own version of the striking colouring he found so irresistible in her mother. Her hair was closer to blonde and her eyes a paler blue than her mother's stormy ones, but they shared the same fine-boned build and heart-shaped faces; the same fierce intelligence as well, he suspected, and some of the mother's stubborn will and pride had been passed on to her child, if Verity's determination to be with her mother at this sad time was any indication.

Luke frowned and decided he must make time to ask Chloe about Verity's father sooner than he wanted to. Until then he'd trust Josiah's sharp eyes and Eve's company as well as his own vigilance to keep the child safe while her mother was managing his house and seemed barely to have time to eat, let alone sleep soundly.

A few hours later Chloe and the maids stopped work and wrapped themselves up in shawls and mittens before going out on the balustrade roof to watch the funeral cortège wind its way towards the church where the fifth Viscount Farenze was buried. The sombre procession went in and out of sight as it crossed the park and Chloe wished she could attend the service. As she was a female and a housekeeper with a house to prepare for cold and sorry mourners to return to, she bowed her head and recited the Twenty-Third Psalm and the

Lord's Prayer in memory of their beloved mistress and silently wished her ladyship Godspeed with all her heart.

When that was done they watched with tears in their eyes when the horses were taken out of their harness so the male servants and estate workers could drag the sombre rig the last stretch to the church instead. Chloe nearly sobbed as unguardedly as the maids at the sight of such love and devotion to a wonderful woman. She took a deep breath instead and handed out snowy squares of soft cotton and salvaged linen to those who had forgotten their handkerchiefs and hugged Verity close as they said a private goodbye to Lady Virginia.

They stayed in the chilly winter sunshine until a crush of nobility and gentry left the tiny church while the tomb was opened inside and Virginia's closest family and friends saw her laid beside her beloved Virgil. Only then did Chloe order the staff downstairs to get Farenze Lodge ready for the mourners' return and all the rituals of this solemn winter day.

Bran's militant look at her former charge told Chloe she wanted her ewe lamb out of the frigid

January air as urgently as she did Verity, but at that moment a robin began to sing as if its life depended on it from the top of an old holly tree nearby. Neither of them could bring themselves to scold the girls for avoiding the ladies who were gathered about the fire in the grand drawing room sighing and reading their prayerbooks after that. They went downstairs with the echo of that joyful song in their ears, a last serenade to a woman who had always lived life so richly and loved so well.

'I'm glad Lady Virginia made it clear she didn't want a grand formal fuss when she died. Miss Eve will miss her too much to want to play hostess to half the county as if she'd only lost her pet canary, with her being as close to her ladyship as she always was,' Bran observed to Chloe over tea in the housekeeper's room several hours later.

'She did it very well, but she's too young to endure much more formality today and Lady Virginia's real friends know it. By leaving as soon as they decently could they took the rest with them by sheer force of will, which is why they were Lady Virginia's friends in the first place, I suppose,' Chloe replied as she eased her aching feet on to the footstool and blessed the comfort of a fire of her own. The demands of the last few hours seemed to crowd in all over again and she wondered if she'd forgotten some small but vital detail. 'I thought Lady Bunting and the Squire and his wife would never leave, though.'

'And I wondered if that dratted Mrs Winterley would ever stop eating,' Bran said with a grimace.

'But, Bran, "in a well-regulated household there would be more sugar in the plum cake and less salt in the cheese scones",' Chloe parodied the lady wickedly. 'That didn't prevent Mrs Winterley eating vast quantities of both while telling anyone who would listen how prostrated she was by grief.'

'Fat old hypocrite,' Bran said as she lay back in her chair and closed her eyes.

'I can't argue, although I know I should,' Chloe replied as the warmth of the room and her own deep weariness tugged at her conviction she still had a deal to do before she dared try to sleep again. 'You're a bad influence on me, Bran,' she said drowsily.

'Someone needed to be,' her new friend declared and opened her shrewd eyes as if she'd only been pretending to be half-asleep. 'It's high time you learnt to live again, young woman,' she said, as if she could see into Chloe's heart and all the bitter memories she didn't want to face.

'I could say the same about you.'

'I did all the living and loving I ever shall with a man before Miss Eve was born. My Joe is buried at sea on the other side of the world and I'll have no other, but you deserve better than life seems to have handed you so far.'

'No, I don't,' Chloe said shortly, even as a picture of Luke Winterley flitted into her mind, laughing and at ease as nature intended him to be and murmured, *But aren't I better than you imagined in your wildest dreams before you met me?*

'Then perhaps he does,' Bran said.

Chloe's heartbeat had accelerated at the thought of him and the way all the longings she wished she could kill shivered through her body whenever the wretched man was in the same room. It must have shown in her eyes.

'He needs more than I can give,' Chloe said and closed her eyes again in the hope it might put paid to such a painful topic of conversation. All her normal defences felt so weak it was as if her emotions were about to spill over in a disastrous flood.

'More tea?' she asked with a brightness they both knew was false and Bran nodded obligingly and let the painful topic of Mrs Wheaton's feelings for her noble master drop, with a look that said this wasn't the time for an argument, but her new friend would have to confront those feelings sooner or later.

Chloe was glad Mrs Winterley and the other ladies favoured the state rooms as the early January dusk began to darken the skies outside and most of the gentlemen congregated in the billiard room. They couldn't divert themselves with a game on such a day ,but seemed comforted by the idea that Virginia would have told them to forget such flummery and get on with it and most of them were avoiding the drawing room and the low-voiced gossip that was all the ladies could indulge in as dusk came down on this solemn day.

It seemed a good time to place the little vase of snowdrops someone had snatched a moment to gather earlier and she had only now found time to arrange with a few sprigs of wintersweet. The gardeners always forced as many spring flowers as they could to bloom early, since Virginia delighted in the bravest of the spring ones to remind them winter wouldn't last for ever.

Sooner or later she would have to stop behaving as if Virginia might walk into a room and exclaim at such a simple luxury and ask about a gardener's elderly mother, or perhaps his wife being close to her time, when one of them came to hand the flowers over. Chloe thought it a shame to kill off Virginia's routine and make her loss even harder to bear. She did her best not to make things worse than they must already feel when the speechless, grief-stricken head gardener came to the door with this tribute to his employer and old friend and simply nodded her sincere thanks and told him how beautiful and hopeful they seemed in the depths of winter.

'Oh, heavens! I didn't see you there, my lord, but why on earth are you sitting in the dark?' she gasped now, shocked when he rose from the chair by the window where Virginia often sat to catch the best light for her book.

'Because I enjoy sitting in the dark?' he replied wryly, but she heard the flat weariness in his voice and somehow couldn't make herself walk away.

'I doubt it,' she said as her eyes grew accustomed

to the gloom and instinct warned her to plunk the vase down and leave.

'You're right,' he said gruffly and she wondered if he didn't want her to see tears in his supposedly steely gaze when he turned his head away.

'How gratifying for me; good evening, my lord.'

'No, stay,' he asked, again in that rough voice as if he couldn't find the energy to smooth it into any sort of gentlemanly restraint right now.

'You know I can't,' she murmured as she sank on to the chair closest to his and folded her hands to stop them reaching to him as if by right.

'Don't speak of "can't" today.'

'I have to,' she argued, gripping her fingers more tightly together to stop them soothing his lean cheek, or ruffling the stern discipline he'd imposed on his unruly raven locks in his great-aunt's honour.

'Virginia wasn't a great one for rules and conventions,' he replied with tension in his voice that said he wanted human contact, too, even if he hadn't moved since she sat down.

'I imagine she was as determined not to be confined by them as a young woman as she was when I knew her.'

'She was a rogue, or so her sisters said before she outlived them all,' he said with such pride and love for his late great-aunt by marriage in his voice Chloe felt herself melting from the inside out.

'So many people loved her for it that it makes you wonder if being correct and ever ready to criticise, as I remember her sisters being when I first came here, is the way to live a good life after all. They used to visit and sniff and carp at her for simply having me and Verity in the house, let alone employing me as her companion-housekeeper.'

Chloe shifted uncomfortably in her seat as she recalled he'd been almost as critical once he found out about that act of kindness himself, but perhaps he'd decided this wasn't the day to have too good a memory.

'I think when she and Virgil wed, Virginia gave up scandalising society one way, so she was determined to find as many ways of confounding its prejudices in other ones as she could.'

'You think of me as one of her rebellions, then?'

'Perhaps at first—later even I could see that you and your daughter were more to her than a whim to infuriate her sisters and any stuffy neighbours she wanted to annoy. She needed you almost as much as you did her. She would have been an excellent mother and would have doted on any grandchildren who followed in her children's footsteps.'

'Instead she was a wonderful friend and mentor to me and so many others society would like to turn its collective nose up at and ignore.'

'You were not a charity cases, but a good and dear friend to her; allow me that much insight today, even if we must pretend to be enemies again tomorrow.'

'I know, I am sorry,' she said softly.

He smiled at her unguarded apology and they sat in companionable silence for a few wonderful moments, as if they understood each other too well to need words.

'Virginia was the product of another age,' he finally said with a sigh, 'but even she wouldn't have been quite so eager to break the rules if she knew it would reflect back on her progeny.'

'No, I suppose she didn't have a daughter of her own to make those rules real for her. It colours everything when your own reputation affects another's whole life so drastically,' Chloe agreed with a hearty sigh of her own.

'As those girls of ours both changed our lives?'

'Yes.'

'Sooner or later we must talk about it,' he warned.

'No, your daughter is your business; mine is hers and mine alone. We have nothing to discuss, my lord.'

'Yet we must talk about it all the same,' he said as implacably as he could, when he sounded as if grief and weariness were weighing him down too heavily to face a confrontation now.

'Not if I can help it we won't,' she muttered under her breath, but he heard her in the intimate gloom of the dark room. Only a glow from the banked-down fire was left to show them their thoughts and feelings now the light had faded, but when he wanted to he could read her like a book.

'Do you remember the day we first met?' he asked sneakily.

All of a sudden the gloom of a January dusk was gone and they were bathed in summer heat again, her most disreputable bonnet was hanging down her back and his bright, curious gaze sharpened on this new phenomenon tramping her way up his great-aunt's drive.

She had just paid a visit to her little daughter at the wet-nurse's neat cottage on the Farenze Lodge

Estate and she was buoyed up by the hope Verity was finally going to be big enough to come home with her next week. The world seemed a light and happy place that fateful summer day, then she had looked up and met a pair of complicated masculine grey eyes and a fluttery feeling of excitement joined the hope that was rekindling in her after a long winter.

'Where are you going to, my pretty maid?' he'd asked as lightly as if he hadn't a care in the world, for once in his too-responsible life, either.

'I'm off to London to see the Queen,' she'd said, suddenly as giddy as a girl as she tossed her fiery gold curls out of her eyes and refused to regret they were wild and tumbling down her back for once.

'Can I come?' he'd said and that was it, her heart had opened to him. Dark-haired, smiling Viscount Farenze's eyes promised her impossible things as they met as the equals they should have been and were no more.

'Too well,' she admitted sombrely now, the memory of all they should have been to each other in her eyes as she stared into the fire to avoid his.

There were no pictures of unattainable castles in Spain hidden in the complex depths of it. She'd spent ten years convincing that hopeful girl there could be nothing between Viscount Farenze and Verity Wheaton's mother, so how could there be?

'If only things had been different for us, then and now,' she added regretfully and thought she heard a gruff groan, hastily suppressed, at the thought of what could have been, without their daughters and their duty to make it impossible.

'It's time we stopped pretending we're nothing to each other, Mrs Wheaton.'

'No, it's our best protection. My Verity and your Eve will always make it impossible for us to be other than master and servant and you know it. Now, if you'll excuse me, it's been a long day and you must be weary and eager to have it over and done with,' she said with a would-be humble nod.

She could only just see his shadowed face and his white shirt and collar and stark black necktie through the deepening darkness. A lot of her longed for the right to move closer; feel cool linen and hot man under her spread palms; offer him comfort nobody else could give on this sorry day and take some in return. It was a right she'd relinquished the day Verity was born, so she hid her hands in her midnight skirts and waited for the words of dismissal that would set them free of this fiery frustration, for now.

Chapter Nine

'I *am* tired,' Luke Winterley admitted with a sigh, as if it was a weakness he was rightly ashamed of, and tenderness for his manly conviction she had no right to feel threatened to undermine her aloofness.

'Despite your attempts to prove otherwise, you are only human, my lord. You need a proper night's sleep after your hard and hasty journey, last night's vigil and all you have had to endure today,' Chloe replied.

'I haven't enjoyed one of those under this roof from the first day I set eyes on you,' he snapped, as if she was an idiot to suggest he might now.

She'd offered him the only warmth and understanding she decently could and he'd thrown it back at her as if it revolted him, drat the man, but he could stand apart from the rest of humanity with her blessing. 'I will get back to my duties,' she said, snatching back the hand she hadn't known she'd stretched out as if he'd scalded it.

'Before God, woman, I could shake you until your teeth rattle,' he gritted between what sounded like clenched teeth.

'Because I speak sense and keep a cool head? If so, you're a fool.'

'Then let's see how idiotic I can be, shall we? Then maybe next time you will take a warning in the spirit it is meant,' he said in a husky voice and sounded so brusque her mouth twisted in a wobbly smile.

He was my Lord Farenze at his most bearlike and made her feel emotions no other man had ever stirred. Her fingers itched to test his athlete's body and fallen-angel features; to curl themselves into that overlong raven mane of his and tug him down to meet her mouth with his kiss; to discover anew he was as addictive to the touch as to the rest of her senses.

Temptation made her senses flex, stretch and luxuriate in the promise of him. How familiar and seductive and dangerous it was. To be part of something with him was almost as irresistible as the physical fact of him and his ill humour at not being able to freeze her out of his life as he clearly wanted to. Heat flashed through her like sheet lightning; her breathing went shallow as her heartbeat raced and she leaned towards him to…

No! Her body was as wrong now as it was ten years ago. She'd felt such yearning need to be passionately loved back then it was little wonder bitter, guarded, dashingly handsome Lord Farenze unleashed wild dreams in her that ought to be dead and done with. He still could, simply by being here, but her world could never be well lost for love. She had a daughter who must come before him, and her, and everything else in Chloe's life.

Anything that smirched Chloe's reputation would make Verity less in the eyes of the world. Yet every time she fought this battle it was harder, as if this darling bear of a man was wound so tight into her senses she would never be free of the feel and look and touch of him, that faint scent of masculine cologne and Luke Winterley. All of him, gruff and smooth, tender and sharp, was caught into her heart so securely that she only had to scent that cologne to be aware of him as a lover until her dying day.

No, she must win her battle one last time and

then she would be free of temptation for ever. The thought of never seeing him again made tears sting her eyes. How could she not pity herself all the long years with not even the sight of him ahead? A voice whispered, *Giving in to what you both need won't hurt this once,* but it lied.

Never to see him again, never to feel him and his mighty body respond to her after they threw caution to the four winds and indulged in the unimaginable luxury of loving for one short night? Verity had been enough to make her step back and say no before and must keep being so, because one night would never be enough.

'No, my lord, we could make a fine pair of fools of each other together, but I've worked hard to be the respectable woman I am now, despite the gossip and doubts you and so many others had when I came here with a babe in my arms. I can't give in to improper advances from so-called gentlemen like you and waste all that effort now,' she said with a careless smile meant to lessen the tension.

'Do you think me such a rake I might take what isn't freely given?' he demanded, refusing to let her joke them out of something that really wasn't funny. 'I have never chased the maids or tried to sneak kisses from a poor governess who can't fight back and I never will,' he snapped and marched over to glare at the glowing fire as if he couldn't endure being so close any longer.

'I'm sure you're all that's noble, but you're the one who has always insisted I'm in danger of causing gossip and scandal by staying here.'

'You're not a servant,' he snapped.

'Try telling that to your guests, or indeed to the other servants.'

'We both know you've been masquerading as a companion, or a housekeeper, or whatever act you and Virginia settled on to fool the world with. If you were truly born to be even an upper servant, I wouldn't have come near you other than as your employer, but you make it open season for me to hunt down the truth and force you to face it. No, wait and hear me out, woman, I must know who you truly are, before someone else finds you out and we must marry to right your good name.'

'I'd never ask such a sacrifice and stop sorting through my life to divert yourself from your grief. Or is that too much for a housekeeper to ask of a lord?'

Despising herself for the wobble in her voice,

Chloe felt a terrible weariness weigh her down. Resolving to resist him until she rode down the drive for the last time on the carrier's cart with all her luggage was sapping her strength, as even the disturbed nights and dark days they'd suffered here of late had not been able to do. It felt as if a cloud of feathers were falling on her as his concerned voice came and went over the beat of her suddenly thundering heart.

'I'm not sure, but sit down before you fall over,' he barked as he dashed over to scoop her up before she could do exactly that.

After last night she knew how seductive it felt to let someone care for her, to feel his gentle touch on her forehead and lean into his powerful masculine body while she regained her own strength after the weary days while Virginia lay dying. She was tempted to let go and simply allow him to hold the world at bay for her for once.

'I'm quite all right,' she murmured, willing away the faint that would make her weak with the very last man in the world she should be weak with.

'Of course, you're so well you snatch sleep in half-hour parcels and nearly faint from grief and whatever else you're worrying about rather than confide in me. I can see how robust you are, Mrs Wheaton. Rude health is written all over your ashen face and painted under your shadowed eyes.'

'Why not make me feel worse and tell me how haggish I look?' she asked, as if her appearance mattered when her whole world was falling apart once more.

Somehow it did though, when he was the one looking at her. Chloe enjoyed the luxury of meeting his gaze, once he was satisfied she could sit up without his help and he crouched down in front of her so she didn't have to crane her neck. It felt as intimate as when he held her in his arms and did his best to scout her demons last night.

'Can't you see that I need to help you?' he ground out as if it hurt to admit it. 'Whatever we can or can't be to one another, I can't let you wander off into the wide world alone, as if it doesn't matter a jot to me what happens after you leave here.'

'I won't *be* alone,' she protested, his gruff sincerity tugging at her resolution.

'Virginia told me she has set aside a sum to cover your daughter's education and a small income to fall back on if she ever needs it. She wouldn't leave you to worry yourself to flinders by keeping that secret, so will you be returning to your family now you don't need to support your daughter?'

'There's nobody to go back to,' she admitted.

'Then you have no family?'

'None who cares what becomes of me or Verity,' she said wearily.

'Someone is damnably curious about your daughter then. Birtkin thought the coach was followed back from Bath,' he said.

Chloe frowned at the idea, then dismissed it as foolish. Her father was dead and her brothers wouldn't bother to track her down, let alone Verity.

'My family would take no interest in us, even if they knew where we were,' she said.

'Tell me who they are and I'll make them take one,' he said with such arrogant determination she only just managed to stop herself reaching up to kiss him.

'They are as dead to me as I am to them,' she said, finding she couldn't sit and let him confuse her secrets out of her any longer. Her turn to march up and down the room now, her faintness forgotten. 'And I will never go where my daughter is not welcome,' she told him when her circuit brought them close again.

'Then she *is* a love child?' he asked with surprising gentleness, and no judgement in his voice, as he stopped her by standing in front of her and making it impossible to go on without brushing against his muscular strength in the shadows.

Chloe ached to avoid his question by taking that step, but Verity and all the reasons why not forbade it. She hugged herself defensively instead, not sure if she was keeping hurt out or the pain of denying them in. 'I don't know,' she said unwarily, so agitated by the hurt of forever denying them each other that the truth slipped out unguarded. 'No, that's wrong, of course I know. I know only too well,' she said too loudly.

'She's not yours, is she?' he said with all the implications of that fact dawning in his now furious gaze. '*Is* she?' he demanded harshly, as if lying to him was a bigger sin than bearing Verity out of wedlock, as he'd always half-suspected she had done, would have been.

'Yes,' she insisted and it was true. 'Verity is *my* daughter.'

'And I'm the Archbishop of Canterbury,' he scoffed.

She shrugged and turned to stare sightlessly out

of the window, looking from almost darkness into even more of it, as she tried to ignore the furious male presence at her back. Instead of all-too-real Lucius Winterley, she saw a dark mirror image of him in the shining panes in front of her.

Even the small amount of light in the room made a sharp contrast to the darkness outside and their reflection showed her a plain and pale female of very little account and the mighty man she could have had in her life, if she didn't have a child to put before everyone else. He was brooding and intense and utterly unforgettable; the shadow image of the man she didn't want to love. Nobody would ever need to search their memory to remind themselves if Lord Farenze was at a certain event; he was someone you couldn't ignore even when you wanted to.

'I don't care who *you* are, Verity's my daughter,' she lied.

'As Eve is Bran's daughter in every way but fact, I know Verity is yours,' he said with that new gentleness in his voice. 'You took on even more than Bran when you accepted Verity as your own, for whatever reason you felt you must.'

'There *was* no choice. She is my child.'

'Don't take me for a flat any longer. I've been one for the ten years I stayed away from you for her benefit as well as your own. Now I see why there was such fury in your eyes when you first told me to take my dishonourable intentions straight to hell all those years ago, such a steely need in you to keep you and your child safe at whatever cost. I suppose going back home would mean admitting you'd failed.'

'No, there is no going back. Verity would have been left on the doorstep of the nearest foundling hospital on a bitter night like this one if I let them get their hands on her. If I even wanted to go back now, they would find a way to rid themselves of her the moment I took my eyes off them,' she told him, the defiance, hurt and grief she'd felt after their reception of the fact Verity had survived her rough birth sounding harsh in her voice at that terrible truth.

'I doubt they would have brought themselves to carry out such an inhuman scheme, whatever threats were made in the heat of the moment,' he said as if she had taken Verity and stolen away on some childish whim.

'Exposing unwanted babies to the elements,

given even the slim chance they might be found and raised to some sort of life by the parish, is an everyday sin in a world that despises tiny children for the mistakes of their parents,' she said bitterly. 'So, yes, they refuted her as coldly as an unwanted kitten and would have dealt with her as lightly if I had let them,' she said, refusing to spare him when she had all the details of Verity's terrible beginning etched on her memory, to live with for the rest of her life as best she could.

'Why did her mother sit by and let you take her babe?' he prompted so gently she let the information past her numb lips before her mind could leap in and argue he should not know so much about them.

'Her mother was my twin sister and she died in childbed,' she told him, the sorrow of it heavy in her heart, memory so vivid it could have happened yesterday.

He knew so much she hadn't wanted anyone to know now, at least until Verity was old enough to hear the truth. She wondered if that day would ever come when all it could bring her was sadness at the fact Daphne refused to name the father of her child, even as she lay dying.

'The other half of you,' Luke said, as if he knew the bond of twins was tighter than that between ordinary siblings.

'We weren't identical,' she said with a wobbly smile as she recalled the many differences between herself and Daphne, despite that shared birthday. 'I can't tell you how shocked everyone was when it was the quiet and angelic twin who threatened to disgrace the family name, not the one they always predicted would come to a bad end. From the day we were born Daphne was the sweet little angel to my devil, although she was as capable of mischief as I was. We argued and fought like cat and dog at times in private and she sometimes let me take the blame for our sins because I looked as if I deserved it. I supposed one of us might as well be punished as both.'

'And yet you truly shared your sins about equally?'

'More or less,' she admitted cautiously.

'You were the dog with the bad name being hanged for it, were you not?' he asked as if he already knew she'd taken curses and blows for her sister more often than for herself, because somehow she needed the good opinion of others far less than her sister had done.

'What if I was? We had each other and precious little attention from anyone but our nurse after our mother died. Daphne made it up to me by bringing food and books when they were forbidden me, or thinking up a new adventure to distract us from my latest punishment. I wasn't a saint and we were both heedless and unruly. I expect the aunts were right to say we were a sad burden to them and our brothers are much older than us. They blamed us for our mother's death, although Mama didn't die until we were five, so that's about as logical as blaming Verity for whatever sins Daphne committed. Oh, don't look at me like that, I'm not so innocent I don't know she had a lover, but I never caught her out in an assignation, saw a love note passed to her, or overheard a furtive greeting to give me a clue who he was.'

Hearing herself saying far too much again, Chloe forced her mind back into the present and glared at him for luring her into a past she still found it hard to revisit.

'What of your father?' he asked blandly, as if

they were engaged in polite conversation instead of talking about the upending of her young life.

'What of him?' she said, wondering how different hers and Daphne's lives might have been if their father loved them half as much as Luke did his daughter.

'Where was he in all this?'

'Away. He used to claim he couldn't abide the sight of us because we were such a painful reminder of our mother, but I found out later he'd installed a mistress in his town house before she was even cold in her grave. Whatever the truth, he spent his time in London or Brighton, or at his main seat in Northamptonshire where his daughters were not permitted to join him. Until we threatened to bring such disgrace on him even he couldn't ignore us, we rarely saw him from one year to the next.'

'What did he do when he recalled the twin daughters he'd left to raise themselves as best they could?'

Oh, but he was good at this, Chloe decided, even as she heard herself answer as if nothing stood between her ears and her tongue. 'He came back,' she said with a shudder. She hugged herself even tighter to ward off the terrible day of his return.

'I suppose he would have to, once your sister was with child.'

She rounded on him to rage at his insensitivity, but he bewildered her before the words could leave her mouth by stripping off his viscount-warmed superfine coat and wrapping her in the heat of his body by proxy.

'You'll be cold,' she protested even as she snuggled into the seductive smoothness of the silk lining and warmth of him and breathed in the unique scent of clean man and lemon water and sandalwood.

'I'm a tough northerner, don't forget,' he argued with a wry smile.

How could she *not* want him when he stood there, so completely masculine and would-be cynical, and made her heart turn over with wanting this unique man in her life? In his shirtsleeves it was impossible to ignore the width of his shoulders and the lean strength of his mature body. She could imagine him at twenty, the young husband of a silly little débutante without the sense to see what a fine man she'd wed, and wondered how they would have gone on if they had met when she was young and impulsive and silly and married each other instead.

Impossible, Chloe; he's almost nine years older than you are and was a father and a widower before you left the schoolroom, she chided herself, yet she couldn't get the idea out of her head that, if he'd only waited for her to grow up, everything could be so different for them now. At six and twenty to her seventeen and steady as the rock his northern eyrie stood upon, he would have been steadfast as granite when Daphne's loneliness and need for love and approval brought the world tumbling down on the Thessaly twins. A pipe dream, she dismissed that fantasy of love and marriage with him, and did her best to see them as others would. She shivered again at the thought of the sneers and jeers that would greet the revelation they'd been closeted in this room so long and only talked of past sins, not committed a whole pack of new ones.

'Come closer to the fire,' he urged gently at the sight of her apparently still feeling as cold as charity.

He couldn't know it was the temptation of him

that made her seek occupation for her hands, lest they reached for him. In his pristine white linen shirt, with that simply elegant black-silk waistcoat outlining his narrow waist so emphatically by the glow of the fire he had stirred into stronger life for her, he was temptation incarnate.

How she longed to wrap her arms about him and be held until the pain and grief abated. She told herself it was nothing more than the concern he would feel for any girl left so alone that was softening his hawk-like features. He had a young daughter and felt for her plight when she faced such a stark choice between her old life and Verity's death.

More than likely he would have opted to rescue Daphne if he'd met them in their hour of need. She was appalled by the jealousy that blazed through her at the idea of him in thrall to her sister's angelic blonde looks and easy smiles. Apparently there *was* something that could make her hate her sister for being so lovely and needy after all, or rather *someone*.

Chloe felt ashamed that Luke Winterley meant more to her than her twin had done. Until she met Verity's furious gaze the first time and became a mother, despite the facts, this man could have meant more to her than any man should to a girl of such notoriously rackety lineage as hers.

Chapter Ten

'Do you think that just once during our acquaintance you could be sensible and come here to get yourself properly warm, Mrs Wheaton?' he barked in fine Lord Farenze style and set her rocking world back on an even keel. It felt so familiar, his lord-of-all-I-survey guise, that she came back to the present and found she liked it a lot better than the past that had haunted her for so long, despite not being able to be more to him in it than she already was.

'I should give your coat back and leave,' she managed with a weak smile for the man now glowering at her with such impatient concern he could break her heart.

'Flim-flam,' he asserted with a wave of his hand that dismissed convention and the rules of master and servant as if they didn't exist. 'The important thing is for me to know who you really are, so I can make your idiot of a father realise what he's done and put it right. He should at least grant you an income so you may bring up your niece as the lady you truly are, instead of standing by with his hands in his pockets. Virginia may have relieved him of the need to provide for his grandchild, but he has a duty to his remaining daughter, whether he likes it or not.'

'He proved my sister and I were dead to him when he sent us to the remotest place he could think of so she could have Verity alone and unseen. Anyway, I saw a notice of his death in the papers over a year ago, so even you can't harry him to do his duty in his grave, Lord Farenze.'

'Luke,' he corrected impatiently and how she wished she *could* call him so. 'If the rogue was alive, it would be, "Behave as a gentleman should or else", and think himself lucky he was my senior so it was not, "Before I kill you with my bare hands,"' he said, the gruff rumble of his voice coming to her as much by feeling as sound.

'Thank you.'

She couldn't help the wobble in her voice as she tried to find words to say how it felt to know he cared. She'd lost so much she could have had if fate was kinder, but told herself Verity outweighed it all. Chloe knew her youthful choices would not have been wise if she had made her début in society.

She would have scandalised the *ton* with her wild ways and headlong temper, but she was banished to a remote farm with her pregnant sister before either of them had been properly noticed by the polite world and saved them the task of disapproving of her. According to her father and the aunts, one twin could not be introduced to society without the absence of the other being remarked. She wondered how they accounted for the disappearance of both Thessaly twins, but doubted anyone recalled their existence now.

'I don't want pity,' she made herself add.

'Should I pity a slip of a girl who refused to turn away from a helpless infant because a killer told her to? Or be furious you were forced to renounce all you should have had before you could grasp it? If I heard this sorry tale at second hand I might pity you, I suppose, but as it is I can't offer you aught but my respect for your courage, as well as my lack of surprise at finding out you're as stubborn with everyone else as you have always been towards me.'

'Thank you, I think. Your family and friends must be gathered in the drawing room by now, though, and wondering where you are, so I suggest we abandon this topic and get on with the business of the day. You have more pressing matters to deal with than a weary housekeeper with a sad past,' she said as she did her best to renounce the fairytale of him admiring her.

'Eve is my family and I only have one true friend staying here to concern myself with,' he informed her dourly.

'I have a ten-year-old daughter and my reputation to guard,' she replied and it seemed to jar him out of his king-in-his-own-country frame of mind.

'We both know that's not true now,' he said as he crossed the room to loom over her instead of walking away, as she told herself she wanted him to.

'Verity is my niece and not my daughter in the strictest sense of the word, but you knowing the truth changes none of it.'

'Does it not?' he swung round and demanded, direct and passionate as she had always suspected he was under the icy self-control he tried to fool the world with. 'Is that truly all the difference you make between the "us" of today and of yester- day, Mrs Wheaton? Today I know you have never loved a man so wildly you had to bear his child alone when you were barely out of the schoolroom; never gave yourself wholly and completely to an- other man's passion and need and haste for com- plete possession of you, one lover to another. If you think that's nothing, I'm as mistaken in you as I was ten years ago, or yesterday afternoon when I saw you sad-eyed and pale at the loss of my great- aunt and your home of ten years and wanted you so urgently across all that frost and stone I've burnt like hot iron for you from then to now.'

Chloe stood dumbstruck and searched her mind for some phrase that could turn them back to lord and upper servant and came up blank.

'Cat got your tongue?' he mocked her silence.

She struggled against the weary impatience in his voice as he waited for her to produce a glib ex- cuse. 'No,' she said quietly, 'you leave me noth- ing to say.'

'Not even, "No, never even look at me again with all this in our heads to remind us of what you just admitted?" Can't you even bring yourself to deny it as you have since we first met and longed for each other as lovers?'

'No, it's as true for me as you say it is for you. From the first moment I set eyes on you and let myself regret for a second I must put Verity before my own wants and needs. Her existence makes sure I can't be what we both want.'

'My mistress?' he insisted ruthlessly, as if he must get the words out of her to repay the weary frustration of a decade.

'Yes,' she admitted at last, as polite lying was impossible today.

'I could have seduced you back then if I'd persisted, but I didn't.'

'Oh well done, Lord Farenze, how very noble of you,' she forced herself to half-sneer and half-praise him, as if his chilly, and true, résumé didn't hurt.

'Luke,' he corrected as if determined she should learn a name she could never use. She found him cruel for that and let her glare tell him so.

'I didn't seduce you because you were so young and vulnerable and it would lessen us both too much. You have no right to reproach me; we both know I would have ruined a virgin if I'd ignored my scruples. Back then I had a young daughter to raise on my own as well and I wanted her to respect her father when she was old enough to know what the world said. I couldn't face her with you on my conscience when that day came,' he insisted as if it was important she understand he had his own version of her impossible situation to struggle against.

'Don't you know half the world already thinks me an unnatural monster whose coldness drove his poor vulnerable little wife to ruin herself with every buck and roué in town?' he went on as if finally willing to open himself up to someone and why did it have to be her, when she was still bound hand and foot by the decision she'd made on another cold and starry January night all those years ago?

'That was before I somehow forced her to flee with half a dozen of them to the Continent in an attempt to avoid my terrible lack of wrath towards them for taking her away, of course,' he said, as if mocking himself was his way of protecting the young man he had been from the humiliation his wife had heaped on him. 'What would the rest of the world think of a rogue who seduced his great-aunt's housekeeper when she was doing her best to bring up a child alone?'

'I'm amazed you care a snap of your fingers for such fools,' she said simply. What else was there to say about those who couldn't see his wife must have been insane to whistle a husband such as Luke Winterley down the wind?

'I try not to, but I do have a daughter to consider.'

'Only introduce me to them and I'll say it for you.'

'I wouldn't dare,' he said as if he admired the wild spirit that had been raging for release for so long, rather than condemning it as unfeminine and graceless as her aunts had always done.

'No, they would be sadly offended to be harangued by Mrs Wheaton or Lady Chloe…' She stuttered to a halt as she realised where her unwary tongue was about to take her.

'What a day for revelations this is almost proving to be,' he said as smoothly as if he'd never raged and prodded and challenged her and had stumbled on this latest truth by pure accident.

'You accused me of being a lady in disguise at the outset of this unsuitable conversation, if you recall?' she reminded him crossly.

'So I did. Maybe I have the instincts of a gentleman after all and we should be proud of them.'

'And perhaps we should not,' she returned, reluctantly unwrapping herself from the warmth of his coat and handing it back to him with a haughty look meant to put him in his place. If he wanted Lady Chloe to make a brief return to his world, who was she to deny him the dubious pleasure of her acquaintance?

He grinned like an unrepentant schoolboy as he shrugged back into it and made a show of appreciating the scent of her on it, as she had more secretly when he put it round her with the heat and spice of him still lingering on the fine cloth. 'Have you never wanted to kick over the traces with me as dearly as you wanted your next breath then, Lady Chloe?' he invited as if it was even a possibility, with ten years of not doing so between them.

'Mrs Wheaton has no right to when she has a child to bring up and the kindness your great-aunt granted her when she needed it most to live up to.'

'And yet she wants to?'

The lie formed in her mind, but somehow she couldn't bring herself to say it. Instead she met his eyes with her pride and ten years of isolation hot in them. 'Yet she still says *No*, to both of us,' she said as coolly as she was able.

'And I say, *Not yet, but soon*,' he told her as if, because he willed it so, it would be in the end.

'Only in your dreams, my lord,' she argued, but how she longed to be his dream. No, it would be a nightmare if they succumbed to the sensual passion raw under the aloof politeness lord and housekeeper had tried to maintain.

'Don't promise more of those, Lady Chloe. You haunt mine and have done far too long,' he warned her with a look that would have burned his way out of an ice house, if they were careless enough to get trapped in one.

'I'm not Lady Chloe now and wish you good evening, Lord Farenze. Your dinner awaits and I regret I am unable to join you for a delightful evening of housekeeper-baiting tonight,' she managed to tell him, before sailing out of the room as if her dignity and secrets were all intact.

She was amazed to find only half an hour had passed since she found him in the dark and nobody seemed to have noticed they'd been together far too long.

* * *

Luke stared at the space Lady Chloe Whoever-she-was had occupied and forced himself not to shout out a plea for her to stay. The revelations he'd drawn from her like a barber-surgeon pulling teeth left him feeling raw and furious on her behalf, but the essentials hadn't changed. He'd always known she was gently born, but couldn't help wondering now which nobleman had managed to mislay twin daughters without a scandal he would have heard about even at Darkmere.

Apparently he urgently wanted to bed a noble virgin and couldn't do so with an iota of honour unless he actually married her. He wondered if he dared take such a wife without loving her with every fibre of his being. Chloe and her sister were left to grow up wild as ponies on a moor, so she wasn't just a virgin, but pitchforked from school-room to motherhood without much pause, or any idea how her beauty and bravery could tear a man's soul until he was a danger to himself and her.

Now her innocence loomed between them instead of the mythical Mr Wheaton, he ought to be glad he'd listened to his conscience years ago and walked away from the unfledged girl she'd really been back then.

Luke ran a distracted hand through his dark hair and went back to pacing like a restless wolf. He frowned at the bookshelf where a *Peerage* sat, tempting him to track down any earl or above with twin daughters. He doubted she was in a rational enough state when she told her sad tale to lie to him and who would expect a Lady Chloe to pose as an upper servant in order to save her baby niece from the poorhouse?

It astonished him two such beauties could disappear from any local society without a great many questions being asked. Either their father was a powerful man, or such a reprobate nobody expected good of him. Luke paced on, clenching his fists against a need to lash out at whoever should pay for the isolation and terror Chloe endured after refusing to abandon her dead sister's child.

Unable to bring himself to smash Virginia's personal treasures to relieve the frustration roiling in his gut, he snatched up his empty brandy glass and dashed it into the fireplace instead. Feeling not much better, he marvelled at himself for expecting he would. A day's headlong ride on a half-broken stallion, or a long bout with one of the professional pugilists at Gentleman Jackson's Boxing Saloon might take the edge off it, but a broken glass wasn't going to lessen his urge to wrench a dead man from his grave and dance on his corpse.

Breathing deeply to calm himself, he reminded himself he'd lived through an appalling marriage and humiliating legal separation without breaking up furniture or violating graveyards. Then he'd thought Pamela had done everything she could to test his temper to the edge of insanity. Now he knew otherwise and what wrenched most was the fact Chloe thought it was her fault for some ridiculous reason.

Could she have stopped her perfidious twin sneaking out to meet a lover and getting pregnant in the first place? No—it was obvious to him Daphne expected to dance her way through life, laying blame for her sins on her sister's shoulders before she flitted off to make more. The last one killed her and left Chloe more grief and worry than any young girl should carry alone. Even the pleasure of begetting a lover's child was denied his Chloe and he cursed the unworthy curl of satisfaction in his gut at the thought no man had touched the woman he wanted so badly it was a chronic ache of need that never quite went away, however many miles he put between them.

With a wry twist of a smile it was as well he couldn't see for the tenderness it might show, he decided he was in danger of making her a plaster saint. Nothing could be further from the truth of stubborn, defiant, contrary Lady Chloe—warrior and termagant.

If her life had been different she would be as famous, or notorious, by now as Virginia was before she wed her last husband. Luke recalled the portrait his Uncle Virgil had commissioned of his wife in all her splendour after their wedding and mentally put Chloe in silks and satins, let them drop from her glorious white shoulders so her firm high breasts were only half-covered and desire boiled at even the thought of her lounging on the sofa in the Blue Saloon, not quite wearing a scandalously revealing evening gown for his exclusive pleasure.

If posterity wanted an image of *his* viscountess to envy him by, it would have to make do with one of Chloe sternly buttoned to the neck. No hot-eyed young artist was going to glimpse *his* lady in such a state of sensual abandon, ever. He gasped at the place his imagination had taken him to then froze as every cell in his body locked on that revolutionary idea. His mind might want to scream a panicked negative, but the rest of him was very happy with the notion of spending the rest of its life with an extraordinary woman.

He couldn't ask her to marry him simply because she was Lady Chloe and not humble Mrs Wheaton. Whatever his eager senses had to say, he'd promised himself never to marry for what Pamela called 'love' and why else would he wed Verity Wheaton's supposed mama? Yet he couldn't ask her to live in a quietly scandalous neighbourhood in London either; forever on the wrong side of every town and village he chose to inhabit for the rest of his life. The idea of never seeing her again, of living life as if he'd never met and wanted her so achingly hurt like hell.

Left with the conclusion he couldn't let her walk away, or be his mistress even if she would consent, that left marriage or the madhouse.

'What a confounded tangle,' he grumbled aloud, a frown pleating his dark brows until he knew he must look the very picture of forbidding Lord Winter he knew the wags of the *ton* had christened him last time he glowered at them across a London ballroom in Virginia's wake.

He cursed fluently as he marched up and down the library as if he might find an answer in a shadowy corner. If he was reckless enough to ask the woman to wed him, she'd lead him a dog's life. Passion driven and beguiled by her enchantress's body, fiery hair and the infinite mystery in her blue-violet eyes, he might forget himself in idiocy for a while, but what use was such a besotted idiot to his daughter and all the others who depended on him?

For a moment he nearly fell into the fantasy, but it was too much like Pamela's constant pursuit of 'love' for him to stay there long. He shuddered at the idea of need turning to hatred as it had between him and Pamela when their youthful delight in each other wore off, when the honeymoon was over and he couldn't spend every waking moment pandering to his new wife's whims any longer. He should restore Lady Chloe to her family, then find that convenient viscountess he'd promised himself as soon as Eve was ready to find her own path through life.

Fool, he told himself, then bent to coax the dying

fire back to life, *your life will be cold and dark as this room if you let her go.* He shuddered at the very idea and a faint waft of Chloe's unique scent beguiled him anew as he savoured the knowledge she'd shared his jacket as if it was one intimacy she couldn't resist. Dash it, he didn't want to live without her and he needed a wife. Somehow he'd persuade her to marry him and they'd live every day as it came. Each of them would feel as bleak as the January night closing in outside without her, so what did he have to lose?

'Now the preliminary part of Lady Virginia's will has been read, we can get to the main business,' Mr Poulson, senior partner of Poulson, Scott, Poulson and Peters informed his audience with the flair of a masterly performer the following afternoon.

Chloe pictured him putting on matinee performances of the wise family lawyer in libraries up and down the land and wondered why she was still here when the rest of the servants had been dismissed after hearing their late mistress had not forgotten them.

She eyed the assembled gentlemen and wondered what they thought of Virginia's housekeeper being included in such an exclusive gathering. Mr James Winterley, the Marquis of Mantaigne, Lords Farenze and Leckhampton had every right to be here, so she exchanged glances with the only other misfit, a seemingly nondescript young man she judged to be in his late twenties.

The stranger looked a modest professional man of middling rank, until his cool gaze made you to take a second look. He was a shrewd gentleman, she concluded, wondering why Mr Poulson needed his junior partner here to assist with Virginia's estate even so. Mr Peters smiled faintly to admit his senior was pacing his speech for dramatic effect and Chloe wondered why she'd thought him nondescript.

She gave a faint nod to admit they were the outsiders and felt Lord Farenze's glare as if it might burn her through the pristine white-lace bonnet she'd put on this morning, now Virginia was no longer here to forbid it. Never mind respecting her late employer's wish she should dress as befitted a valued companion; she needed all the camouflage she could get after admitting too much about herself to him last night.

Chapter Eleven

'Get on with it, man,' Lord Leckhampton, Virginia's old friend and one time suitor urged querulously, 'we haven't time or inclination for an oration.'

'I need to be on my way before night draws in, I suppose,' Mr Poulson said with a frown that told them a master craftsman was being told to botch a job as if he was a mere day labourer.

'Not at all, Poulson, you must stay,' Lord Farenze said with a hard look at Chloe to order she confirm his hospitality.

'Your bedchambers are prepared and we have a footman very happy to act as valet for the evening, gentlemen,' she agreed, hoping Carrant hadn't scorched their linen in his eagerness to take up a career as a gentleman's gentleman.

'You are very kind, Lord Farenze, ma'am,' Mr

Poulson said with a seated bow Chloe thought old fashioned and charming, even if Lord Leckhampton snorted as if heckling a fine performance. 'But to proceed, since it *is* a complicated document and needs some explanation—Lady Virginia leaves the residue of her fortune to Miss Winterley, but her ladyship made a series of unusual bequests to all of you...' He paused to gauge the effect of his words.

'Don't need a penny of her blessed money,' Lord Leckhampton said.

'Just as well, my lord. Her ladyship left you the contents of all the bins in her late husband's inner wine cellar,' the little lawyer told him and Chloe saw an impish smile on the elderly peer's face.

'That's Virgil's finest burgundy and the best cognac. God bless her. I'll think of them both whenever I tap a bottle,' he said and blinked determinedly. 'Dare say you don't need me any more, then?' he said with much harrumphing and a pretend cough into a black-bordered handkerchief.

'If these other beneficiaries refuse to take up their parts of the estate, you are to administer Miss Winterley's fortune until she marries or attains the age of five and twenty, my lord, but if you wish to leave, no more of this unusual document purports to you,' Mr Poulson replied.

'Good, good, something in my eye, y'know?' Lord Leckhampton said and left the room to come to terms with that proof of Virginia's deep affection.

'Now, Mrs Wheaton and gentlemen, we come to the core of her ladyship's will and most eccentric it is as well, but it was what she wanted. Lady Virginia has left a series of letters to be delivered to four people one by one. The first letter is to be handed over today, the second when that first gentleman has fulfilled his request from Lady Virginia or handed it back to the trustee and so on, until the last letter has been given out. Each stage of these tasks is to take no more than three months of your time and, on completion of the quarter of the year allotted to it, the next task will begin. I trust you understand so far?'

'Dashed if I do,' James Winterley said with a glance at Chloe that told them he would not come out with such a mild expletive if she wasn't here.

'Lady Virginia thought we needed to keep out of mischief, Jimmy,' Lord Mantaigne said with a careless shrug.

'I'm a busy man,' Lord Farenze muttered grumpily and Chloe wondered if that was the reason her late mentor demanded he spend three months not being the viscount in possession.

'Hence a provision her ladyship made for the time each of you will spend on your allotted task,' the lawyer replied smoothly. 'Peters here will be available so each of you can put his talents to good use in turn. In your case, Lord Farenze, perhaps he could turn land agent so you can concentrate your energies elsewhere. My junior partner has accomplishments I cannot always approve of, but he recently assisted the Duke of Dettingham with a series of confidential investigations as well as managing to bring the perpetrators of the Berfield outrage to justice.'

'You must be very unpopular in certain quarters, Peters,' Lord Mantaigne observed with a gleam of respect behind his easy smile.

'Only if they know about me,' he said with a long look at his senior partner that made the little lawyer shift in his chair.

'I'm sure no whisper of it will leave this room,' Mr Poulson blustered, but from his blush was conscious he'd let himself be carried away by a desire to impress.

Chloe flushed under the combined gazes of four interested gentlemen. 'Of course I shall not reveal a word,' she promised, wondering why she was here again.

'Which brings us to your role, Mrs Wheaton,' the lawyer said as if he'd read her mind. He pushed his eyeglasses up his nose and glared at the parchment in front of him as if will-power alone might change the words on it.

'Lady Virginia left you her personal jewellery not already covered by bequests to family or friends and all her personal effects not likewise left elsewhere.'

Chloe allowed herself an audible sigh while she fought the urge to weep over such a magnificent gift. As a housekeeper she could never wear the exquisite pieces designed for a famous beauty in her scandalous prime, or use the delicately wrought *objets d'art* Virginia's lord delighted in showering his love with, but owning them meant so much.

'How kind and generous of her,' she said, puzzled why she'd been allowed to hear so much before being told this, then dismissed.

'Stay, Mrs Wheaton, I am not done,' Mr Poulson said and she sank back into her chair and looked quizzically back at him. 'There is a gatekeeper for this odd affair of one gentleman, then the next, taking up Lady Virginia's quests. That person controls the allotted monies and letters for the next twelve months and will receive a generous stipend in return. I am to tell you that you have the role and must not argue.'

'Me?' Chloe managed faintly.

'If you would take a look at this part of the document and confirm your true identity?' he asked and Chloe sat open-mouthed.

'How did she know?' she managed to mutter numbly.

'Your confirmation, if you please?' he prompted, pointing to a passage in the closely written script that said Lady Virginia's housekeeper-cum- companion was the Lady Chloe Bethany Thessaly, eldest daughter of the seventh Earl of Crowdale and late of Carraway Court in the county of Devon.

Numbly she nodded, then realised that wasn't enough for the law. 'Yes, that is my name,' she affirmed and raised her chin, 'What else did her ladyship tell you?' she let herself ask.

'Only that she had been very slow at putting two and two together and couldn't imagine where her wits had got off to. Indeed, who knows what she knew and didn't know about any one of us? I should not like to hazard a guess.'

'Do either of you intend telling me who has been housekeeper here for the last decade?' Lord Farenze demanded crossly.

'Not now,' she said.

'Later, then,' he promised, or was it a threat?

'Who is the lucky recipient of Virginia's first bombshell?' Lord Mantaigne drawled.

Chloe was beginning to see past his assumption of lazy indifference and sensed he was both diverting attention from her and adjusting his own expectations in case he must start Virginia's year of imposing her will on her favourite gentlemen.

'Lord Farenze is first on Lady Virginia's list, but he is at liberty to delay his task until later if he needs time to settle his affairs,' Mr Poulson said with a glint of what looked like humour in his eyes.

'I have no need; what is my so-called quest to be?' Luke demanded and Chloe let tenderness quirk her lips into a betraying smile at the scepticism in his deep voice that he could be any-one's hero.

Luckily the rest of them were watching him as if not quite certain if they were sharing a room with a primed incendiary or an occasionally un-civil nobleman.

'You forget I'm not in charge of that part of the instructions, my lord. No doubt Mrs Wheaton will inform you of your task, once she has read Lady Virginia's letter to her and understands her own role in this business a little better.'

If I ever do, Chloe added under her breath, trying to shrug off the feeling too many powerful males were focused on her as she tried not to squirm in her seat.

'It might prove difficult to maintain a disguise with us happy band of adventurers to keep in order, Mrs Wheaton,' Mr James Winterley cau-tioned with a wry smile she found rather charm-ing when she caught echoes of his elder brother in his grey-green eyes.

'Nevertheless, I am Mrs Wheaton for now and ask you all to respect my privacy,' she made her-self reply steadily, dread of the scandal if she made her true identity public making her shudder.

'Am I never to know?' Lord Farenze asked, frowning as he bent to stir the fire into a blaze.

'If it ever seems safe for me to be other than a housekeeper, you will be among the first to know, my lord,' she said briskly. 'Now could I have my letter?'

The little lawyer bowed respectfully. 'Here you are, ma'am,' he said gently, offering the sealed letter as if it was a crown jewel. 'I'm told this will cover the most salient points and expect any details can be discussed later.'

'There's one you managed to skirt round,' Luke said with a long hard look Chloe admired the man for not flinching under.

'My lord?'

'Who is your fourth Knight of the Round Table, or do you intend keeping him secret until we spot some fool dashing about searching for dragons to slay for my late great-aunt's heavenly amusement?'

'I fear I cannot tell you who he is at the moment.'

'Say you won't rather and why not for heaven's sake?'

'Because I don't know myself,' the lawyer said.

Chloe thought he was telling the truth, but given Mr Poulson's acting skills it was difficult to tell.

'Then it will be impossible to recruit him to Virginia's happy band of heroes.'

'I was given four envelopes, my lord. Three have your names on and they will be handed to Mrs Wheaton when she asks for them. Lady Virginia included one with a question mark on and told me Mrs Wheaton will tell me who is to have it when she has instructions to begin his part of the task. You will be the first to have that secret in your keeping, ma'am, and I'm sorry to hand you so much responsibility,' Mr Poulson said with a frown of what looked genuine concern.

'Lady Virginia would never leave me with a task I couldn't carry out.'

'She did insist you would succeed in any venture you set your mind to,' he admitted.

Lord Mantaigne laughed, then smiled wryly to invite her not to take offence. 'I suspect that's a tactful way of saying you're stubborn as a mule and sharp as a knife, Mrs Wheaton,' he said with a knowing nod at Lord Farenze's thunderous frown.

'If I was that clever, I wouldn't be working as housekeeper here, Lord Mantaigne,' she told him with a repressive frown, but he let his smile stretch into a mocking grin and shook his head.

'Nobody found out you were here though, did they?' he said as if that was an achievement in itself. Chloe supposed it was and held her head a little higher.

'Never mind fawning on her, man, let Mrs Wheaton read Virginia's letter so I can get this fiasco over and get back to everything else I should be worrying about instead,' Lord Farenze grumbled, but his eyes met Chloe's with a myriad of complex emotions under the cool control he was trying to show the rest of the world.

'And the sooner I read my letter, the sooner you can have yours, my lord.'

'Eager to be rid of me?' he murmured as he rose to walk past her, indicating to the others it was time to let her and Mr Poulson begin this rackety affair.

'Of course,' she said with eyebrows raised as if it was obvious.

'Liar,' he whispered so intimately she felt his tongue flick shockingly into the intricate curls of her ear before he stood watching with all sorts of threats and promises in his darkened grey gaze.

'I know,' she let herself mouth once he'd finally

left the room with his half-brother, his best friend and the mysterious Mr Peters in his wake.

'I shall leave you to read this missive, Lady Chloe,' Mr Poulson said with one of his best bland looks. 'I trust you will not be disturbed.'

'Little chance of that,' Chloe muttered as the echo of the door softly closing behind the little lawyer died and she eyed the thick packet dubiously.

No point sitting here and hoping the whole business would go away if she avoided it long enough. She broke the familiar seal of Virgil and Virginia's entwined initials and peered at the closely written missive, half-longing for and half-dreading whatever her late employer had to say to her.

'*Dearest girl...*' it began, in Virginia's familiar, elegant hand and tears blurred Chloe's eyes until she forced them back and made herself concentrate on what her late employer and friend had to say, instead of missing her so deeply a gulf yawned inside her that would never be filled.

You have become the daughter of my heart, or perhaps I should call you my grand-daughter as you are so much younger than

*I am. I never could give my Virgil a child,
but with you and Verity in the house these
last few years it has felt as if he approved of
your presence here. Would he was truly here
to play great-grandfather to your daughter,
for he would have delighted in her quickness
and mischief even more than I have done.*

Chloe blinked and stared blankly out of the window for several minutes until she had control of her emotions and could carry on reading.

*I knew you were born to a higher sphere than
the country vicarage you admitted to when
you first came to the Lodge. Since I disliked
all the other candidates the agency sent me,
I overlooked the fact you were clearly lying
and settled down to be amused by you and
your babe, when Verity came back from the
wet nurse. That really was a giveaway, by
the way, my darling Chloe, since you would
never let your child be nursed by another
woman unless you had no milk yourself and
you certainly didn't have any of that, now
did you?*

Again Chloe had to stop reading with a shake of her head at the turmoil her late employer's words sent racing in her head. She'd suspected Virginia had doubts about her made-up ancestry at times, but never Verity's.

You have been very wary about giving me the smallest clue to your true identity and it wasn't until I took notice of a tale Lady Tiverley whispered to me a few months ago about Rupert Thessaly's outrageous brood that I realised who you really are. Now, if I happened to be a good woman, I would have delved deeper there and then and found a way to force your brother to admit he and his father and that milksop brother of his conspired to throw his own flesh and blood to the dogs three times over, then make restitution to his surviving sister and niece. I fear I am not that noble and have come to love you and your supposed child far too much to find the idea of living without you at all comfortable, so I managed not to see how I was compounding damage already done to you both for as long as I could.

During the last few weeks I have come to realise how deep an injury I did you by not doing or saying anything to restore you to your true place in life. I love you and my great-nephew as far as I am capable of loving anyone, but apparently I love myself more than both of you. I can see you shaking your head and refusing to believe Luke has anything to do with you even now, my dear, but take a deeper look into your stubborn heart and I pray you'll see there what you two have ignored far too long.

Since Chloe was shaking her head at the very moment her late employer accused her of being stubborn, she stared round the room as if her wraith might be watching. If Virginia was born in another age to poorer parents, she might have been accused of witchcraft, she decided with a shudder. Dare she look hard at her feelings for Luke Winterley? Something told her she might have to soon, but for now she had the distraction of Virginia's letter to shake her head over instead. Not that it did much good, since every other word seemed to be of him.

If you ever do decide to lay down that stout armour of yours and consider what you and dear Luke could be to one another, please forget the petty details and seize your happiness at last, my dear Chloe. It is for your brothers and the Thessaly connection to talk their way out of what they did, or didn't do, by leaving you to raise your sister's child as your own. Such things have been managed well enough in other noble families for centuries. Since it sounds as if you two girls were left to more or less bring yourselves up, such neglect was sure to end in trouble.

I hope your brothers have spent the last ten years feeling deeply ashamed of themselves after you proved better and stronger than either of them, but somehow I doubt it. You have a tender conscience and a good heart, Chloe, and the rest of the Thessaly family were ready to commit murder by leaving poor Verity on a freezing doorstep well away from their own nest. I'm quite sure they would have done so if you hadn't stolen away like a thief in the night as well.

Penelope Tiverley is a sad rattle-pate, but

she was your sister's godmother and I'm sure she has told her tale to nobody else. She only wanted to ease her conscience by telling her mother's old friend how uneasy she felt about the affair. My years seem to bring confidences, whether I want them or not, and please don't think the story is common currency in society. I know it is not so and have kept the promise I made Penelope not to repeat it. Given she did not see who was under her nose, I doubt you were ever close to your sister's godmother, but I wish your mama had picked one for you who might have helped when you had to disappear.

Chloe impatiently undid the strap that held her fussy cap in place then threw the constricting thing into a dark corner and rubbed her temples against the headache it had caused. She looked ruefully at a red-gold curl escaping from her tight chignon and wondered if its colour explained the differences between her and her angelically blonde twin sister. Even her mother must have decided Daphne needed a sweet-natured godmother and Chloe could make do with a chilly and puritanical distant cousin, who disowned her as godless and ungovernable long before she walked away from Carraway Court with Verity in her arms.

Chapter Twelve

Chloe reminded herself of Virginia's opening words and decided she had been given the best godparent ever born and felt as if her mentor's hand stroked her fiery curls for a moment to confirm her true place in Virginia's heart.

So there it is, child. I confess my part in you being misplaced for so many years, not so much from your family, who don't deserve you, but from wider society. I am a wretched old sinner and the more I knew you, the less I wanted to live without you and Verity. Now I sense my race is almost run, and about time too, so don't you dare mourn and mope over me, my girl. I have set my conscience to consider my sins a little more seriously than I quite like of late and will do my best to atone for the worst of them. It has to start with you and darling Luke, because I have finally re-alised why he avoids Farenze Lodge as if it were a noxious pest house. That selfish little cat he wed convinced him he was a heart-less monster because he wouldn't fawn on her, but I was wilfully blind to his feelings for you for too long.

How very much I wish I had used the brains God gave me sooner, dear Chloe. Of course Luke is attracted to my beautiful young com-panion housekeeper and won't let himself stay more than a couple of days in this house I love because you live here as well and he's an honourable fool. Don't shake your head again and wonder if I've gone senile. Look deep into your heart and his before you risk breaking them both. I suspect Luke also thought both your daughters would suffer if he made an unequal marriage. The poor dar-ling clearly has no idea you're his equal and possibly superior in rank. Legend has it the Thessalys were princes in Byzantium before they landed in England and settled for being warlords instead.

Chloe did shake her head this time, not because Virginia raised the mirage of love binding her and Lord Farenze together, but because she knew the Thessalys were descended from a Barbary pirate who captured, then fell in love with, the widow of a crusader, on her way back home to claim her husband's lands before the king could seize them. Apparently the lady captivated her captor, married him, then brought him home and set that legend about to baffle those who might take Crowdale from them. Chloe was torn between pride in her adventurous ancestor and doubt the Winterleys would consider it a wonderful connection if they knew. Descent from a pair of bold adventurers and a long line of gamblers, opportunists and downright thieves wasn't much to boast about.

Anyway, that is all by the by—I have been a wilful fool about you and Luke for far too long. Lately I have taken the chance to observe the two of you on his fleeting visits to Farenze Lodge and believe you are as besotted with him as he is with you, even if you don't yet know it. It would be a far darker sin to turn away love than to leap straight into the joy of it. Age comes on far too soon, so grasp your youth and beauty and reach for the happiness you deserve. I beg you not to fail yourself and Verity by letting the sins of others stand between you and a man truly worthy of you. Society would accept Verity as your adopted child, if Luke does the same. He is a truly noble man, so please don't hurt him even more than his wretched wife managed to during that ill-fated marriage of theirs, dear Chloe.

By now you will know there are more things to put right than this, even if this tangle concerns me most, but I beg you not to refuse the role I allotted you. I am forcing your hand and making you reveal things to my great-nephew you would rather keep secret, but those things need to be out in the open.

Chloe gasped and found out she was nowhere near as strong as she hoped when it came to Luke knowing the full details of her ancestry. She tried not to notice how sadly her hand shook when she took up Lady Virginia's letter again to read the last page.

Stubborn independence is all very well, but it's terribly lonely and for you I fear it might also be dangerous. Your brother Crowdale has fallen into bad company since he inherited, so be wary if he pretends repentance and wants to take you and Verity home. Please don't push Luke away when he comes to ask you about yourself, as he must once he's reads the letter beginning my year of wonders. I hope and pray it will be wonderful. There are four wrongs I must see righted and thank God I was granted time to realise they cannot stay quietly wrong for ever.

So there we are. I trust you to do your best to make sure my sins of omission are put right. You are a better woman than I ever was, my love, and you have a fine mind to go with that soft heart. Remember Luke is nothing like the harsh recluse he would have the world believe and look how he loves and indulges his daughter if you doubt me. If the worst comes to the worst, at least you now have a year's grace to decide what you want to do, but I hope and pray you will reach for a better future and a fine man instead.

Goodbye, my dear, live well and be happy; nobody deserves a blissfully argumentative marriage more than you and my stubborn great-nephew.

Chloe let the letter drop into her lap and stared out of the nearest window, surprised to see twilight outside when she hadn't noticed she was straining to read the last few words of Virginia's letter. She wondered how she was supposed to face Lord Farenze with this epistle in mind and decided the best thing to do was to give him his letter and leave him to read it.

'Here is your task from Lady Virginia, my lord,' Chloe told Luke, her composure so brittle he wondered if she might shatter if he breathed too hard.

Luke left it in her outstretched hand and waited for her to meet his eyes with a challenge in her own—ah, that was better. There was his Chloe, furious and ready to fight the world with any weapon she could lay hands on if it threatened those she loved. Somewhere along the long line they'd walked towards each other these last ten years he'd come to know her, despite his resolution never to expect more than hot passion and a few nights of mutual pleasure from any woman when he found out what Pamela had done for 'love'.

'I suspect my great-aunt of plotting to push us together as well, Mrs Not-Wheaton, but so far I've barely seen you,' he said, holding her eyes and wishing she would trust him.

'Read your letter,' she said with a resigned gesture that might be designed to show off her long-fingered hands and elegant wrists, if she wasn't his contrary Chloe and convinced there was nothing worth showing.

'Stay,' he ordered, wrapping her slender capable hand in his own larger paw and pulling her down on to the elegant little sofa by the fire they had stared into last night. 'You're half-frozen,' he reproached as he rubbed her chilled fingers to get some warmth back into them.

'Never mind me; you must read your letter. It's my job to make sure you do, don't you see?' she asked and the blank look in her eyes tore at his heart.

'Just this once I think we can let duty go hang, don't you? Sit with me, Chloe, let someone take care of you for once in your life.'

'I don't want to be a cause you champion because nobody else will.'

'Apart from our daughters; my late great-aunt and Mantaigne, I suppose? I thought Tom was too idle to bother with anyone but himself these days, then he ups and tells me I should look after you properly before another man leaps in and does it for me. Even my self-absorbed brother wants to make sure you come out of this odd affair un-harmed and I thought Poulson was going to adopt you himself if you refused Virginia's original offer of employment for the coming year.'

'That's very kind in all of them.'

'I tell you people around you have come to care for you and you call them kind? You must always be the one who gives, must you not?'

'It's what mothers do,' she said with a shrug.

'And fathers,' he said and decided, since he had her hands locked in his, he might as well put his free arm about her stiff shoulders and offer her some of his warmth and maybe more, if she would only let him.

'I'm not your daughter,' she argued with a mil-itant stir in his embrace he gloated didn't go far enough to shake him off.

'Does it feel as if I look on you as other than a fully mature woman totally unrelated to me, Mrs Wheaton?' he asked and let the heat of her next to him run under his skin like wildfire wherever their bodies touched, despite her bombazine armour and that truly absurd cap she had jammed back on her head any old how.

'Um, no,' she admitted and he waited for a militant objection.

She surprised him by sighing deeply, then snuggling into his embrace as if she'd needed him to hold her all day. Something like triumph roared through him, but caution came in its wake. She was looking for comfort. Only yesterday they had buried the woman who had given her security, shelter and love these last ten years, while the rest of the world turned its back on her and twiddled its thumbs.

Perhaps his friend Mantaigne could have offered her a broad shoulder to lean on and share some human warmth with on a dark day and been just as welcome. Grief and injustice had ruled her life for too long and the world must seem out of kilter to her now Virginia wasn't here to keep it at arm's length. Maybe wily old Poulson would have done equally well to offer comfort, or even, Heaven forbid, his brother James?

He would have wanted to kill every one of them if he'd found them sitting in his place like petrified granite, trying to give what she wanted and not what he needed so badly it hurt. Except for the extraordinary fact they would probably offer comfort and no more, whether from male stupidity or fear of him he wasn't quite sure. He seemed the only one deeply aware of her beauty and potential for passion, but he lusted after her so rampantly it made up for them. He squirmed in his seat to shift her so she wouldn't be terrified by the evidence, fully awake and roaring for satisfaction as it was when she was in the same room, let alone in his arms.

'I don't want a stand-in father,' she murmured and he could hardly believe his ears.

'Good, I want you so badly I can't remember my own name,' he admitted with shaken acceptance she was looking at him as if the sky might fall on her head.

'Kiss me, you idiot,' she ordered.

'Willingly, my lady,' he agreed with a sense of inevitability in his heart and did it anyway.

To leash his inner beast he framed her face with his hands, noting the contrast of pale feminine skin with his calloused hands—he was so impatient of wearing gloves he often rode without them. Her lashes swept down to hide her thoughts from his fascinated gaze so he studied them instead. Tipped with fiery gold, they were darker than her hair and ridiculously long, almost sweeping down to touch high cheekbones he wanted to explore in the finest, most intimate detail.

No good, he was making himself more outrageously male rather than less so by lingering over every detail of her face like a miser. She was a lovely woman; not a secret cache of inanimate gold. He sighed a whisper of intent against her pert nose and felt the precipice they were walking narrow under his feet and still couldn't make himself draw back from the brink. He gloated over the perfection of her rosy lips before he met the slick softness of them with a gasp of awe and they stepped off the cliff together and who knew where they would land?

Let me not hurt or shock her, his inner lover begged as she seemed to have to remind herself to breathe under the onslaught he was holding so carefully under control. *Let her be caught up by this endless storm of wanting too much to fear it.*

'Delicious,' he heard himself whisper as if testing a fine wine and a flush of mortification almost burned away the one of fierce arousal already scorching his cheeks. *Idiot*, he chided himself and heard the word slip from his lips as he held a little away from her tender mouth and sucked breath into his aching lungs. Somehow he had to stop himself plunging into her shy welcome like a boorish great bull.

'If I'm one, you are too,' she informed him crossly and so close he felt the movement against his aching mouth and her breath on the tongue he used to slick moisture on to his dry lips.

'Not you, me,' he managed to rasp and heard her chuckle, felt her chuckle and it threatened to turn him completely feral.

'My idiot,' she argued, sounding nearly as ambushed by need as he felt. 'Kiss me properly then, you great fool. I won't break.'

'No, but I might,' he breathed and did exactly what they both wanted until he could hardly remember his own name for wanting Chloe Wheaton with every fibre of his being.

* * *

Chloe tumbled into mysteries that had been beyond her wildest imaginings even after their first, disastrous kisses all those years ago. Not even longing for him so badly it hurt had prepared her for this. Her wildest fantasies; dreamt of and half-recalled with a blush when she woke, hadn't said how it felt to be kissed so deeply by this unique man. Those wild dreams, she supposed now, were brought on by lack of *this*. Lack of him; Luke Winterley; the only man she would ever love. It jarred through her in a long, hot shudder as he used touch and taste to fit them closer, strove for unity deeper than flesh on flesh. It opened up huge chances for pain as well as promises, added the feel of falling through vastness, tumbling into loving him as if her life might depend on it, to the already novel feeling of walking on fire.

He was the *one*—her Luke; her love. Of course it didn't hurt, his mouth on hers, his gentle, fascinated touch as he padded sensitive fingers through her loosened hair as if he loved the feel of it and when had he done that?

Her mouth kicked up in a smile even as he teased her lips apart. The rogue had more seduction in his fingertips than a hardened rake had in his whole armoury. He'd disposed of her hairpins so neatly she hadn't even spared a breath to ask why he'd let her heavy hair hang loose down her back and now seemed to adore the heavy weight of it against his skin. The thick mass felt wild and undone, just like her.

The hand he hadn't kept free to weave her ever deeper into his spell, learning her features by touch, was smoothing her back through the waves and weight of it. The bane of her younger life was being gloated over by her lover; a shiver of joy slid through her as he reminded them both he liked her carroty hair far more than she'd ever dreamt a man could, but he also adored her eager mouth and had work for it.

Oh, never mind her hair, he'd thrust the tip of his tongue into her mouth as if asking if he could. Chloe gasped in a breath and opened on an un-mistakable *yes*. He would be a fool not to read surrender in every inch of her and she spared a thought to chide herself for that, before he cindered it by deepening his kiss. This was *him*, the man she had longed for and lingered over in her head for so long passion and need and love stuttered down her supple spine and warmed her toes. *Yes* wound a little tighter, she wriggled closer so she lay against the cushions and felt him shift to follow her down with a smile of satisfaction he read on her lips. She used her freed hand to pull him after her and still his hot, deep kiss never hesitated on her willing mouth.

Wasn't it amazing what ten years of trying to live without a man she'd cried for far too often could do? Fire shot through her everywhere they touched and she found out how to shiver with sensual heat in mid-winter. Still he held himself away to shield her from the full force of his arousal. *Bless the man; doesn't he know his rampant need makes me melt from the inside out?* If he wanted her this much, it must be possible to play with fire, now she had the lick of it deep inside her to remind her there was more to making love than kissing.

A snatch of uncertainty nibbled at her conscience, but she loved the tightly muscled fact of his powerful torso tensing under her hands, as if he felt her touch and wanted to take her deeper. All the reasons she couldn't loose her gown or rip off his neckcloth and push away his snugly tailored coat to insinuate herself closer screamed in her head. She tried to ignore it as every inch of hot satin-smooth skin over hard muscle fascinated her; for a precious few moments he was her Luke.

She wanted to be naked with him, was almost ready to find allure enough and even some feminine enchantment she hadn't recognised in herself until today. All the reasons that couldn't be were stronger now; Verity was full of life and promise and must soon dream as a young girl should, without her hopes being smashed before she had time to grasp the bright promise of all life might give her.

Meanwhile Luke was kissing his way along the pared-down curve of Chloe's jaw, as if it was uniquely fascinating to feel his mouth there. *Ah, just one more minute,* she promised her inner woman as her breasts seemed to swell and kick up against the buttons of his waistcoat and the leashed strength of him, begging for release from the demure gown and very correct corset she'd imposed on them for some reason that eluded her right now. Somehow her nipples felt as if they had a life of their own, needs they hadn't fully told her about until this moment and now they were hard and tight and begging to be satisfied.

Under their disguise they pouted and longed, then made her sigh when she shifted against the cool silk and jet of his black waistcoat, fine buttons and him, then felt them tighten even more. Far better with his bare skin over taut muscle to writhe against her, her wildest instincts whispered sneakily. Chloe moaned at the very idea and almost wished it hadn't sprung into her head that to feel his fingers explore her might go beyond pleasure into something desperate and driven and even needier.

Maybe he read her mind because he rolled a little closer, lay half over her and she felt those wanton breasts of hers bloom with satisfaction against a hard wall of muscle and her almost painfully hard nipples tightened even more mercilessly. He raised his head to look down at her with so much in his eyes she had to blink and decided there was no point trying to hide her arousal from him. She held his hot grey eyes with steady acceptance they wanted each other more than she'd known a man and woman could. No use guarding herself from him any longer, no point pretending he was only a man just like any other. Luke was *the* man; the only one who could build a universe for her; spin stars and planets into the sky, and if only this world was different, go on doing so for the rest of their lives until it was vast and beautiful and all theirs to explore together.

'I want you so much,' she murmured as reason slammed back into his dear grey eyes and she finally saw his beloved northern skies, clear cool moorland air and the full depth of his fine mind and loving heart in them.

'You know I'm on fire for you,' he muttered, endearingly gruff about the fact, so explicit now even she could hardly help but know it.

'I want it all with you, Luke Winterley, everything a mature woman can share with a very well-grown and mature man,' she murmured with dreams in her eyes and far too much love in her heart to hide it from him. He'd awoken a wicked sensuality she hadn't even known she was capable of until now and it whispered of endless delight and satisfaction to be had, if they were not who they were.

'But?' he whispered and the knowledge there was always a 'but' for them was deep in the clear depths and complex shadows of his gaze.

'You know why,' she said with Verity's secrets misting her gaze with tears.

'Aye, I do,' he acknowledged roughly, as if saying so hurt.

'Not because of you,' she said as if that might make it right.

'Yes, because I'm me,' he argued and it nearly broke something in her when he levered himself away to put distance between them. 'If I wasn't a titled aristocrat with more houses than a one man can decently live in, you would give yourself to me heart and soul, Lady Chloe Whoever-You-Are. If I could offer you decent obscurity and a full heart, you would marry me and be my love for the rest of our lives, but because I'm Farenze and will be until the day I die, you won't see what we could be.'

'Oh, I see,' she argued shakily, 'but I won't do. You don't believe in love and swore to marry again only for convenience. In your wildest dreams you could never describe me as convenient.'

Chapter Thirteen

'Marry me anyway,' Luke asked, stubbornness in his intent eyes.

'You don't even know who I am,' Chloe objected even as joy sang in her heart and a flock of butterflies seemed to take up permanent residence in her fluttering stomach, then fly lower to whisper of delights unmapped and infinitely pleasurable.

'I know you're Chloe; Verity's aunt and mother in all but giving birth to her. I know you would give everything for someone you love, let alone your sister's child, a girl you love deeply for her own sake. I'd be a fool to try and part you from her. How can I not want that for our children, Chloe? How can you refuse it to the red-headed, mule-tempered brats we could have between us, if only you would let go of your pride and allow them to live?'

'Who I am would come back to bite you and our black-haired, dark-eyed wild things, the ones we can't make because of me,' she argued sadly, feeling the air chill between them. They sat upright on the graceful little seduction of a *chaise*, designed for two lovers to while away a long winter evening together.

'Don't I deserve to even know why not, Chloe?'

Of course he did, even though he would know she was right as soon as she told him. She had no reason to prolong the sweet moment when she might reach out and grab her wildest dreams, if only she loved him less.

She delved in the pocket no fashionable lady would have permitted to spoil the line of her high-waisted gown and silently held out the letter, addressed in Virginia's elegant sloping hand to *Lady Chloe Thessaly.*

Watching him read those three damning words, she waited to see all she dreaded cloud his face and make him frown with revulsion, but there was only mild interest in his eyes. Hadn't he heard her family name under all the notoriety her father and brother heaped on the title until it stank like three-week-old fish?

'My father was Lord Crowdale,' she made herself admit.

'Mine was a fool, but it doesn't prevent us marrying,' he insisted.

She was shocked into meeting his gaze and saw anger deep in the silver-and-gold-rayed irises and clear black pupils; besotted Chloe mused how she might lose herself in such complication for hours on end, if only she dared and he'd let her.

'Don't you realise what a scandal my resurrection from whatever early death they made up to account for losing two daughters would be? Far better for Verity to remain the daughter of an obscure housekeeper who might or might not have been widowed tragically young. Nobody will care enough to argue the birth of a girl of the middling sort as they would about Lady Daphne Thessaly's child.'

'And you would narrow all her choices to that? Being a nondescript girl of the middling sort? Oh, no, Lady Chloe Thessaly, you can't make a nonentity out of a girl who carries all the promise of being as inconveniently beautiful as Virginia once was. Haven't you noticed she has the fine bones, character and colouring that will take the world by storm in a few years' time? Foolish of you if you haven't, but as the child of a mere housekeeper she is going to have a terrible time without a father to protect her from the storm her looks and grace will bring down on both of you as soon as she's old enough to attract the wolves to your door.'

'I...' Chloe ground to a halt and wondered if he was right.

'Yes, you...?' he insisted mercilessly, temper now sparking in his grey eyes and knitting his brows in a formidable frown.

It made her want to love him even more. His fury was part on Verity's behalf and part because he seemed, wonder of wonders, to want to be her daughter's father.

'I can't simply change my mind and say yes because it suits me to have a noble husband, that wouldn't be right.'

'Oh, Chloe,' he said on a choke of unwilling laughter that chased the thunder clouds from his stormy gaze. 'My Chloe,' he said as if nothing would ever change that fact, whatever she did to argue him out of it, 'I would say never change, but I'm not quite sure I could mean it when you're keeping us apart with such idiocies. I promise to cherish your daughter as if she is truly my Eve's little sister. Please accept me and admit we'll never stop wanting each other this side of the grave. I vow I'll do my best to track down your Verity's father and make him honour his obligations towards her, if he still lives. She is a Thessaly when all is said and done, Chloe, and that means something to me, if only because you are one too.'

Chloe would have argued, but he shook his head.

'No, don't insist on reeling off a list of your father's and now your brothers' sins to blight both your lives with. Yours is still an old and loyal name and the title was won by better men than the current holder or your father. Thessaly women have defended castles and led soldiers in their husbands' absence; tramped across battlefields to find loved ones and guarded fortunes so their sons wouldn't have to go to the devil in their father's footsteps. Stay in hiding and you will oblige your brothers even more than you have already by staying away, as well as robbing your Verity of her heritage and all the fierce warrior ladies she has a right to know about.'

'No,' she denied. 'How can you sit there and condemn me for doing what was right? Are you accusing me of being less than all those rash and outrageous Thessaly women, because I ran instead of letting them put Verity out to freeze to death in the depths of winter?'

'I don't need to, you've done it to yourself,' he said so quietly she stopped in mid-rage and stared up at him with her mouth open. 'And now you're doing it to me and both our daughters as well,' he added ruthlessly.

'No, whatever happens they will be safe from harm.'

'That's not true, Chloe. Unjust as it may be, they could still suffer for the sins of their fathers,' he said bleakly and how could he call himself a sinner when he had been so desperately young when he became a father himself?

A boy of twenty seemed unlikely to have a pocketful of sins to carry around, let alone the vast burden he looked as if he had on his shoulders as he said it with a heavy sigh that spoke of mysteries and secrets she wasn't sure she even wanted to think about right now.

'And their mothers?' she said, thinking of Daphne dying in agony as she strove desperately to give her child life. 'Birthing them ought to wipe out all of them in one blow,' she said with a shudder.

'Would that it did,' he rasped as memory seemed to suck him back into the past as well. 'Not that your sister had time to bank many sins in her short life,' he added, as if forcing himself to slam the door on whatever his wife had done before she met her end in a carriage accident in a far-off country, too many miles and years away from her husband and daughter to matter in their lives any more by then.

'No, and I refuse to believe Daphne died as a punishment for what she did to bring Verity into the world. I can't pretend many wouldn't say that was so, then go on to blame Verity for being born the wrong side of the blanket. We must think of her, Luke. I might not like it, but there's no point pretending the world won't point the finger and speculate endlessly who her father is if the truth comes out,' she said gently, his name openly on her lips for the first time and would it wasn't to find another way of saying no to him. How she wished for the right to squirm back into his arms and forget the past in loving him now.

'Aye,' he said with a heavy sigh, 'so it might,

but if we have each other it won't touch us. That's what I've learnt from being Eve's father and you need to learn it as well. As long as there is love and strength inside our home the evil and pettiness outside can only touch us if we let it.'

'You can't stay shut away in that bleak castle of yours for ever though, my lord,' she half-teased and half-warned him, wondering how he would cope with the fuss and attention of Eve's début in a couple of years' time, if he had a stepdaughter with no apparent father and a wife who had sensationally returned from the dead with an orphaned niece at her side to make them all a seven-day wonder.

'It's not enough any more, thanks to you,' he said dourly.

'There's no need to sound quite so cross about it.'

'Why not? I was almost happy living with what I could have if I didn't think too hard about what I truly wanted, until I learnt to hope. You're the one who taught me, Chloe, so do you really think you have any right to take it away from us now I've learnt the trick of it at last?'

'I'm not sure.'

'Then be sure, be so certain you could carve it

into rock and display it in the Strand, Lady Chloe Thessaly, because until you can, I won't give up.'

'Can you imagine it in the announcement, my lord? Lady Chloe Thessaly, whom the world thought dead a decade ago, is to marry Viscount Farenze, who deserves our profound sympathy.'

'And can you imagine what the world had to say about me and mine when my wife dragged my name through every muddy puddle she could find and the odd boggy swamp or two along the way? I don't care what they say; the people who matter to me will know the truth and those who don't can do as they please. It's of no consequence to me what the wider world thinks.'

'But it is to me.'

'That is your cross to bear, don't make it mine as well.'

She met the challenge in his straight gaze once again and nodded to admit it was a problem she must worry at until she knew if she could accept such notoriety for them all or not. Wasn't it asking too much of any man to take her and Verity on, but could she and Luke endure *not* to take that risk? Could she live without him; wait every day to read of his marriage to another woman; the birth of his children and not hers? Wouldn't it drive her mad to stay in her narrow little existence as house-keeper in some house she didn't want to learn like she knew this one and long uselessly and bitterly for my Lord Farenze for the rest of her life?

'I have a set of tasks to carry out, whatever you and I could be, Lord Farenze,' she reminded him and rose to her feet.

'So Lady Chloe Thessaly puts her disguise back on to be Mrs Wheaton again. I'd be more im-pressed by that if you didn't look so thoroughly kissed and rumpled, madam. I suggest you rear-range the housekeeper if you want her to be taken seriously,' he said with a look that admitted he was being harsh. 'Go on then, leave me with Virginia's missive to soothe my pride. Rebuild your defences for me to knock down again, because I will find the weak points in them and tear them away.'

Not sure if it was a threat or a promise, she shook her head and felt the unfamiliar weight of her hair about her shoulders with a distracted frown. 'I'm sorry,' she said numbly then gathered up her scat-tered hairpins and discarded cap. The words *I love you* almost got on to her tongue and into the evening air, but it would be unfair to say it and walk away, so she bit her lip and went.

'Read your letter,' she'd said. Luke opened his last missive from Virginia with less reverence than he would have half an hour ago, then held it unseeingly instead of reading.

How could he take in Virginia's words as if nothing much had happened? Impossible to let her words glide into meaning now, instead of dancing across the page as if written in code. All he could think of was *her*—Lady Chloe Thessaly; Mrs Wheaton; the woman who kissed him like a heated dream. The dream he'd refused to have for so long.

He wondered what life would be like if he wasn't a coward. Pamela had treated him like a wooden effigy without feelings, but why had he let her spoil so much that could be good and right about his life once she was no more than a bitter memory? If he'd forced his way through Chloe's barriers when she was young and wild and daring, they could have been happy together for years.

Instead of seizing the happiness he could have, he'd clung to his wrongs. Pamela said he was a cold-hearted martinet, so he'd become one—not with his daughter, but to the world outside the castle walls. He was nineteen when he made that disastrous marriage, twenty when Pamela taunted him with what she'd done and walked away. His hands fisted involuntarily, but he made himself open them, then laid Virginia's precious last letter aside until he was fit to read it again.

It had come to him when he kissed Chloe that his future felt right with her in it and those wasted years weighed heavy. He might have had Chloe at his side, could have seen his second wife flourish and flower as their closeness grew, if he wasn't such a fool. Even when she eyed him hungrily as a half-starved wildcat at a banquet ten years ago, he had not taken his advantage.

He'd been such a *boy*, that unformed youth Pamela took in lieu of the rich, titled and sophisticated man of the world she'd really wanted. The hurting youth she made of him went on lashing out every time his precious isolation was in danger. It really was high time he grew up, he decided, with a wry smile to admit to himself that he'd left it a little late.

'Nothing ventured, nothing gained,' he told the

small and exquisite marriage portrait of Virginia
and Virgil that hung in their favourite room, 'and
any other cliché I can think of to get me where
you two sat so smugly contented with each other
all those years ago.'

For a moment it seemed as if the lovers took
their love-locked gazes off each other, focused on
him with mocking approval and whispered, 'About
time.'

'Must be more tired than I thought,' he muttered
as he blinked and looked again.

No, they were as they'd always been, so absorbed
in each other he could imagine the exasperated artist demanding they look outwards and let him do
what he was here for time after time, until he gave
up and painted what he saw instead of what they
did. Of course they were still lost in each other's
eyes, every idea in their heads focused on one another, painted lovers caught in an endless moment
of loving and wanting each other.

'A trick of the firelight,' he assured himself and
his great-uncle and aunt's painted likenesses, then
bent down to light a taper from the glowing fire to
light a branch of candles. 'You'll have to do better
than that if it wasn't,' he told the oblivious lovers,

glad Chloe had closed the door behind her so there was no risk of being overheard talking to a picture.

'She might not have me anyway,' he argued with a stretched canvas and a few layers of expensive paint. 'Little wonder if she's curious about what she missed and responds to me like a man's wildest fantasy. Maybe she wants to know what her sister risked so much for.'

He could feel a huge gap opening up inside him at the very idea he might love Lady Chloe and she could not love him back. He shook his head to try to reason it away, or accept the full echoing emptiness of that future.

'You could give me a clue,' he told the youthful image of Virginia with so little of her attention on the world beyond her lover's gaze.

It seemed to his tired mind Virgil spoke this time, 'You did tell the boy to read that letter, not use it to line his hat with, didn't you, love?'

Since he'd be a fool not to, he did as he might have been bid, if his conversation with two dead lovers wasn't impossible.

'Lady Farenze was very specific, my lord,' the portly little lawyer said a few minutes later and took off his spectacles to peer at Luke with apparently mild eyes. 'We went over her will in minute detail six months ago and I can confirm that her ladyship was of sound mind and very clear about her wishes.'

'I dare say, but this scheme of hers is ridiculous. No, it's beyond ridiculous. You must find a way to set this part of Lady Virginia's will aside and allow me administer the estate instead of Lady Chloe.'

'Lady Virginia was very specific—either the whole of her will is proved and enacted or none of it. Naturally you will receive this house and the Farenze Lodge Estate under the terms of your great-uncle's will, but the rest of the provisions of her ladyship's will must be rendered null and void. Her personal fortune will then go to her blood kin as her legal heirs. By the time it has been fought over and split between all the DeMayes and the Revereux family entitled to a share it will do little good to anyone, but if you fight this document, that is what must happen.'

Luke swore as he paced the room angrily, raging at the devil over the few words Virginia left him to fume over echoing about in his head.

Darling Luke,
Your task for the next few months is to track
down Verity Thessaly's father. I only wish for
your happiness, my dear boy, but I suggest
you start out by visiting Crowdale's Scottish
estates to look for clues to the man's identity.
All my love,
Great-Aunt Virginia

Chapter Fourteen

So that was his last letter from Virginia; a couple of lines and a cryptic reference? Now he was supposed to do what Chloe least wanted him to do—dig into her sister's past as carelessly as if excavating potatoes. Curse it; he'd always thought Virginia loved him, despite his faults and managing ways. Now she'd left him an impossible task and expected him to be happy at the end of it. Chloe would curse him up hill and down dale, then refuse to have anything more to do with him if he found out her sister had cavorted with a married man to beget her child.

How could he not suspect Verity's father was an adulterer when he'd abandoned a seventeen-year-old girl to carry his bastard alone? If so, the damned rogue would have left no trace of himself in Daphne Thessaly's life, except the unarguable fact of his child and who could prove one way or the other who her father was on the strength of hearsay and rumours? If Chloe didn't get the truth from her sister, it couldn't be uncovered when Lady Daphne Thessaly was ten years in her grave.

'What if I can't do it?' he barked at Poulson when he came to a halt.

'What if you cannot do what, my lord?'

Luke sought a reason for that confusion and found it in the challenge he'd offered to Virginia's will and her damnable scheming.

'This ludicrous quest I've been given,' he snapped impatiently.

'Oh, that's simple enough. Then you must inform Lady Chloe you are not willing to carry out your task and she will subtract a quarter of the sum put aside to purchase a manor and estate for Mr James Winterley at the end of the twelve months, if enough of you complete your quests, and forward it to the Prince Regent.'

'That's devilish,' he ground out, Virginia was giving with one hand and taking away with the other.

'Perhaps the word ingenious describes it better, my lord.'

'However you look at it, my great-aunt has me tied up so tight I'm surprised I'm not screaming. I'd give a great deal to see my brother decently occupied and financially independent of me. Happy is probably beyond him, but at least he deserves a chance to prove me wrong. James won't accept a penny from me to set himself up in a new life, but such a bequest could change his life.'

'Mr Winterley might surprise himself and everyone else if he had the means to do so,' Mr Poulson suggested as if he thought there were hidden depths to one of the most notorious rakes of the *ton* as well as Tom Mantaigne. The lawyer shook his head as that idea played through it and he realised how much looking it demanded. 'If he was better occupied, it would divert his resentment from your inheritance of the family lands and titles.'

'What a fine prospect you do dangle before me,' Luke said, wondering why James's dislike still hurt after all these years of mutual distrust, 'but it still begs the question whether I can do what Virginia asked me to.'

'Lady Virginia had more faith in you than you do in yourself, Lord Farenze.'

'I assume you don't know what she asked, unless

you managed to undo this letter and reseal it without leaving a single trace, Poulson, so pray don't imagine you understand the task she set me until I come back and admit it can't be done.'

'I'm sure you won't do that, Lord Farenze,' the lawyer said with a smile Luke didn't trust one bit.

The man eyed the legal documents he'd been working on to transfer the estate and various other pieces of property to their new owners, as if he could imagine nothing finer than burying himself in wheretofors and howsoevers until dinnertime and Luke sighed impatiently, then left him to it.

By the time Chloe left the library it was nearly dinner time and she was soon caught up in the rush and urgency when Cook burned her hand and the cook maid dropped a pint of cream on the kitchen floor. She felt a sadly neglectful mother by the time the family and their guests were all served and the kitchen was calm again and she was free to make her way upstairs to spend a few minutes with her daughter.

'There you are, Mama,' Verity exclaimed, looking up from the much-crossed and amended first attempt at an essay her headteacher had set her. 'I was never more pleased to see you in my life,' she admitted with a quaintly adult shrug and mischief in her bright blue eyes.

'Because I am an exceptionally wonderful mother, or because you need help with whatever fiendish task Miss Thibett set you this time, my love?'

'Both, of course,' Verity said and Chloe wondered if her father had been a charmer as well—if so, it seemed little wonder poor Daphne had found him irresistible.

'What have you been afflicted with, then?'

'It's geography, Mama,' Verity said tragically, as if she had been asked to visit Hades and report on the scenery.

'Oh, dear me, that's certainly not your best subject,' Chloe sympathised and wished she had more than a scratch education. 'There must be some clue in one of Lady Virginia's books or on one of the globes.'

'I can't find the Silk Road on a globe,' Verity said with a pout that told Chloe she hadn't tried very hard.

It was a trait that reminded Chloe of Daphne and, whilst she would always defend her sister fiercely if anyone else criticised her, she refused to let Verity grow up with the same belief she only needed to cry or bat her eyelashes to get unpleasant tasks done for her.

'Then you will find it in the new atlas Lady Virginia purchased last year for times like this. Once you have a list of the countries it passes through you can look up the history and trade it carries in the books the last Lord Farenze collected about the more exotic corners of the world. You should be grateful to have such knowledge at your fingertips so you can answer your headmistress's questions when you return to school next week.'

'Oh, Mama, must I?'

'Yes, Verity, you must.'

'I thought you might help me. It would be so much more interesting than wading through a lot of dry-as-dust philosophising about the savage ways of peoples those dreary old travellers considered less civilised than their own kind on my own.'

'You must have been looking in the wrong ones. Find a book by someone who loved exploring new places and meeting new people and read what he has to say instead of some person who probably never went to the places he wrote about. There must be writings like that in such a collection. Lady Virginia's husband doesn't sound the sort of man who was happy to be bored witless every time he picked up a book.'

'Then I must plough through every book in the library to find out a few facts that will satisfy Miss Thibett I didn't idle my time away this week?'

Chloe was tempted to snap an easy reply and go back to her housekeeping accounts. She knew an unsaid question about where her daughter now fitted into the world lay under her Verity's fit of the sullens and she must set aside her not-very-tempting household accounts to deal with it.

'You need an occupation, my love. Miss Thibett is a wise woman who knows far more about life than you do and she knows Lady Virginia stood in the place of a family for both of us. That is why she let you come home to say farewell to her ladyship. I was wrong to try to shield you from the pain of loss, my love, and your headmistress was right to let you grieve for the person who meant so much to you.'

Suddenly her daughter wasn't a young lady, or the mischievous urchin who had torn about on her pony and worried her mama with daring exploits until Lady Virginia offered to send her to school. Chloe tried not to let her own tears flow as Verity turned into her arms to be comforted.

'I miss her so much, Mama,' she wailed and wept at long last.

'I know you do, my darling,' Chloe whispered into the springing gold curls making their escape bid from Verity's fast-unravelling plait. 'You have every right to cry at the loss of such a good friend. Lady Virginia loved you very dearly and I know how deeply you loved her back.'

For a while Verity wept as if her heart might break and Chloe rocked her gently, as she often had in her early years, when Daphne's child sometimes went from happy little girl to a sobbing fury in the blink of an eye, as if she wept for all she had lost at birth. All Chloe could do back then was hold her until Verity calmed and slept, or Lady Virginia managed to divert the little girl from her woes with a joke or a funny story about her own misspent youth. This time there was no Virginia to make light of such woe and Chloe felt terribly alone and as bereft as Verity.

'Where shall we go, Mama?' the desperate question stuttered from Verity's shaky lips as she battled dry sobs and looked tragic, as if all Chloe had been worrying about for the last weeks was crushing her, too.

'Oh, my love,' Chloe responded with tears backed up in her own throat as she realised she should have had this conversation with her daughter as soon as she came home. 'I don't know if we can stay here, but Lady Virginia left me a full year's salary in return for a trifling charge she laid on me. I have enough saved to live comfortably on for a year or two after that, if I should choose not to look for a new post yet, and Lady Virginia left you an annuity, so you will never starve. Please don't run away with the notion you're an heiress, though, will you?'

'Then I shall not. I love her even more though, now I know I shall be able to look after you one day, Mama, when you are too old to do it yourself.'

Chloe went from the edge of tears to fighting laughter. 'We probably have a few years before I'm too bowed with age to work, darling,' she said with a straight face.

'You're laughing at me, aren't you?' Verity accused.

'I'm sorry, love, but I'm not even eight and twenty yet. That might sound as if I could shake hands with Methuselah on equal terms to you, but I feel remarkably well preserved when my daughter is not making me out to be an ancient crone.'

'That's what age does to a person, Lady Virginia told me,' Verity informed her with a solemn shake of her head, as if she saw through her mother's ruse.

'Lady Virginia was at least fifty years older than me, Verity love, and that was only what she admitted to. Her age varied every time someone was rude enough to try to find it out. I'm unlikely to follow Lady Virginia into the grave for a great many years yet and you must stop fretting about me.'

'But what if you die in childbed, Mama? I can tell Lord Farenze wants to marry you and ladies die giving birth, particularly when they're old.'

'Why would Lord Farenze want to marry me?' Chloe asked; shocked that her brain picked that rather than thinking how to reassure Verity ladies gave birth safely time after time at much more than seven and twenty.

'Oh, Eve and I realised ages ago,' her daughter said, as if it was so obvious she was amazed anyone could miss it.

'I hope you kept that conclusion quiet then, as you couldn't be more wrong.'

'Bran and Miss Culdrose agree with us.'

'And whatever would the rest of the household make of such a silly idea?' Chloe asked faintly, dread at facing even the smallest scullery maid eating at her lest they were already speculating about it.

'They think Mrs Winterley will put a stop to it, but Eve says her father takes no notice of what his stepmother says and even less of what she thinks.'

Chloe sighed and decided she could put off telling Verity the story of her own birth no longer, if only to scotch any false hopes of becoming Eve's stepsister, but her niece's eyes were red and tired after her crying bout and the sad tale of Daphne's love affair must wait for another day.

'Lord Farenze is a viscount; I am his housekeeper and lords do not marry servants. Forget such wild flights of fancy and get into bed, love. Your Miss

Thibett would be the first to say you need a decent night's sleep before you're ready to face world trade and the laden caravans of gold, jewels, silk and spices that will be winding their way through far-off, exotic lands even as we speak.'

Her imagination caught by the idea of those processions of camels laden down with fine cloth and exquisite treasures, Verity allowed Chloe to walk her to her room and help her undress, then get into bed. Verity asked for a story and how to resist when she usually insisted on reading herself to sleep and this might be the last time Verity let her be her mother? Chloe dreaded telling her the tale of her birth and felt like crying herself by the time they wandered a little way along that ancient road in their imaginations and Verity's eyes got heavier and heavier until she slept at last.

Chloe let her voice trail away, then gazed at her precious child as if she had to fill her mind with Verity as she was now. Tomorrow Verity might hate her for a pretence begun when nobody else cared enough about Daphne's child to save her from death or a lonely life at the mercy of the parish.

Shaking her head to keep back the idea that things

were better as they were, Chloe went to her own room earlier than usual to struggle with the knot her life seemed tangled into all of a sudden. Someone had lit a fire for her and she knew exactly who had ordered it. Luke's thoughtfulness at a time when he had hundreds of other things to think about made tears sting as she gazed into the glowing flames and wondered how he'd ever managed to fool anyone he was an unfeeling recluse.

She loved Luke Winterley and finally admitted to herself she had loved him far too long. The fact of it, fresh and vital in her heart as she knew it would be to her dying day, made her content and full of hope for all of a minute. Yet if she emerged from whatever fate her family had told the world she had met to wed my Lord Farenze, Verity would be exposed as the reason Lady Chloe was supposed to have died with her sister in the first place.

Her brothers would walk through fire rather than publically admit they'd let one sister give birth with only her twin to help her and a rapidly sobering midwife, then forced Chloe out to starve with her dead sister's child after even that ordeal didn't kill the poor little mite and they had to rid themselves of her by other means.

Chloe sat watching the fire with tears sliding down her cheeks as she bid farewell to a dream she hadn't let herself know she had. She had Verity and a secure future many a woman left with a child to bring up alone would envy her. Verity's future was secure as well and she ought to be dancing on air. Instead she must fight the heavy weight of grief and an urge to sob her heart out on the threadbare rug she had decreed good enough for her bedchamber, so at least nobody could accuse her of gilding her own nest.

Luke could condemn her thrift and look at her scratch bedchamber with offended distaste, but she had lived among the cast-offs of a bygone age most of her life and was used to making do. Carraway Court had been neglected and down at heel for as long as she could remember and the older servants would shake their heads and say how different it was in her grandfather's day, before their mother wed her lord and he took all the rents, then left the Court to go to rack and ruin.

Even then they whispered of gambling and extravagant mistresses and how even an earl couldn't bring such low company to his late wife's home with her daughters in residence. Chloe wondered bitterly why her father and brothers cared so much about the family name when they blighted it so enthusiastically.

A sentence from Virginia's letter slotted into her mind as if her mentor had whispered in her ear and a possible plan formed. Lady Tiverley was an amiable feather-head, but she was the daughter of a far richer and more respectable earl than Chloe's father had ever been and moved in the highest social circles. If such a lady whispered the truth in a few well-placed ears, could Daphne and her romantically mysterious child become the heroines of such a sad tale? It was a faint hope and her heart beat like a marching drum at the idea she and Luke could love openly after all.

Then she remembered Daphne lying in that rough bed, dying and feverishly demanding that Chloe promised her never to love a man so recklessly. She wasn't Daphne, or a vulnerable seventeen-year-old girl with no protector now, though. Anyone who wanted to take advantage of her would have to get past Luke Winterley first, even if he was the one wanting to take it. She smiled at the thought of him holding aloof from Farenze Lodge for so long, because she had said *No* and they each had a daughter who would be damaged if she didn't. He could deny it as often as he pleased, but her love was a noble gentleman from the top of his midnight locks to the tip of his lordly boots and how could she not love him? It was admitting it she had trouble with.

First she must talk to Verity and insist Luke told his own daughter the truth about them as well. Lying in bed, torn between wild hopes and abject terror, the weight of four people's hopes and dreams seemed to press her into the mattress. Even as the wonder of 'perhaps' made her heart lift with joy and her toes and a good many other places tingle with anticipation, Chloe couldn't bring herself to believe her impossible fairytale might actually come true.

Fumbling Virginia's letter from the pocket of her neatly discarded gown, she jumped back into bed and relit her candle. She had talked Verity to sleep; now she let Virginia do the same for her. Chloe was very glad in the morning that her candle had sat firmly in a night stick, since it had gutted without her even being aware she had gone to sleep with it alight and slept peacefully the whole night long.

Chapter Fifteen

'I need to speak with you privately, Mrs Wheaton. Meet me in the Winter Garden in half an hour if you please,' Luke demanded when he tracked down his housekeeper to the linen room, where she seemed to be having an urgent consultation with the head housemaid about torn sheets, of all things.

From the flash of temper in her magnificent eyes at his order he felt lucky he hadn't come across her alone and she had to keep to her role in front of the maids. He smiled like a besotted idiot as he ran down the backstairs, as if it was what a viscount did, and went out to the stables to speak to Josiah Birtkin about travel arrangements and how this place could be kept safe and cautious whilst he was away. The thought of being parted from Chloe, Verity and Eve while he carried out Virginia's quest added a bite of nerves to his elation as he finished his conversation and went to seek a far more crucial one.

It could be another clear morning, if only the mist would clear. Instead it hung about this sheltered valley and he wondered if he should have asked Chloe to meet him outside on a day when frost seemed to hang in the very air, waiting to crystallise their breath. The wintery statue at the heart of the place was still staring into the distance, but Luke resisted the urge to confide his thoughts to his unresponsive stone ears. Some things were so private they should only be said to the person concerned.

'There you are,' Chloe's pleasantly husky voice observed from so close it made him start and her frown turned to a satisfied smile.

'As you say,' he drawled as annoyingly as he could manage and from the flags of colour burning across her cheeks he'd succeeded a bit too well in rousing her temper this time.

'How dare you order me to meet you out here in the middle of my duties like this? What do you imagine the household will make of such a hole-and-corner encounter, Lord Farenze?'

'That I wish to speak to you in private and can hardly do so inside with so many eager ears tuned to our every move, I expect,' he replied with a shrug part of him knew was wrong when he was master and she was playing the upper servant.

'Why would you need to be private with me?' she demanded haughtily and Luke took a deep breath of frosty air and prepared to tell her.

'So I may ask you to marry me again, of course,' he managed to say casually, as if it was what viscounts always did of a foggy morning, when they employed housekeepers as magnificent as this one.

'Just like that?' she demanded and he wondered if he'd miscalculated by stirring her into enough fury to be her true self instead of Mrs Wheaton.

'No, not just like that,' he said with a stern frown of his own. 'After a decade of denial and deception—' he heard her draw breath to annihilate him with negatives '—I'm done with pretending it doesn't matter that we wasted ten years because I was too stupid to see past your disguise and my wife's shoddy little love affairs to the woman you truly are, Chloe Thessaly.'

'You can't call me that here,' she argued with a

shocked look about in case old Winter at the centre of the garden might pass her identity on.

'Nobody is in earshot and there are eight-foot-
high hedges all about us, but are you ashamed of
me then, my lady?'

'Never that, my lord,' she shot back so urgently
he had to hide a satisfied grin.

'Then when do you intend telling the world who
you truly are?'

'When the time seems right,' she muttered
crossly and shifted under his steady gaze. 'Oh,
I don't know,' she admitted with a heavy sigh.
'Soon,' she added as he continued to watch her as
annoyingly as he could manage when all he really wanted to do was kiss her speechless and a
lot more it was as well not to go into right now.

'When Verity is of age, or has run off with the
boot boy perhaps? Or when hell freezes over and
I'm so old and grey even you don't want me any
longer?'

'I shall always want you,' she said unwarily and
he couldn't help his broad grin at the declaration
he most wanted to hear on her lips.

'Marry me, then,' he managed to say before

he could launch himself at her like a lovestruck maniac.

'You could do so much better,' she said, avoiding his eyes as she watched the stony statue as if he fascinated her and Luke found he could even be jealous of inanimate objects now.

'I could ask nobody better suited to be my wife,' he assured her as he cupped large hands about her face, so she had to look up and let him see the doubts and questions in her amazing violet-blue gaze, as well as the heat and longing that made his heartbeat thunder with exhilaration and desire. 'I never met a woman I honoured so much or wanted so badly, Chloe,' he told her shakily and hoped he had managed to put all he was feeling into his own gaze, for once. 'You've made me into me again,' he said and grimaced as all the words he couldn't put together clogged up in his head. 'I don't have the right words. I've been trying not to admit it for a decade, but I love you and I won't stop doing it, even if you walk away.'

'I can't marry you, Luke.'

Chloe let herself gaze up into his fascinatingly hot grey eyes and saw pain and anger there before he decided *No* wasn't enough this time. It felt as if the frantic beat of her heart might choke her as she gazed up into all she'd ever wanted and had to say it anyway. Love *was* there in the flare of gold about his irises, the hidden depths of green at the heart of his gaze that looked back at her.

Luke, Lord Farenze, was finally showing her the tender places in his heart, the hopes and dreams in his complex mind and she was hurting him all over again. Tears swam in her eyes as she thought of the young man he'd been—scarred so badly when his dreams were trampled in the dust by his shrew of a wife. He needed her to love him back, and love him back she truly did, but it didn't mean she could let him marry her and make Verity into a bastard again.

'Why not?' he breathed, so close she wondered how she could still be so cold.

'I have a daughter,' she said sadly.

The blighted hopes and dreams young Chloe once wept over so bitterly while missing stubborn, noble, infuriating Lord Farenze in her bed seemed as nothing, now she had to renounce everything mature Chloe wanted to give her lover.

'Oh, Luke, don't frown at me and shake your

head. I know you're a good man and I'm a coward, but I can't let Verity grow up with Lady Daphne Thessaly's shame blighting her life. You need a pristine wife with an innocent heart, not me.'

'Why would I want a tame little tabby kitten when I can have a lioness who'd fight for our cubs with her last breath?' he said with a refusal to be fobbed off that made temptation tug so powerfully she had to look away.

'I am fighting for one of them now.'

'No, you're denying we could fight the world for her together. I won't accept this as your final answer, Chloe Thessaly,' he said with a determination that made her knees wobble and her breath come short. She loved him so much she felt herself weakening and turned to watch the foggy garden to stop herself admitting she would only ever be half-alive without him.

'Virginia's quest for me is to find out who Verity's father was. I will do my best to do so, but after that I'll wed you, whoever he turns out to be,' he told her.

It sounded as much a threat as a promise, until he ran an impatient hand through his sable pelt of hair and let out a heartfelt sigh. 'Lord above, but you're a proud and stubborn wench, Lady Chloe Thessaly,' he informed her with exasperation.

Chloe sighed at the angry intimacy of them here in this foggy garden and longed for a forever after to spend with him. She spared a thought for Virgil, begging Virginia to wed him rather than be his scandalous lover as she would have offered to be. They must have realised after two previous marriages bore no fruit there was a strong chance she was barren, but even that didn't seem as huge a barrier to love and marriage as Verity's future happiness was to her.

'I'll wed you or nobody,' Luke told her so stubbornly she almost believed him and her unhappiness seemed about to double. 'Although heaven only knows why I'd saddle myself with such a steely female for life,' he grumbled.

'How charming. You look very much like a grumpy mastiff denied a juicy bone right now, my Lord Farenze.'

'What a sad pair we are then; you look like a queen about to have her head cut off,' he replied, eyebrows raised and a challenge to deny it in his sharp look.

'Nobody else would want us if they knew what a sorry pair we are,' she agreed.

'They'd better not want you, but if we're not to be united in marital disharmony, I suppose I'd best be off about Virginia's business,' he told her with a look that said it was her fault. They could be married inside the week and have a wedding night before he went, if not a honeymoon on the way.

'Wait for a better day,' she urged, all the imaginings of a woman terrified that her lover might never come back taking shape in her mind.

'If I wait out one more night under the same roof as you, Lady Chloe, I shall either run mad or break down your door from sheer frustration. I need to be gone, but first you have to tell me everything you can remember about your sister's visit to Scotland all those years ago.'

'I don't know much, she never told me.'

'Tell me what you do know, then, for it is sure to be more than I do.'

'Daphne went off to our father's Scottish estate to stay there with his sister while her husband was in Ireland, supposedly to be instructed how to go on in polite company, then make a début of some kind in Edinburgh society. My father was deep in debt by that time and had secretly agreed to marry her off to a pox-ridden but very wealthy old duke as soon as they could fool the world she chose such a fate of her own free will.

'Papa was furious when his plan went awry and the old man wanted his money back and Daphne was sent home in disgrace. We were sent away so she could have Verity at a remote and tumbledown property on Bodmin Moor that my father had won in a card game and couldn't sell, but Daphne still refused to tell me who her lover was. She said it was best I didn't know, then I wouldn't be embarrassed when I was presented and had to meet his relatives.'

'He must come from a gently bred family at the very least then; she could have met one of the neighbours during her time on your father's estate, I suppose, properly out or no,' he said with a preoccupied frown.

Chloe thought fascination with his quest was already overtaking his frustration that she'd refused to marry him, but she put that grief aside for later and did her best to help him with what was probably an impossible task.

'Daphne was desperate to escape marriage to that dreadful old reprobate, but she had always dreamt of a gallant hero who would come and rescue her from the lonely lives we lived at Carraway Court. I wouldn›t be surprised if she took any lover happy to have a sixteen-year-old girl in his bed in a desperate attempt to get herself with child and escape marriage to such a man.'

'She was no older than my Eve when your father tried to sell his own child to the highest bidder, then? What sort of a father would consign his own child to a life of such misery and frustration?'

'The Thessaly sort,' Chloe said sadly, regretting the gaps in hers and Daphne's lives and contrasting them with my Lord Farenze's fierce love for his only child. 'He was no sort of father at all and only wed my mother because she was heiress to the Carraway fortune. I don't suppose he was faithful to her, or even particularly kind. Such a hard-hearted man can do a fearsome amount of damage to his children, so Daphne and I ought to have been grateful he favoured our brothers and despised us as mere girls, I suppose.'

'He was your father and ought to have been proud of his spirited and beautiful daughters. But why did he send her to Scotland with his sister and not you?'

'Because I was openly rebellious and Daphne always chose the course of least resistance, then did as she wanted to as soon as his back was turned. He thought she was meek and tractable and would do as he told her, in so far as he thought of either of us as beings and not his chattels to be disposed of as he chose.'

'Miserable old fool.'

Somehow his round condemnation of her late father made her smile, even if it wobbled and flattened at the thought of all that cold idiocy had cost the Thessaly twins.

'He was, but you can see why Daphne longed so desperately for a lover when she had so little affection from anyone other than me in her life, can you not?'

It came out more as a plea than a demand, he understood her twin and she was grateful for the warmth of his hands as he folded her cold ones in his and watched her with a mix of admiration and exasperation in his intent gaze.

'And what of Lady Chloe Thessaly? Was she supposed to stand alone and become the prop for her weaker sister whenever a lover let her down? You must have felt so alone, my love, so forsaken, when your sister and companion was bundled away like that.'

'I always knew that one day we would be parted. Daphne needed to be loved and supported and I had to hope she would meet a man strong enough to do both, until Papa came up with his plan to wed her to a monster. Every day we were apart I was scared she'd do something dreadful to evade what he had in mind for her.'

There, she had almost admitted it for the first time in her life. She had been terrified her sister would find the prospect of that marriage so impossible to endure she would choose death over it.

'It was almost a relief to me when she returned to Carraway Court unwed and with child by a lover she refused to identify even to me,' she added, because he might as well know all her secrets now the worst one was out in the open.

'Oh, my love,' he said, everything she longed for and couldn't have in his dear eyes as he watched her without condemnation. 'What a heavy burden your wretched family made you carry when you were too young to bear even half of it.'

'I grew up very quickly,' she said with a would-be careless shrug, but he drew her closer instead of letting her stand further off and clasped their hands between them as if he never intended letting her go for very long.

'No wonder you thought me such a paltry creature when I made you that dishonourable proposition ten years ago,' he almost managed to joke, despite the pain of that driven declaration spiky between them even now.

'I didn't, Luke, I thought you were the only man I might ever love enough to accept it. Then I thought of Verity and had to say no for all of us.'

'Aye, and you were right to do so, but if only I'd let myself delve deeper then, looked a little harder at Mrs Chloe Wheaton and all the witchy secrets you didn't know and I thought you did.'

'I wouldn't have told you anything back then.'

'Probably not, but it would be good to remember that I tried.'

'I think you did,' she almost whispered and somehow it sounded so loud on the freezing air she looked about and wondered how they must look to a casual observer, this potent lord and his encroaching housekeeper.

'Whereas I think I was a fool until very recently. Now stop distracting me with might have been and let me get this confounded quest over and done with, before I decide to consign it to the devil and stay here and lay siege to you until you finally agree to wed me after all, my Chloe.'

'None of it will go away,' she warned.

'Maybe not, but life and hope must win out over history and gossip. I have to believe it and so ought you, my darling. Coming to terms with our future will keep you out of mischief while I am away.'

'As if I need any sort of occupation with your house to spring clean and put back in order for you,' she said brusquely, but suddenly all the barely hidden energy of nature in January felt as alive in her as it was in the bulbs pushing through the cold earth even here, in the frozen realm of Winter.

'I'll return to you,' he promised, all that life and promise in his dear eyes as he held their clasped hands up to show her they were pledged on a level even she couldn't deny,

'To us?' she offered as a sort of compromise, since they agreed Eve should stay here while he was away and Verity would become a weekly boarder for now and it felt as if a family was forming between them whether she wanted it to or not. 'Will that do?'

'For now, and that brings me back to my quest—what sort of lover would your sister have favoured?'

'A young Adonis, such as my Lord Mantaigne might have been ten years ago, if he was less cynical, which I doubt,' she said after thinking clearly about that lover for the first time since she realised her twin was with child by him.

'He was never so and had better keep away from this Thessaly twin if he wants to keep a whole skin,' Luke said crossly and she smiled.

'I prefer dark and brooding Border raiders.'

'Stop trying to hold me here with half-promises, woman. I'm off to find this idol of your sister's with his feet of clay. After I confront him and beat him to a pulp, I shall be able to come back and wed you at long last.'

'As if that will solve anything. I said no and I've got work to do,' she told him huffily and pulled out of his arms to walk away with the sound of his surprised laughter echoing in her ears.

'Insufferable, stubborn, impossible man,' she

muttered as she marched inside, then darted into the flower room when she thought she heard someone coming downstairs.

Chloe splashed frigid water from a jug waiting to warm up enough to be used to refresh the few vases of flowers available at this time of year and gasped in a deep breath. The impossibility of it all threatened to suck the elation and hope out of her, but this time it wouldn't go. That had been her last no and they both knew it. He was a risk she had to take when he got back from Scotland, whatever the result of his quest might be. She was going to take that risk on love Daphne warned her against with her dying breath. Risk or not, she was going to have to jump right into it and trust him not to let them both drown.

She felt a little less convinced he'd manage it when she came down the elegant front stairs of Farenze Lodge on a fine spring morning six weeks later, ready to begin the grand clear out of hatchments, black veiling and all the other trappings of mourning Virginia had ordered must take place as soon as possible after her death. Chloe knew she should be as happy as she ever could be here without her beloved employer and mentor, but somehow knowing she was a coward took the joy out of the spring sunshine and dulled the sight of a flurry of primroses and violets brightening the edge of the still-leafless woods.

She still hadn't found the courage to tell Verity who she really was. She felt weighed down by her own folly as she helped the maids take down the dark veiling from gilt mirrors and statues and open the blinds in all the rooms kept half-dark until today. Holland covers were removed from the furniture in Virginia's splendid boudoir and the last bequests were matched to the list Mr Poulson left, ready to be sent to new owners with a note or a personal visit from Eve, her father or the housekeeper to hand over a memento of a much-loved lady.

Life was going relentlessly on all round her and Chloe felt the past threaten her happiness like a pall. She looked the same soberly correct housekeeper she'd been for so long, but felt nowhere near as serene and composed as she appeared while she awaited Luke's return and the end of his quest to find Verity's father.

Luckily, none of the neighbours knew Luke enclosed long letters to her with the sealed packet he sent to his daughter every week. Eve always handed them over with a lack of expression that said more than Chloe wanted anyone to know about her relationship with the girl's father. Yet with Eve's middle-aged governess here now to keep her pupil busy and all of them respectably chaperoned, Chloe knew Luke was making her own continuing presence here as unremarkable as possible and could only love him all the more for it.

'He's courting you,' Bran had pointed out when the latest letter came and Chloe hastily hid it in her pocket to read as soon as she could make an excuse to be alone.

When she did, she sat pouring over every word and could almost imagine he was here, telling her who he'd met and what he thought of the part of Scotland where Daphne stayed at first, then some sharp observations about her paternal aunt, Lady Hamming, that the lady would certainly not enjoy if she read them.

'His lordship is keeping me informed of some business he undertook for me whilst he is in Scotland,' she had retorted as briskly as she could when

Bran made that accusation, knowing her blush was giving her away so badly they both wondered why she was bothering.

'His lordship is a good man, but not so good he'd write at such length to someone he was doing a favour, Mrs Wheaton,' the shrewd little woman told her.

'He can't court me, I'm a servant,' Chloe said numbly.

'Are you now?'

'Of course I am.'

'The nobility and gentry might see what they expect to when they look through any of us as doesn't slop their bathwater or knock over the silver, but you won't fool the rest of us that easy, my dear.'

'For all that, I'm still a housekeeper.'

'And a very good one you are, too, but it's not what you're born to.'

'As if most ladies of birth and expectations are not brought up to keep house, when they're not too busy bearing heirs. Even if I was born a lady, why would I want to become a brood mare for some chilly lord?'

'Because he's a man in every sense of the word and would be whether he was born a lord or a labourer, perhaps? Don't you go judging Lord Farenze by any other noble devils you've come across, Mrs Chloe. He suffered enough grief from a woman who wouldn't see he's got a good heart under that abrupt manner of his. Why don't you ask yourself if he'd grumble and glare at those as wants to poke about in his life to pass the time if he hadn't a wild, romantic yearning inside him to protect? He needs you, my girl, so are you going to make him happy or kick him aside like that heartless young madam he married when he was too young to know any better did, as if he was nothing?'

'You'd trust me with the happiness of such a good man? I'm not sure I would. I come from bad blood, Bran, best for him if he has no more to do with me.'

'Your girl's bad then, is she?'

'No, she's as sweet as a nut all the way through, which makes her almost a miracle considering the nest of vipers I hail from,' Chloe replied with a shrug.

'Speaking for myself, I don't judge a book by what's next to it and you should try looking in the mirror sometimes.'

'I do. How else can I be sure I look neat and tidy every morning?'

'Look closer and you'll see a stranger looking back—bad blood indeed.'

'I'm not worthy of him, Bran,' Chloe whispered as if to say it aloud admitted Lord Farenze really was courting his great-aunt's companion house-keeper.

'You won't be if you cower behind that cap and your blacks for ever and won't see what could be if you was to let it. He deserves better.'

'That's exactly what I'm telling you.'

'No, you've come up with a cartload of reasons why not, when he's set his heart on you. He deserves a woman who'll say yes to him and damn the devil.'

'I have a daughter to consider,' she argued stubbornly.

'And he doesn't? Don't you trust him to be a good father to your Verity?'

'Of course I do,' Chloe admitted, then sighed with relief when Eve came to find out why it was taking them so long to count napkins and write down an order for more and saved her from even more uncomfortable questions.

Looking at herself from where Bran stood, Chloe wondered why anyone would believe she'd been the bold, bad Thessaly twin, who defied anyone who stood in the way of what she or Daphne wanted or needed now. When her father decided to sell off his more tractable daughter, she recalled how cleverly he'd whisked Daphne away so Chloe had no idea where she was and found she wanted to lash out at him as fiercely now as she had then. How that fiery young Chloe would stare at the subdued woman she'd become. She had kept herself and Verity safe by refusing to live fully and love Luke for years and it was time to let that pent-up fury go and learn to live without it.

Lady Chloe Thessaly learnt young that love was a snare. It left Daphne dead and her with a child to bring up. Little wonder if she refused to trust her feral longings for my Lord Farenze a decade ago. He'd been gruff and hurt then and must have resented wanting her until he glowered at her more often than he smiled. The battered and cynical aristocrat he pretended to be back then was so unlike the ardently romantic young lover she'd once dreamed of that it was little wonder she'd been horrified to discover he roused passions in her she'd thought stone dead.

Chapter Sixteen

As a delicate and vulnerable baby Verity had needed Chloe to concentrate all her energy on her, but did she truly need it now? She considered how a mother could cope with her child growing up. Mrs Winterley had treated Luke like a cuckoo in her nest his entire childhood because she wanted her own child to inherit, but now that James regarded his own mother as sceptically as his brother did, how must it feel to be rejected by the very being you adored? Chloe felt a moment of motherly sympathy with the woman before she disliked her all over again for doing her best to make the half-brothers hate each other. Little wonder it took years for Luke to recover his faith in human nature with such a stepmother. Then his self-centred fool of a wife did her best to convince him he was cold and unlovable and compounded the damage before running away.

She recalled how warm-hearted and passionate he could be and blushed. Telling herself to keep her obsession with the master of the house a secret, Chloe set her maids the tasks of washing and cleaning the paraphernalia of mourning, then storing it in the darkest attic they had. When they were all busy, she took a half-hour of peace and quiet for herself and sneaked into the library to shut the door on the world.

No need for the entire household and Brandy Brown to know she always kept one or other of Luke's letters in her pocket to re-read when she wanted to feel he was close by; or that sometimes she just wanted to set out for the north to find him and to the devil with appearances and duty. She sat back against the cushioned comfort of the little *chaise* in front of the unlit fire where they had sat one memorable January afternoon and let herself hear his deep voice in her head while she read the words he seemed more able to put on paper than bring on to his tongue to woo her with when they were together. Wasn't that just like him? Yet would she love him half as much if he was glib and care-less and ready to pour forth his every emotion?

Here on the West Coast of this fair land the gorse is in blithe flower outside my window, and the sight and heady, astringent scent of it reminded me so sharply of my prickly Lady Chloe that I had to set pen to paper in order to dream of you as I write and wish we could be together again, but this time in every way that word knows how.

Typical of him to begin with an insult, then turn it into a charm, she decided as she fingered the paper where his pen had scratched, then been mended and refilled with ink, bringing the scene to life so vividly it was almost as if she had been sitting nearby, shaking her head at his impatient curses, while all that had to be done before he could continue.

As dreaming of you is all I seem able to do at the moment, I might as well sit here and suffer the frustrations of the damned, while I imagine you with your knitted brows and

*a quick shake of that clever, unwise head
of yours as you wonder if I have finally run
mad from missing you in my life and especially in my bed.*

She stopped as she read that once again and
stared unseeingly at the wonderful portrait of Virgil and Virginia over the mantelpiece. As always,
it showed two lovers so lost in love they couldn't
spare their very expensive artist friend time to look
anywhere but into each other's eyes. When her
heart stopped racing at the very idea of Luke here
with her, saying things like that and holding her as
if he couldn't bear to let her go, she focused on the
painted likeness of those other lovers and frowned.

Was taking all your lover had to offer part of
the true generosity of love? How would she know,
never having been one in any sense until now?
Even if it took a daring leap of faith and imagination, the risk could be well worth taking though.
Sinking a little deeper into the cushions of the
chaise she'd shared with him the day Virginia's
will was read, she took up Luke's letter again and
let herself imagine him writing it with such un-
Luke-like candour it made a tender smile lift her

lips at the very thought of him putting so much on paper for her.

This is such a beautiful land, full of contradictions and surprises, so really it's a lot like you. I'm sure you'll like it when I get you here for a visit with no lost lovers to unmask at the end of it and, I sincerely hope, no forced politeness to a relative of yours I couldn't warm to if lost in an icy waste alone with her. I would rather snuggle up to an icicle than your once so famously beautiful paternal aunt, my Chloe.

Lady Hamming is still outwardly attractive, but not even her close family dare touch her, presumably fearing her chilliness is catching. I'm surprised she hasn't given poor Hamming frostbite or turned him into an ice statue after so many years of marriage, but he seems to consider her a marvellous curiosity it's best not to try to understand rather than his comfortably familiar companion through life.

Chloe smiled fleetingly at his vivid picture of an aunt she had no desire to know after she had conspired to sell Daphne to a depraved old lecher. Luke had laid her aunt's character open to her without any need for them to meet and she knew he was protecting her again. Chloe frowned and wondered why she wasn't offended by the notion— especially after swearing never to let another man shape her life the day she left Carraway Court for the last time.

'Is it part of love; learning to let someone make your burdens lighter?' she mused out loud. 'I really wish you two would pay attention and answer a few of my questions,' she told the painted lovers across the hearth crossly. 'What can I be expected to know about true love, after being brought up a Thessaly?'

As if they had answered, which was clearly impossible, the portrait of the first 'princely' Earl of Crowdale and his devious countess in an exquisitely painted book of hours, before her father sold it, seemed to sparkle before her mind's eye. Little doubt those two rogues adored one another, she decided, recalling them turned towards each other and holding hands as if that was the bare minimum of contact they could endure. The Thessaly family made a good start on loving immoderately and against the odds. *What a shame so few of their line carried on the tradition,* she felt she was being told now and wondered if Virgil and Virginia would scold her wariness if they truly could see her now.

'Good point,' she conceded, 'although I never actually *knew* them.'

'You knew me.' Virginia's voice, even richer and more full of suppressed laughter and devilry than Chloe remembered, seemed to echo in her mind and add weight to lying, loving Lady Crowdale and her pirate lover. 'I'm one-half of us two, my dear Chloe, and a love like ours doesn't fade and die when facing a challenge,' the imaginary Virginia added.

'Death is quite a challenge,' Chloe replied out loud, very glad she had shut the door behind her when she came in here to read and dream of her love.

'Only if it stops you living in the first place,' Lady Virginia's voice seemed to add before she withdrew from their non-conversation and was only a painted image again: fabulous Lady Virginia, Comtesse, Marquise and now Lady Farenze, sitting for her third marriage portrait and unaware of anyone but the man she'd married for love.

Luke's letter continued, and how could she miss a voice in her head when his loving words were right here in front of her?

The only way Lady Hamming reminds me of you is in how opposite you are to her in every way. It's been like trying to chip away at granite to get anything about your sister out of her or hers, but at last Hamming let fall something about the 'sad business' as he called it last night, while we dipped too deep into a bottle of aged malt whisky he'd managed to hide from his wife and her equally frosty butler; it cost me the devil of a head this morning, but at least this visit north of the Border hasn't proved a wild goose chase after all.

I'm sure Hamming could have been a decent man with more will-power and less frost in his life, but he was busy on his Irish estates that spring, so her ladyship was unchecked by any softer impulses her lord may have. He knows something was done in his absence, but it will probably cost me a few more sore heads to get the whole tale out of him.

I really don't know how you manage to think yourself unimportant to me when I'm risking my poor Sassenach constitution to find the name and fate of your sister's mystery lover. Apart from that, and being parted from you and Eve when I least want to be, I must admit that I have an easy enough role in all this.

Poor Peters seems to be faring less well in London, since he had to treat with some of the worst rogues the place can hold and visit its lowest hells to find the true depth of your elder brother's decline. It truly is a decline, Chloe, in every sense of the word. The wider world appears to think your younger brother more led into evil than devoted to it, but the current earl would make Francis Dashwood and his silly Hell Fire Club blush.

Nobody in Crowdale's inner circle would be surprised to hear how deplorably he and your father treated you and Lady Daphne and little Verity, but Peters tells me a very wealthy City merchant is rumoured to be about to permit Crowdale to marry his only child, a seventeen-year-old, naïve school-

girl available to pawn for a title at just the wrong moment. Any whisper of his heartless conduct towards his little sisters and niece until that alliance is sealed will blight the whole plan.

Chloe gasped with pity for the very idea of that unfortunate girl being left at the mercy of such a man. Her brother certainly wouldn't balk at wedding an innocent for her father's money when his father had done the same thing to her mother. She resolved to do whatever she could to stop the marriage, but not even her disgust at such a scheme could dim the glow of happiness she felt at being loved by such a fine man as Luke Winterley. Most men who lusted after an upper servant would have schemed to get her dismissed, or forced her to become his mistress ten years ago, but even now Luke had gone away and let her be when she begged him to, while he waited for her to believe the unbelievable.

For years he'd avoided this house when he clearly loved it, in order to make sure an upper servant of his great-aunt could raise her child in peace. Bran was quite right; he was an exceptional gentleman.

She recalled how brusque and bad-tempered he'd been about it with a smile. The promise of such a rare love was so breathtaking she could hardly bring herself to believe it was within her reach. To reassure herself it was, if she dared accept the wonder, she re-read the ending of his letter.

You must take every care of yourself whilst I'm not there, love. I have sent Josiah to stay at Miss Thibett's school, with that lady's full knowledge and permission, so your girl can be kept safe whilst I gather the whole tale of your sister's adventures. Then Peters can give it verbatim to that ambitious alderman and even he won't be able to dismiss it as a warm story thought up by one of Crowdale's detractors. Peters seems to have some surprising connections of his own, so one or two vigorous and wary rogues will be joining the staff at Farenze Lodge soon to outfox anyone intent on harming you to keep me quiet, if it should come out I have been asking questions about Daphne and Chloe Thessaly's disappearance.

Please say and do nothing reckless in the

meantime, since yours and Eve's welfare are crucial to me and your brothers are clearly desperate for the girl's dowry and will do anything to make sure this sad tale and their appalling treatment of their very young sisters never comes out, or at least not until the marriage is safely over and cannot be revoked.

Believe me a blind fool if you like, but I bitterly repent a decade of refusing to look into my own heart and find you there tonight, love. I'd rather live without a limb than endure another ten years without you, so even if you can't return my feelings, please don't run away again and disappear as you did from your father's house all those years ago. I'll run mad fretting about your safety and happiness if you remove me so completely from your life. I shall stop now, before I sink myself for ever in your eyes by begging pathetically for anything you feel able to offer me. You must give that freely and I must turn into a patient man.

I think of you with every other thought and

for a curmudgeonly old bear like me to say
that you must know I mean it,
I am, now and always, your Luke Winterley,
whether you want me to be or not.

Chloe caught herself staring into thin air and smiling broadly at a mental picture of him as he signed his name at the end of her letter. When she read his words again it all seemed so simple. She could echo her love back at him across the miles between them without a second thought.

'Oh, I want you all right, Luke Winterley,' she told the place where he'd signed his name as if it might bring him back all the sooner, 'And I wouldn't love you half so well if you were more charming and less bearlike,' she whispered softly. Then went to make sure her maids were setting about the spring cleaning whilst the master of the house was away, to stop herself from sitting and dreaming the whole day away.

Several days later Luke urged his weary horse onwards and fought his frustration that this was as fast as he could get to Farenze Lodge. He'd had the best horses money could buy under him all the way, but he still wasn't getting there fast enough. It was asking too much of this poor beast and he was weary to the bone, but fear drove him on relentlessly and he'd bid his head groom goodbye when the man had almost fallen from his saddle some time yesterday.

Nearly there, the words seemed to echo in his head with every step, but he still felt as if the devil was on his tail, his rank breath hot on the back of Luke's neck and the chaos of hell at his back. He'd racked his brains all the way south to work out when Chloe's wicked aunt began to watch him with active malice. He hoped he'd outrun the messenger she must have sent south as soon as she realised he was in Scotland to track down a pair of star-crossed young lovers, not to buy one of her husband's precious racehorses, or marry the last unwed Hamming daughter left on her hands.

In the end he'd realised Hamming must have told her about Luke's interest in Lady Daphne Thessaly's tragically early death and he cursed the woman's ability to prise information from her amiable but shallow lord. It wasn't hard to see where Chloe got her brains, but thank heaven she and her sister got their warmth and sweetness from their mother as well as their distant Thessaly ancestress.

His love could say what she liked about bad blood, but everything about her screamed her difference from her father, brother and icy aunt. If Lady Hamming was ever presented with a tiny baby to cast into the world alone or protect with her last breath, she would place it on that frosty church step, then walk away without a second thought.

There, at last, the Lodge was in sight and he asked his tired horse for one last effort as the urgency that brought him south as fast as he could get here needled him. At first glance all seemed serene and hope stirred that he was in time. As he rode into the stable yard and nobody came out to welcome him or take his weary horse, it was clear he was wrong and Lady Hamming was as coldly efficient in getting messages to her disreputable nephews as she was at everything else.

'Take him,' he barked at the stable boy who ran breathlessly into the yard and stood with his mouth open as if he'd forgotten who Luke was. 'Put him in a box and rub him down, then let him rest.'

Weariness forgotten, Luke jumped from the saddle and dashed towards the house, wondering what the hell had happened. He went through the back door and into the kitchen to save all the fuss of rousing Oakham and explaining why he had no luggage and looked more bearlike than ever.

'Ah, here's his lordship at last. Now we can relax and worry about you and your injuries while he sorts everything out, sir,' he heard Chloe say calmly as if she was welcoming a late guest to a party and he felt his temper snap.

'What the devil is going on?' he rapped out as he surveyed the crowd cluttering the kitchen with what he felt was excusable irritation.

'Mr Revereux has been shot,' Eve informed him calmly.

The man's name punched through the haze of weariness dragging at him and he blinked to bring the Adonis wilting on the scrubbed kitchen table into sharp focus.

'Has he now? I've been searching the length and breadth of Britain for the man and find him lying on my kitchen table? Good day to you, Revereux, do make yourself at home, won't you? Perhaps you'd enjoy a few covers and the odd side dish when you're done and the rest of my house and gardens are of course available for your enjoyment when you're not reclining on the kitchen table.'

'I think Papa is tired and hungry. He certainly looks as if he hasn't slept for days,' Eve explained his lack of hospitality with a furious sideways look for him and a sage nod for everyone else. Luke felt as if even her presence might not prevent him swearing long and fluently if someone didn't explain what was going on very soon.

'Of course he is. I dare say he's found out something crucial and travelled here far too fast to inform us of it, so do go and sit by the fire and rest for a moment, my lord.' Chloe finally spared the time to turn from her patient and soothe him, as if he were a dangerous wild dog she was trying to see the best in before he bit someone.

'Yes, I have,' he thundered, quite unappeased. 'I found out he was it,' he said with an accusing gesture at the pale and interesting-looking blond god trying to fight Verity Wheaton off without hurting her. She refused to be diverted with a hardy determination that reminded Luke strongly of her aunt.

'Then you are Verity's father, sir?' The question seemed to tumble out of Chloe's mouth before she could silence it and first she stared at the stranger, then had the gall to glare at *him,* as if he should learn to guard his tongue. Luke felt another check on his temper snap.

'I am,' the pale and interesting hero gently pushed his daughter's hands aside before he sat up to confront Luke with that knowledge, and what a fairer side of his nature told him was excusable pride in his daughter, as well as a challenge in the clear blue eyes Verity had inherited from him.

'My papa is dead,' Verity insisted with a frown nearly as fierce as the one Luke felt pleating his own brows on her face. At that moment he felt a deeper kinship with the bewildered, belligerent girl than ever, even as another man claimed her as his own.

'So some would have you believe,' the man muttered darkly and shot Chloe a look of angry dislike that made Luke's ire boil over like the saucepans he could smell doing the same in the background.

'If you weren't being physicked for that injury and lying on my kitchen table already, I'd knock you down for that,' he bellowed at the prone figure of his latest unwanted guest. 'Lady Chloe gave up everything to keep Verity safe and happy and you lie there and accuse her of usurping your role and scheming to keep the child to herself? You'll meet me for that insult as soon as you've recovered from whatever wound some worthy soul has inflicted on you to teach you some manners before I could do it for him, sirrah.'

'No, he won't,' Chloe said flatly, glaring at him for defending her integrity and he turned a blazing challenge on her instead.

'Why the devil not? He's the idiot who ruined your sister's life.'

'My father and brother did that. He saved her from a marriage that would have been hell on earth and I can't bring myself to think what they might have done to make me miserable if I'd stayed home to be bartered off to some rich roué as well. If Captain Revereux loved my sister even for a week or two, it was more than either of us had from any other human being after our mother died and I'm thankful for it.'

'Thankful to lose your twin sister? To endure what you have done? To be left alone with her in that shack in the hills Peters reports they consigned you to like a pair of unwanted puppies while she waited for her child to be born? Why forgive the sins of everyone in your life who wishes you harm and never mine, when I want only the best for you, woman? Well, I give in, I'll finally accept you don't want what I do and leave you to your happy family reunion while I take myself somewhere I can endure being regarded as a devil in human form more easily,' he said with a hitch in his voice he didn't care to hear at all.

Chapter Seventeen

Turning to stamp out again and ride as far as a fresh horse could carry him this late in the day, Luke stumbled over the doorstep, then righted himself like a drunkard. Just as well he did, considering Chloe rushed into the yard to confront him with her cap sadly awry and her auburn locks tumbling from under it. She would have tripped over him if he had tumbled on to the cobbles.

'Don't you dare say that, then walk away from me, you lubberly great coward,' she spat at him. 'How dare you come home, looking like something the dog didn't want, then snap and rage at the man who saved my daughter from the very men you were supposed to be protecting her from?'

'I suppose he has some excuse for being here.'

'Yes, and I have the good manners to thank him

for it, whoever he might be. You challenged him for no good reason that I can see.'

'If you can't see why I would, then I'll leave you to your touching family reunion. The man is clearly everyone's hero but mine and you have no need of me.'

'You're jealous, aren't you?' she asked and gave him a smug smile that made him squirm, but at least temper made him face her challenge with one of his own.

'Of course I'm not, the man's obviously an idiot.'

'How can even you say so, let alone believe it? My brother hatched a wild plan to abduct Verity, to keep me quiet about his past sins until his wedding was over and the poor girl bedded so it could not be annulled. Captain Revereux foiled it, then rode here with Verity up behind him and a bullet lodged in his arm, until Josiah recovered consciousness after being knocked out and he and Mr Peters rode to the rescue a little too late to be a great deal of use.'

'Then he is clearly your hero and I have nothing to do or say here.'

'And you're going to turn and walk away in a fit of pique? Go out of my life for another ten years…'

Words failed her for a moment. 'How could you, you ridiculous, thick-headed, bad-tempered great *idiot*? You wrote me all those wonderful letters; full of love and hope, and let me dream of you loving me back. Now you're going to throw it all away because you're tired and you've lost your temper? Oh, go away then, you stupid great oaf. How could I ever think I loved you? I must be an even bigger fool than you are.'

He stood reeling when she turned on her heel with a huff of impatience and prepared to storm off and leave him there gaping after her like a stranded codfish.

'No, you don't,' he barked as he snapped out of his shocked stupor and grabbed her by the waist to physically stop her walking away from him. 'You're not going anywhere until you've explained yourself,' he told her gruffly.

'I'm not saying anything,' she informed him and tossed her head so the awful cap finally fell off and the sight of her glorious copper-gold locks down her back like hot silk nearly mazed him into slackening his grip and letting her go.

'Good,' he said huskily and snatched a hungry,

explicit kiss square on her mouth at the instant she opened it to hurl some new insult at him.

She resisted angrily and a rational, gentlemanly part of him stood aside and tutted as the rest of him deepened the kiss. His grip on her softened, but he had to persuade her to need him back before he dared raise his head and admit she was right and he was a damned fool to even dream of walking away from her and this.

His inner gentleman was about to win the battle and let her go if this wasn't what she wanted desperately as well when she wriggled insistently against him. His heart in his boots, he waited for her to wrench out of his arms, then rage at him and demand he never came within a hundred miles of her ever again. Instead she flung her arms about his neck and held on to him as if she never intended to let him go. Fierce joy sang in his heart even as the appalling weariness of his forced ride threatened to wash over him and send him into a very unmanly faint.

'I missed you so much,' she informed him tearfully as she stood on tiptoes, meeting his tired eyes with a blaze of passion in her own. 'I love you, Luke Winterley, and don't you dare walk away,' she threatened fiercely. 'If you do, I'll walk in the opposite direction and *you'll* have to chase *me*, because I am a Thessaly and I do have some pride,' she told him; all they could be together in her mesmerising gaze.

'Oh, my Chloe, whatever would I do without you?' He breathed and hardly dared blink unless he was imagining the feel and fact of her against him and the wondrous promise she'd just made, in public, in front of rather a lot of witnesses as half his staff were standing in the kitchen doorway grinning like idiots.

'I feel the same about you, you great unshaven, smelly brute of a man,' she murmured, then kissed him as if he was her perfect pattern of a gentleman.

'It might be best if you came back in, Lord Farenze, ma'am,' one of the men Peters had sent to protect Verity interrupted them from the back of the crowd. 'Yon Captain Rever—whoever you said he was—has fainted and the cook's beating the kitchen maid with a soup ladle.'

'Oh the romance of it all,' Luke whispered against Chloe's lips as he forced himself to stop kissing the love of his life and met her laughing eyes instead. 'Life seems to await us in all its rich variety, my darling. Don't forget me whilst you deal with it in your usual inimitable fashion.'

'As if I could, my scruffy, disreputable lord,' she whispered, 'now let me go before I kick you in the shins as I should have done the instant you laid disrespectful hands on me, you great barbarian.'

'Virago,' he replied shakily.

Scandalously hand-locked, they went back into the once spotless and beautifully ordered kitchen and Chloe snapped a series of concise orders. Within minutes the hysterical kitchen maid had been sent to lie down in a darkened attic, Cook was sipping tea in her chair by the fire and looking sheepish while the footmen hauled quantities of water onto the hot plates to hasten the bath Luke knew he needed rather badly.

Eve somehow stopped Verity plucking the feathers out of the head housemaid's best feather duster to burn to revive the patient. Revereux woke from his faint of his own accord and was now insisting on getting down from his undignified perch as if he would never do anything so unmanly.

'Don't be an idiot, man,' Luke urged him roughly as Revereux tried to stand tall and accept the challenge Luke had thrown out in his flash of overwrought temper after finding Verity safe and sound and his mad dash south more or less unnecessary. 'Lady Chloe explained about your rescue of Miss Verity and told me in no uncertain terms that we are all deeply in your debt and I owe you an apology.'

'I was protecting my own,' the man stubbornly insisted, as if he could think of nothing he would like more than a good fight with his uncouth host.

'Shame you weren't about when the child needed you most then, isn't it?' Luke rebuked him grimly and met the man's pained blue eyes, so like Verity's there really was no questioning his claim to be the girl's father.

'Aye,' he replied with a deep sigh and looked easily as weary as Luke felt.

'I am here, you know?' Verity intervened even as Chloe sent Luke a warning glare to inform him he was making things worse for the poor man.

'Something I trust Lord Farenze and his daughter are about to remedy,' Chloe said and Verity looked as if she was about to argue. 'This is not the time for anything other than making sure poor Mr Revereux is made comfortable as he can be with a bullet wound in his shoulder—explanations can come later.'

'I don't know about that, but would you mind finding out how my poor horse does, Miss Verity?' the gentleman asked faintly. The girl still hesitated and Luke's admiration for her courage increased.

'Very well, but please don't think I'm too young or stupid to know what's going on,' she said sternly and managed her exit a great deal more gracefully than the master of the house had done.

As soon as Verity was out of earshot Luke watched Chloe ruthlessly uncover her patient's wound, despite his protests this was too public a space for a gentleman to remove so much of his clothing.

'Pray stop being such a baby,' she ordered the strapping sea captain, who bit his lip, then fainted again while she examined the wound for stray fragments of cloth and lead, then cheerfully pronounced the ball had passed along the fleshy part of the gentleman's upper arm and avoided any major veins or arteries.

She frowned in concentration while doing her best to remove every shred of fine linen threads from his wound then clean it with a solution of what smelt to Luke like rosemary and brandy, before binding it up with a pad soaked in herbs and honey and bandaging it in place.

'It's as well we're still only in March,' he observed as Chloe sat in one of the kitchen chairs with a relieved sigh and accepted a cup of Cook's best tea. 'The poor man would be mobbed with bees and wasps if he set foot outside later in the year.'

'It will stop infection, although Captain Revereux must have the constitution of an ox to manage to ride here from Bath with a wound like that draining him of energy all the way,' she said.

'True, although it would be as well if we wait to get the whole tale out of him before we declare him a hero. He doesn't strike me as being the type to dwell on his good deeds and he is a little late in rescuing his daughter from the wolves,' Luke said, glad he hadn't been called upon to test his limited knowledge of herbs and doctoring in his current state of travel-stained weariness.

'And Mrs Wheaton is quite right, Papa, you really do need a bath,' his own daughter told him with a fastidious wrinkling of her nose at the smell of sweat, road mud and horse so strong on him it almost drowned out the astringent herbs.

'I'm a trial and embarrassment to my womenfolk at the best of times,' he said with an unrepentant smile and went away to remedy it with an energy he'd have thought impossible, before Lady Chloe Thessaly admitted she loved him.

'Why did Lord Farenze call you Lady Chloe when you were arguing, Mama?' Verity asked even as she accepted Chloe's help to don a fresh gown and sat still for her to comb out her tangled mane of wheat-blonde hair.

'Because it's my real name, my love.'

'Then you are the daughter of an earl or marquis or duke?' Verity said as she held Chloe's gaze in the mirror.

'An earl,' Chloe admitted with a sigh.

'The men who tried to make me go with them, then attacked Mr Revereux, said the Earl would have their hides if they let us escape. What an odd coincidence.'

'I'm afraid not, love,' Chloe admitted, wishing Verity was less intelligent for once.

'He is the same one, then? My own grandfather

paid those men to kidnap me and attack anyone who got in their way? What kind of man would do such a thing to his own flesh and blood?'

'The earl who wanted to capture you is your uncle and not my father and I don't really want you to know what kind of man he is now.'

'I want to know why he thinks I would want to live with him when I'd rather be your next scullery maid. He had poor Mr Revereux shot because he stopped those bad men carrying me off.'

Chloe was unsure how much Verity had heard or understood of the arguments in the kitchen, so she took a deep breath and told Verity how she and Daphne grew up together on a rundown estate in Devon. How their father and brothers ignored them until they decided Daphne would net them a fortune as a beautiful and biddable young lady they could sell to the highest bidder. She couldn't describe Daphne's visit to Lady Hamming in Edinburgh because she didn't know about it herself, but she also admitted that her father, the Earl of Crowdale, thought their aunt should introduce his prettiest and most docile twin daughter to Edinburgh society before she married the old man he agreed to sell her to.

'Rumours that my father was in debt were probably flying about London and a London Season is very expensive. My aunt has always doted on her brother and nephews, so they knew she would do as they asked her to at no cost to them.'

'It's a sad story and I feel sorry for Aunt Daphne, but what has she got to do with that man who says he is my father?' Verity asked.

'Well, instead of marrying her to an elderly duke, your grandfather and uncles brought my sister back to Carraway Court in disgrace. They ordered me to pack enough for both of us, because we were going to live in the most remote place they could find since she refused to marry that rich old man. So I packed all I could in the time they gave me and was glad to quit the Court with my father and brothers stamping about there as if every breath we took was costing them dear.

'Our things were bundled into a farm dray and we were taken to meet the stage coach, then thrown off it at the turning leading up to a farmhouse high on Bodmin Moor, where no tenant would stay because it's so isolated you can only walk there or ride a single pony across the moor. It was miles from our nearest neighbours. The roof leaked in places and the wind howled across the moor as if the hounds of hell had been let loose to roam the earth. We were often cold and hungry as summer turned to autumn, then winter, and the local people would leave scraps of firewood and any vegetables they could spare us where our narrow track left the road. They had the kindness our own kin lacked and we might have died of cold and hunger if not for them.'

'Why did they turn on you because Aunt Daphne didn't want to marry some horrid old man, Mama?'

'Because she was with child,' Chloe admitted reluctantly.

'How old were you both then?'

'Seventeen at the turn of the year.'

'Then you must have been the one who was pregnant, Mama, since you had me when you were seventeen.'

'I'm sorry, my love, but your true mother was my twin sister, Lady Daphne Thessaly.'

'Then I'm a bastard,' Verity whispered blankly, the full nuances of that word seeming to hit her like a blow.

'A love child,' Chloe corrected her gently.

'And you lied; you pretended I was your child.'

'I admit there never was a Mr Wheaton, love. I had to make him up, so we could both be respectable and I could keep you with me while I worked to feed and clothe us both. I couldn't let my father take you away after your mother died and there was nobody else to look after you but me.'

'Where was he going to take me, then?' The question was without inflection and Chloe hated to go on with her story when Verity was already so shocked by it.

'Your mother was buried at a tiny church on the Moor where the vicar was a good Christian. I was so glad when my family sent for us so you would be fed and warm. I didn't ask what they intended to do until we were back at Carraway Court and I overheard an argument about which church to leave you at on the way to London.'

'Poor little baby,' Verity said as if talking about someone else.

Chloe longed to take her in her arms, but Verity looked as if the last person she wanted close to her now was the one who had lied to her and everybody else about who they both were for so long.

'I stole every coin I could lay hands on that night and took what was left of your grandmother's jewellery. I'm sorry, Verity, but I sold it when I got to London and used the money to support us until I managed to get work. I'm a liar and a thief and you must hate me for pretending to be your mother.'

'You could have left me somewhere safe.'

'Abandon my twin sister's beloved child to an orphan asylum? No, I couldn't. I loved my sister dearly, but I already loved you more.'

'If not for me you would have a family of your own by now. Grandfather was too stupid to see how beautiful you are, but some fine gentleman would have married you long ago, if you didn't have me.'

'Nonsense, I was quite content to be the carroty-headed quiz of the family, my love, and I have loved being your mama, even if I am really only your aunt.'

'No, you're truly beautiful, Mama. Oh botheration, I know you're not my mother now, but I can't call you Aunt Chloe after all these years.'

'Then don't, but you do have a father after all, Verity. Until today all I knew about him was he was young and handsome and Daphne loved him, but from all appearances he is quite the hero and seems very ready to own you as his daughter.'

'Mr Revereux?'

'So it seems and the rest of their story is his to tell, since I don't know it and your mother kept him a secret even from me, for some reason best known to herself.'

'Would Grandfather and my uncles have kept me if they knew he was a gentleman?'

The comforting lie trembled on Chloe's lips for a moment, but she bit it back and shook her head. 'I suspect they did know and forced them apart. My father was a cold man and my eldest brother isn't much better. '

'Then I've had a better life than you did, Mama,' Verity astonished Chloe by saying practically. 'Lady Virginia loved us and I had you. I much prefer being me to living the kind of life you two had to at my age.'

'It wasn't so bad, our mother's aunts descended on us every summer to make sure we didn't grow into a pair of savages.'

'So you two ran wild, yet I endure algebra, logic and geography?'

'Such are the injustices of life.'

'You and Lord Farenze could have married years

ago if you weren't Mrs Wheaton for my sake. That's an injustice and a shame if you ask me.'

'Since his lordship doesn't go into society and I can't see my father paying for me to come out even if he did, it's highly unlikely we would have met in my true guise, darling.'

'He has met you, though, and I think he loves you, Mama.'

'And I love him back, Verity,' Chloe admitted quite calmly now it was out in the open.

At times, she reflected, she could wish her precocious niece was a little less perceptive about the adults around her. It was probably because Verity had spent so much time with Virginia that she saw through social pretence. In a few years' time the beaux of the *ton* would need to watch out when Miss Verity Revereux-Thessaly was launched into their rarefied world.

'You two are going to get married like Lady Virginia and *her* Viscount Farenze did, are you not?' she asked bluntly now.

'Lady Virginia was fabulously beautiful in her youth.'

'And so are you. Eve and I think this Lord Farenze

loves you easily as much as the last one loved Lady
Virginia,' Verity persisted stubbornly.

'I have had to work for my living, Verity. He really shouldn't wed a housekeeper.'

'He can do as he likes and I think you can, too,
if you want to badly enough.'

'And I think you need your dinner sent up and a
good night's sleep after all your adventures today,
young lady,' Chloe said as Verity's eyelids began
to droop. 'Why not climb into bed and I'll see if I
can persuade Cook to send up a tray for you just
this once.'

'I'm not ill.'

'Maybe not, but you've had a busy day, even by
your standards. It won't hurt if you play the young
lady and lie abed until noon if you choose to tomorrow either.'

'But I *am* a young lady, if all you have told me
is true and my father intends to own me as his
daughter.'

'Indeed, Captain Revereux seems the very model
of a heroic gentleman,' Chloe said and managed
to hide a nasty little stab of jealousy. Heroic and
handsome Captain Revereux would soon win his

daughter's admiration and love and where would that leave Lady Chloe Thessaly?

'I still like Lord Farenze best, though. He will never let anyone hurt me if he's my stepfather,' Verity argued sleepily and Chloe was glad the under-housemaid knocked at the door with the tray Cook had sent without waiting for an order.

She let her niece finish her soup and a syllabub, then sit up fighting sleep, as she had to let it all go down before she could curl into her warmed bed with a guard set before the fire and a weary sigh of relief.

'I'll stay with her, you're needed elsewhere tonight,' Brandy said, as she swept into the room with a bland smile while Chloe wondered if she should stay in case Verity had nightmares after such a day.

'Give me time to make certain all's well and Miss Thibett has been told Verity's safe and I'll be back to sit with her myself,' Chloe whispered and Bran shook her head and shooed her away like a farmer's wife chasing hens from her kitchen.

Chapter Eighteen

'Managing female,' Chloe muttered as she stood outside Verity's room, glaring at the blank and highly polished closed door.

'It takes one to know one,' Luke grumbled as he rose from his seat just along the corridor, then tugged her further away so they wouldn't disturb Verity.

'You think I'm overbearing, then?' she asked absently. It was wonderful to feel all that warmth and strength and maleness so close again.

'Of course I do, love. It's been your job for the past decade or more to be a managing female. You wouldn't be much good as a housekeeper if you weren't a little overbearing at times, now would you?'

He understood her and still wanted to spend his life with her. It was odd and unaccountable, but it felt dazzling to know that stubborn, clever, complicated Luke Winterley was indeed the wild lover of young Chloe's dreams, as well as his slightly gruff, everyday self to make it all real and possible.

'You don't mind that I'll never be able to turn myself into a meek and biddable little wife if you marry me, then?'

'I'd be deeply disappointed if you did, my fiery, short-tempered love. Does that mean you're thinking of saying yes to me at long last?'

'I refuse to discuss it when you're weary half to death and should probably be in bed instead of prowling about the place like a restless wolf. You clearly rode south so fast you nigh killed yourself and the poor horses you rode along the way.'

'My bed here never holds much attraction without you in it, Chloe, but I can't tell you how often I have wished for a faster way to get to you these last few days.'

'Or how many times I wished you were here,' she told him with promises of all they would be heady between them. 'How is the patient?' she asked absently, doing her best to tear her fascinated gaze from his smoky dark one in the dim light at the top of the stairs to the nursery wing they hadn't got round to descending yet.

'Revereux refuses to sleep. Unless we convince him Verity's quite safe until he can guard her like a mastiff with a bone again, he'll be running a high fever by morning.'

'Exasperating man,' Chloe said, fear that the Captain would insist on claiming his daughter still haunting her like a bad dream.

'As you have accused me of being one of those so often, I hope you don't expect me to condemn him for it. You do know Virginia's elder sister wed a Revereux though, don't you, my love?' Luke asked gently.

'I thought his name sounded familiar. Then I'm surprised he hasn't visited whilst I've been here, although I'm very glad he didn't. It would be hard to deny my daughter is related to him now I've seen the strong resemblance between them. Do you really think Virginia knew who she might be and didn't tell me, Luke?'

'I doubt it. Can you see my darling great-aunt resisting such a wonderful chance to interfere in so many lives if she did?'

'Not really—it does seem an odd coincidence, though.'

'They do happen and Virginia and her eldest sister never did get on. Lady Revereux was rigidly respectable and even I have to admit Virginia was outrageous in her youth. Virgil was no saint either and I doubt the stiff-necked old stickler approved of their marriage. The current earl is a downright prig, so we'll have to wait and see if this fellow takes after him or has a bit of humanity in him to leaven all the Revereux starch he's probably inherited. Until we know how Revereux found Verity we won't know if Virginia knew or not, though, so we'd better keep the man alive for now.'

'Don't even joke about it, Luke,' Chloe replied with a shudder at the thought of Verity losing her father as soon as he'd found her.

'It was in poor taste, but what do you expect from a barbarian? It'll be your job to civilise me.'

'Maybe I like you as you are,' she said with a witchy smile.

'Hell cat,' he responded with a hot glitter of masculine interest in his eyes she'd thought he was too weary to feel after his epic journey south.

'Wolf,' she countered huskily, all the temptations

of loving him fully running like a hot tide through her heart and mind.

'Mr Revereux refuses to take the potion the doctor left for him,' Culdrose interrupted them from the bottom of the next flight of stairs and Chloe stared down at the ladies' maid blankly for a moment.

It was a timely reminder there were other things to do than find Luke Winterley's faults fascinating and his wonderful qualities even more unique than she'd realised.

'It's quite like old times for Culdrose, I suppose,' she informed the patient crossly when she entered his bedchamber with Luke sauntering in her wake and openly enjoying the view.

'Why so, ma'am?' the patient asked with an impatient frown.

'Our late employer was every inch as stubborn as you are proving to be.'

'Sensible woman,' he muttered glumly.

'There are those who would argue, but did you never meet the lady yourself, sir, related to her as Lord Farenze believes you to be?' Chloe couldn't help asking.

'Only as a boy and I've been at sea since I was

thirteen with very little leave spent in this country. I recall her telling me then that she might like me better if I didn't have such a high opinion of myself. She said if Bonaparte was to be defeated by vain boys I would be an admiral before I was thirty.'

'That sounds very like her; I should try not take it too much to heart, sir.'

'It's very difficult to remain a spoilt brat as a midshipman in the senior service, your ladyship,' he admitted with a rueful smile that tempted Chloe to like him more than she wanted to.

'Then why not take your medicine and prove it, Mr Revereux?'

'Slyly done, Lady Chloe, but if those rogues could get so close to abducting Verity in Bath, how can I risk fogging my wits when she's in the middle of an isolated country estate miles away from authority?'

'Because I know how to protect my own, Revereux,' Luke stepped forward to tell him and there was enough challenge in his deep voice to tell the man he was on shaky ground. 'Our enemies are now too busy avoiding their creditors to bother scheming against us.'

'Foreclosed, have you?' Revereux asked as if he understood the true facts of the matter far better than Chloe did.

'This very morning a friend of mine delivered a detailed account of Crowdale's past sins to the City merchant who almost let him wed his only child.'

'Heaven knows, they're heavy enough,' the Captain said with a restless movement against his pillows, then a quickly suppressed gasp at the pain it caused him that made Chloe flinch in sympathy.

'Heavy enough to finish him in this country; he'll have to flee if he's to avoid being imprisoned for debt, as well as various sins we won't broadcast for the sake of Lady Chloe and your daughter. '

'Since we're being so protective of my sensibilities, why don't you take this draught, sir, before I succumb to hysterics after such a long and trying day?' Chloe asked, glaring at both men as she tried to understand their veiled references.

'You don't fight fair, do you, Lady Chloe?' the patient asked with a wry smile that made her see why Daphne fell so deep in love with him.

'How can I when there are so many unfair advantages on the other side, sir? Gentlemen have a monopoly on dashing about the country engaged on adventures you refuse to explain to us dim-witted females. If I can wait until tomorrow to find out the facts of my sister's tragic love story, you can sleep and recover from your injuries and show a little patience as well. Verity and I wait on the whims of annoying males who feel they have a right to dictate our lives without asking us.'

'I feel sure half that tirade was directed at me, Revereux. It would be diplomatic to restore your strength before she takes you on again though,' Luke cautioned.

'And you'll swear to me my daughter is safe?' he asked with such painful anxiety that Chloe softened a little and even smiled when he directed his question at her, instead of dominant, masculine Viscount Farenze.

'I kept her so when nobody else cared a tinker's curse what happened to her, Mr Revereux, I will do so for as long as she needs me to,' she promised.

'Very well, do your worst then,' he murmured grudgingly and finally allowed himself to feel wretched.

Chloe nodded at the waiting Culdrose, who managed to tip a healthy dose down the gentleman's throat when he opened his mouth to argue he'd do it himself.

'No better than a stubborn babe,' Culdrose muttered grimly.

'Nor much more use than one right now,' he admitted wearily.

'Then you'll sleep like one if you know what's good for you,' Culdrose told him severely and sat in the chair by the bed as if settling in for the night to make sure he did as he was bid.

'I think we can safely leave her to it,' Luke whispered as he urged Chloe out of the room. 'The poor fellow doesn't stand a chance of stirring from that bed until he's healthy as a horse once again.'

'Would she could keep him there,' Chloe murmured and met his steady gaze with a shrug. 'I know, he's Verity's father. What if he wants to take her away, Luke?'

'We're still at war, Chloe, and I doubt he could leave the sea right now even if he wanted to. Verity has a perfectly good family to love and care for her and, in his shoes, I wouldn't even try to prise the child away from a woman she has no intention of being parted from.'

'Thank you for being ready to take us both on then, but I can't pretend he doesn't exist, can I?'

'Hardly, but come downstairs and dine with me, my darling. If I manage to stay awake long enough, we can talk about where we shall live and love and, if we're lucky, raise the rest of our vast tribe of children yet to be born.'

'I haven't officially agreed to marry you yet.'

'Then you'd better do so, Lady Chloe Thessaly. I've waited long enough to be your lover and refuse to be gainsaid much longer.'

'You're too tired to make love to Venus herself, if she bothered to step down from Olympus for such a disagreeable bear as you are tonight,' she told him as he took her hand and tucked it into the crook of his elbow. 'But I'm saying yes anyway,' she added.

'Good, I've waited over a decade for one of those from you, Mrs Wheaton. I intend to hear you say it again and again as soon as I've got my ring on your finger.'

'Not before then?' she asked, all her scruples forgotten as she stared up at him with a scandalous invitation in her eyes.

'In three days if I can get a licence quickly enough, lover,' he said implacably.

'You're turning into a puritan,' she said sulkily, rather insulted he could resist her now their marriage was so close. 'Three *days*?' she asked incredulously as that part of his statement finally got past the heady promises of their marriage bed.

'Our courtship has been quite long enough, we can marry as soon as you've found a gown that isn't made up from black bombazine.'

'I have a very nice grey-stuff gown for best,' she told him solemnly, running through an inventory of all the gowns unsuitable for a housekeeper Lady Virginia had pressed on her over the years in her head and selecting the most unsuitable of all.

Luke did his best to hide his horror at the idea of meeting her at the altar dressed so and Chloe laughed, then met his tired eyes with a teasing smile.

'It's all right, love, the neighbours will be shocked when they see me walk up the aisle in the splendid white ball gown Virginia gave me for my last birthday. As they will already be reeling at the secrets we will have to reveal about my past, present and future by then, I suppose we might as well give them something else to wonder about.'

'True. How do you feel about being the focus of gossip for miles around, my lady?' he asked as Oakham opened the door of the Green Parlour the family used before dinner when not entertaining.

'Indifferent on my own account, but a little worried about how it will affect Verity and Eve,' she replied, then Eve and her governess greeted them with a flurry of questions about the Captain and Verity and even that concern was laid aside for another day.

It took Captain Revereux two days to evade his nurse and make his way downstairs without Culdrose knowing he'd gone. Luke found him ensconced in the family sitting room before dinner and began to dislike him all over again. Eve was busy finding cushions to make the chair by the fire where Luke usually sat more comfortable for the interloper and Chloe was ordering a feast fit for a king in honour of his recovery.

Trying hard to be fair, Luke could see why an impressionable young girl like Daphne Thessaly would fall so hard for the young Adonis Revereux must have been, but couldn't quite suppress a sting of jealousy when Chloe fussed over the man as if he were a fallen god. He felt much better when Revereux fidgeted uncomfortably at so much feminine attention, then wondered if he might even learn to like him one day when the man called a halt.

'I am very well now and have always healed quickly,' Revereux said, so they sat and wondered who would ask the rush of questions they all wanted answers to, but felt too polite to launch straight into as soon as the man was feeling well enough to come downstairs again.

'When does your ship sail, Revereux?' Luke asked, as genially as he could when he was trying not to wish it might be tomorrow.

'In three weeks' time,' the Captain said with a frown and Luke felt a twinge of guilt at reminding a guest he would soon have to depart, but only a twinge. He was feeling very impatient to get on with his wedding. 'She's been in dry dock for a refit, then I am to get her back for sea trials in a fortnight and, all being as it should be, we will embark a week later.'

'And where will you be bound, Captain?' Chloe

asked, looking relieved he would shortly be out of the country, but Luke knew they would have to resolve Verity's future before the man left.

'I'll be sailing under sealed orders, Lady Chloe, so I really don't know.'

'How exciting,' Eve said with stars in her eyes, as if she dreamt of sailing the seven seas in a state of constant adventure and upheaval.

'Not really,' Revereux argued with an indifference to the idea Luke must remember to thank him for later. 'Apart from the danger and upset of a storm and the rush and alarm of battle, life at sea is sadly tedious and the men dread serving on the Caribbean station because of the yellow fever and the like. I hope we're not bound there, Miss Winterley, for I can't like the place for all its warmth and natural beauty.'

'Is it so beautiful, then?'

'Aye, and rich and devilish hot at times and the sugar plantations are worked by unlucky slaves I don't blame in the least for feeling rebellious and running away whenever they get the chance.'

'Oh,' Eve said, looking a little downcast. 'I'm sure I should as well and I'm very glad Papa has no business interests there after all. Will you not tell us how you found out about Verity and tracked her down and rescued her from her wicked uncles though, Mr Revereux? It sounds a very dashing tale and quite fit for one of Mrs Radcliffe's novels.'

'I dare say it was nothing of the sort and anyway it is a story that can wait, love, if the Captain wants to tell his private affairs to such a curious miss at all, that is,' Luke intervened before the poor man felt obliged to recount his ill-fated love story between entrées.

'Indeed, and dining *en famille* is a treat that can easily be withdrawn from young ladies not yet out.' Chloe reinforced his warning with a stern eye on Verity and both girls rolled their eyes at the unreasonable nature of parents, then behaved like a pair of unlikely angels.

'Would you like to take a brandy or shall we join the ladies and be sociable over the teacups, Revereux?' Luke asked at the end of the meal and thought he saw the man pale at the idea of returning to Culdrose's stern rule before he had to.

'I'd best avoid brandy for the time being. I don't want to risk lurching about like a drunkard until I've got my land legs again.'

'Then I'll bring my glass to the drawing room, if you ladies don't object?'

'I think we might bear that much dissipation calmly enough,' Chloe said.

Luke grinned, knowing he'd never find her company tedious if they lived to be a hundred, when she gave him a look that warned him she knew he was up to something and was in two minds about putting a stop to it.

At last Oakham and his acolytes were dismissed and Miss Yorke, Eve's governess, excused herself to write to her elderly parents. It was very close to Verity's bed time, but Luke was glad Chloe didn't send her away. This tale needed to be told and arrangements about her contact with her father and where she would live made before the man went back to sea.

'I think the time has come to tell your story, Revereux. I hope you won't mind doing so in front of Eve and myself, since I'll soon be Verity's uncle by marriage?'

'Neatly put,' Revereux said with a challenging look in those sharp blue eyes of his that said he would be no pushover if his ideas didn't chime with theirs.

'Why, thank you,' Luke said with an ironic bow.

'I will try to emulate you,' Revereux said with a sigh, then watched the fire and seemed to be staring into a past full of mixed blessings. 'I took a bullet in my side at the Battle of the Nile. I was eventually given shore leave to recuperate with my maternal grandfather, a minister of the Scottish church, since even the Admiralty decided they didn't want me back until I had some flesh on my bones.'

'Your poor mother must have been beside herself with worry,' Chloe said.

'She has one son in the navy and two in the army and often says the one who gives her the most worry is my brother Henry, who stayed at home and followed in his grandfather's footsteps. A practical female, my darling mother,' he said with a rueful smile that said a lot about his affection for her.

'I hope we'll have the chance to meet her one day,' Luke put in, to remind them time was wasting and Cully would be down to bear her patient off to bed again very soon.

'So do I, but to return to my tale, I was feeling better and growing restless and bored, as young fools of eighteen often do when they don't have enough to do. Then, one day I met a young lady walking the hills on her own and sadly lost. Not that she minded being so, she told me, since as she didn't know where she was, she hoped nobody else would either. When I pointed out that I now knew, she had a fit of the giggles and admitted I was right. I fell in love with her on the spot.' Revereux smiled broadly at nothing at all and even Luke couldn't help but sympathise.

If only he was heart-whole and still innocent when he'd first laid eyes on Lady Daphne's sister, he'd have done exactly the same. Deep down he probably had, he realised now, then refused to admit it to either of them for a whole decade; which made him more of a fool than Revereux, so he could hardly blame him for diving head first into love with a very different Thessaly twin.

'After that she used to get lost whenever her aunt took her eyes off her long enough for her to get away from Hamming House and I haunted the hills and moors around my grandfather's manse like a lost soul, hoping she would and I could meet up with her. Apparently her aunt had a splendid marriage planned for her and the vast settlements on offer that would set her family back on the road to riches. Daphne told me most of her family could go hang, but she was worried about what would happen to you when we wed and frustrated their whole rotten scheme, Lady Chloe. Her only regret was that our marriage would part her from you.'

'You were married?' Chloe said incredulously.

'I loved her far too much to risk leaving her unwed and with child once I was considered fit for service again and sent back to sea.'

'Then how did she end up in that state and alone anyway?' she demanded fiercely.

Luke thought her magnificent as she defended her sister ten years after her death. Looking away to distract himself from the heady thought of the day after tomorrow he'd been forced to compromise on for their wedding, Luke saw his daughter and Verity were listening to Revereux's tale of star-crossed lovers with round-eyed fascination. Perhaps he should send them to bed? No, the last thing he wanted was either of them thinking a runaway marriage sounded deeply romantic, so far better for them to stay and realise the pain and sorrow that impulsive wedding had caused Lady

Daphne and her impulsive young lover, as well as Verity and Chloe.

'I didn't know she had done so until I cornered your younger brother one night when he had drunk nearly enough brandy to sink a man o' war and threatened to beat the story out of him if he didn't tell it of his own accord.' He paused and sent his daughter and Eve a dubious look and obviously reached the same conclusion Luke had done and decided they ought to hear the sad end of his grand love affair after all. 'I owed him that much for standing by while his brother and the thugs he'd hired beat me within a hair's breadth of my life, then had me carried south and put aboard the next ship leaving for the East Indies.

'Imagine how I felt when I finally came back to my full senses and found out I was halfway to Java with the captain and all the ship's company to convince I was who I said I was, not some poor pressed fool who'd been in the wrong place at the wrong time. They couldn't have turned about and taken me back to my wife even if they had wanted to and I was lucky to have ended up on a good ship. The ship's surgeon treated my new wounds as well as the ones I'd nearly recovered from until the attack and the captain didn't have me shut in the brig for insubordination, or dropped off at the first port as a lunatic. I raged and resisted, but had to accept my fate and serve out my time until the ship sailed for home three years later.'

'Oh, you poor man,' Chloe said sadly.

She looked torn between pity and reluctance to let him off all blame for her sister's sorry plight. Luke's heart went out to her, but she had to accept Verity now had a father who deserved some say in his child's future. He waited for Revereux to finish his story and trusted Chloe to reach the same conclusion.

'Never mind me, Daphne suffered a fate I wouldn't inflict on a dog,' Revereux said, clenching his fists as he had to fight his still-raw feelings for his lost love. 'You know more of that than I do, Lady Chloe. I was a thousand miles away by the time the poor darling bore my child in that apology for a house your father and brothers sent you both to endure, as if that whole greedy scheme was your fault and not theirs.'

'Why did they do so when you were married?' she mused now, puzzlement and pain so dark in her violet eyes that Luke took her hand to show her she wasn't alone with it this time.

'Probably because we were wed, not despite it,' Revereux said gently and waited for her to realise what he couldn't say in front of the girls.

Unwed, Daphne would still be young, lovely and saleable, if shop-soiled; wed she was none of those things and had frustrated them of the fortune the raddled old duke was willing to pay for a virginal wife. Daphne had been meant to die and her baby along with her.

'No! Oh, Luke,' Chloe gasped as that fact finally bit deep.

Chapter Nineteen

'**W**hat happened when I was born?' Verity demanded and there was a wobble of uncertainty in her voice that made Chloe drag Luke in her wake as she rushed to Verity's side to cup her chin in her other hand, then smooth her hair and force her to meet her eyes.

'It doesn't matter, my love, you survived and I loved you from the moment you dropped into my arms screaming at the top of your voice. You were so perfect and so very much your own person, how could I help but love you?'

'I love you too, Mama, but I killed my real mother, didn't I?'

'No, darling, never think that. Your grandfather and uncles did that by abandoning us with not enough to eat and no money to pay for firewood or a doctor when her time came, but she never complained as I did while she waited for you to be born and we scratched a living from the vegetable patch and even resorted to poaching now and again, as well as foraging on the moor for whatever we could catch. She loved you so much she would have endured far worse to see you safe and healthy. Daphne loved you before you were born and I took over when she had to leave you, love. I'm a far better person than I would be if I'd gone on my merry way without you.'

'And when Lady Chloe Thessaly decides to love someone, they stay loved—like it or not,' Luke added with a wry smile.

'Even after ten years of stony silence and gruff discouragement to do anything of the sort from certain viscounts I could mention,' Chloe sniped.

'Even then,' he confirmed.

'You're a lucky man, Farenze,' Captain Revereux told him wistfully.

'Luckier than I deserve.'

'That's what Aunt Virginia said the last time I saw her, Papa. She said you were a lot luckier in love than you would admit of your own accord. I told her I wished you would find a viscountess before I came out, to distract you from growling at any man who looked at me, like a bear who hadn't had enough for dinner,' Eve said.

'Did she now? And did you?'

'We did, and at least now I know that Lady Chloe will stop you making a laughing-stock of me when I make my début.'

'Oh, the joys of fatherhood,' Revereux said with a set look that told Luke and Chloe he was feeling low and wistful about all he'd lost.

'Just you wait until this young lady makes her come out before you dare to be smug about my coming ordeal then, Revereux,' Luke warned him.

'I believe I should like to have a father as well, if you don't mind me staying with Mama and Uncle Luke most of the time,' Verity said earnestly and Chloe looked as if she was about to cry as she watched them assess the sore spots in this new world of theirs and find a way forward, even if it did feel strange and new.

'I don't think I would mind that at all,' Revereux replied huskily.

'Well, that's settled then,' Eve pronounced and nobody argued.

* * *

'Can you bear to part with Verity when Revereux is ashore, love?' Luke asked Chloe when the girls and the invalid were escorted to bed by their mentors and the two of them sat by the fire in the library before parting reluctantly for the night.

'Somehow I shall make myself do so,' she replied, staring into the fire to revel in the love, excitement and security of being held in Luke's mighty arms and dreaming about sharing all she was with him so soon now it was almost in reach.

'Verity will always need you, Chloe,' his deep voice rumbled and she felt the resonance of it as her heartbeat raced at such heady proximity.

'Maybe by the time he is home again she will have a cousin to keep me from fretting myself to flinders about their big sister,' she added, smiling at the thought of a solemn little boy or girl with Luke's complicated grey eyes wondering at the world in her arms. 'It really is hard work trying to sort out all these relationships, isn't it?'

'All that matters is that we love them, but do you think the world is quite ready for another violet-eyed temptress or some mule-headed boy in our image?'

'I do, if you agree to take equal blame, but what if I can't give you children, Luke?' she asked him with the thought of Virginia and Virgil's great love affair, without children to make it complete, heavy on her mind.

'Then we will have to trust James weds a bride with more sense than him, then gives him a tribe of brats. Don't look like that, love, it didn't matter to Virgil and Virginia that they couldn't have a family, as they made one anyway. Mantaigne lived here as a boy and James and I spent our summers with them by rote, since my stepmama couldn't refuse to let Virginia and Virgil have my brother when she wished so badly he was the heir. She wouldn't allow us to come here together though; we might have learnt to like each other and she hoped I'd cock up my toes so he could inherit, so that would never do.'

'She has a cold and calculating heart,' Chloe said and turned to stare up at the wonderful man who'd taken to hiding his vulnerability behind apparent coldness and self-control far too young.

'I was better off on the wrong side of her than

James was on the right one,' he said with a bitter-sweet smile.

'Promise me you won't wed a harridan if anything happens to me,' she said as she had to suppress a shiver, despite the warmth and temptation of him at her back and the glowing blaze in the fireplace to fend off the chill of an early March evening.

'Promise *me* nothing will, then,' he replied with a full-blown shudder she had to find flattering as he pulled her closer and dared the devil to take her away from him.

'You know I can't do that, but I will promise to love you with everything I am and will be for the rest of my life, Luke,' she said, all the love and delight she had in him in her eyes and the hope he could believe he was finally loved as he'd always deserved to be in her heart.

He kissed her deeply and passionately to prove it was mutual and her inner rebel hoped she'd finally broken his silly, gallant notion of waiting another two more interminable nights to make love to her. Unlucky for her that his will-power was as formidable now as it had been for the last decade then; he put a little distance between them and rasped a few deep, shaky breaths as he imposed that dratted iron control of his once more.

'Spoilsport,' she muttered darkly.

'Serpent,' he retaliated.

'Charming,' she sniped back, but the euphoria of finding her viscount had a wild, tender passion for her under all that aloofness of his made her constantly feel about to dance on air. 'I do love you, Luke,' she told him, unable to help herself, despite the drag of wanting and curiosity he'd roused in her once again, and left gnawing at her innards like some bittersweet wild fire.

'A shame it took you ten years to work that out,' he said with his unique Luke smile that sparked her to argue, mainly because he liked arguing with her almost as much as he did making love with her and just now he wasn't allowing them that alternative.

'You're the slow-top, not me,' she accused him.

'I am indeed—how else could I have thought of Pamela when I looked at you and wanted you so much it hurt all this time?' he admitted with a sad shake of his dark head that made tears pool at the back of her eyes, despite her euphoria that they were almost man and wife. This endless waiting really was playing havoc with her emotions, she decided, frowning at the flash of jealousy that streaked through her before she told herself not to be ridiculous.

'You have truly forgotten her now though, haven't you?' she asked and held her breath for the answer, full of hope, but doubting any man could put such a betrayal behind him and truly trust again.

'She was a young man's nightmare, Chloe. Hearing about the one Revereux lived through tonight, mine seems a far lesser one. I got my lovely Eve and he endured tragedy and disappointment, then missed the first ten years of his daughter's life into the bargain. I'm a very lucky man, my darling. In two days' time I'll be far luckier than I ever deserved to be.'

'Now there, my Lord Farenze, I beg to differ,' Chloe breathed as she moved so she was kneeling on the *chaise* and could look down into his wonderfully complex gaze. 'You, my lord, deserve to wed a wife who will adore you, want you and live with you in glorious disharmony for the rest of your days. That's just as well, since that's exactly what you're going to get when I finally get you up the aisle.'

'Before God, I truly am a lucky man then,' he said and, if there was suspicious hint of moisture in his beloved grey eyes, she couldn't bring herself to tease him about it when tears threatened to flood her own and this was definitely not a time for crying.

'Virginia worked a happy ending to your tale then, despite your best efforts to be miserable, Lucius, old friend,' Lord Mantaigne drawled, as if the last months were a play that had been put on by his late godmother to keep him amused and stop him missing her quite so badly.

'No need for you to be so smug about it, you could be her next victim for all we know,' Luke said equably.

'Or me,' James said gloomily.

'Well, it certainly won't be me,' Captain Revereux put in with a grin at the younger of Chloe's two bridesmaids. Verity returned his smile with a confidence Chloe told herself she had to be pleased about.

'I wish Virginia could have been here to see us marry though, Luke,' Chloe whispered as they toasted each other again and all she tasted was his quick, hard kiss on her delighted mouth. 'She would have been so happy today.'

'I'm sure she would.'

'Virginia knew we couldn't stay master and housekeeper for long if she managed to trap us under the same roof for more than the day or so you had allowed us up until then,' Chloe said confidently, sure now that was what her late mistress and best friend had intended all along.

'I like being your husband even better than I did being your impatient master, my lady,' he murmured wickedly for her ear only.

'And being your wife promises to better being your impatient servant, my lord.'

Luke groaned and whispered something very incendiary indeed that brought a rosy blush to the new Viscountess Farenze's cheeks and set her plotting to escape the company of their innocent daughters, before all restraint between them was finally cindered into ashes at long last.

Chapter Twenty

'I love you, Luke. So very much,' Chloe said in a shaky voice, stirring at last as the fog of bliss brought on by becoming Luke's wife in every sense of the word dissipated enough to allow her sufficient spare breath to speak.

'Good, it took you long enough to realise my sterling worth and agreeable temper was exactly what you needed to make your life complete,' he joked, with an echo of her own wonder in his eyes.

'Pompous idiot,' she said with a wifely look he seemed to find fascinating.

'Wife,' he murmured huskily, fascinated by a curl of red-gold hair trailing across her bare shoulder. He tested that word again on is tongue. 'My wife,' he murmured and she opened heavy-lidded eyes a little wider to take him in, naked as Adam and insufferably complacent about life as he currently appeared, and she sighed with contentment.

'What is it?' she asked sleepily.

'*You* are my wife,' he informed her as he kissed the disordered tumble of her wildfire hair over that satin-smooth shoulder, then eyed her as if tempted to work his way downwards and catch her in the sensual web he'd woven round so effectively last night once more. 'Lady Chloe Winterley is *my* wife,' he added, gloating over the fact of her as she stretched her sleek and very bare body luxuriously against his own naked form. 'My lawfully wedded wife,' he added for good measure.

'I think we have already established that fact,' she murmured, still half-asleep, but very willing to wake up to a new and very alert husband in her bed.

'Not to my complete satisfaction we haven't,' he argued, even as the gallant impulse to leave his new-made wife to recover from his amorous attentions seemed to fly out of the window and she put all the provocation she'd stored up over a decade into kissing her one true love back. 'I *love* you,' he distracted himself by saying as soon as he could. 'I love *you*, my Lady Chloe.'

'You haven't leapt out of bed and downed a pipe of port or a cellar full of brandy while I was asleep, have you, Luke? You sound drunk, even if you don't taste it,' she observed with a self-satisfied smile he took very personally indeed.

'I'm only drunk on you, love. Merry as a grig on my first taste of housekeeper and *very* personal companion,' he informed her with a smile that truly freed the wolf in him for the first time in ten years and, oh, but that wolf was *hungry*.

'I like the sound of being employed so intimately by my Lord Farenze—do you think he'll make a hard-working female like me a good master?' she whispered and let her hand wander towards a very rampant piece of evidence he would be a very attentive one, if this newest Lady Farenze ever acknowledged any man her master and they both knew that was very unlikely.

'I know Mrs Wheaton drove him nigh mad with need of her every time he laid eyes on the impertinent female. Shall we see if he can return the compliment?' he whispered in her ear as he taught her the erotic potential of that delicately made organ with his busy tongue. She surprised a groan of delight out of him when she retaliated by exploring his manhood with a delicately curious fingertip.

'Mrs Wheaton wanted you back, Luke; she wanted back you so badly that she used to pace her room at night for the pent-up frustration of wanting you in her bed and not being able to have you there. She cried herself to sleep with missing you more times than she wants to remember right now, poor lonely, lovesick female as she was. I longed for you with every fibre of my being, when I was so young I couldn't imagine how anyone could want a man so much and not have him and for a whole decade after that. On nights when you slept under Lady Virginia's roof for one night, or even a slightly less miserly two of them, I shook with need in my lonely bed and wept for all we could never have.'

'And I had to leave after a few nights because I couldn't sleep for longing for my great-aunt's housekeeper in *my* bed. I wanted you so much I ached with it every time I was within thirty miles of the Lodge and you, Chloe. I had to stay away. There was no other way for me *not* to have you. You had a child to bring up alone and you were my great-aunt's housekeeper and another man's widow. How could I stay when you would have ended up my mistress and I knew that was less than you ought to be?'

'If I'd known you wanted me back like that, I don't suppose I'd have been able to stay away,' she confessed with a blush beyond the rosy flush of need already spread across her cheeks and down to places where she hadn't known she could blush until last night. 'Even for Verity's sake, I couldn't have stayed away if I'd known you wanted me as much in return, Luke,' she said and abandoned teasing for a moment to stare into his eyes with her heart in her own. 'I love you, you great gruff, noble idiot,' she said with wet eyes and a shaky smile. 'I love you so much I won't be able to pretend I married you because you were obliged to right Lady Chloe in the eyes of the world. I can't counterfeit polite indifference and yawn my way through the odd evening when we happen to have no engagements if we spend a Season in London. If you don't want me to give away the fact I feel as if half of me is missing whenever you're not near; that I long for you so deeply that the world is less shining and wonderful when we're apart, then you'll just have to leave me behind. In Somerset or

Northumberland I can be Lord Farenze's besotted wife, who thinks about you every moment of her day, but you and Eve will have to leave me there while you go to London if you want to be fashionably indifferent to me in public, Luke.'

She reared up and dragged the bedclothes with her, since it was still only March and not even love could keep them warm when the fire had gone out hours ago and the chill of an early spring morning pervaded this splendid old bedchamber. Chloe propped herself above him as he lay prone against the bank of down pillows covered in fine and snowy linen and forgot what she had been going to say next in her fascination with watching him, her husband of a day.

'So dark,' she whispered as she swept a fingertip along the stern arch of his brow. 'So determined…' she lingered over the hard firmness of his jaw. 'So tempting,' she gasped as his lips parted to nibble that fingertip and his grey eyes heated to silver and steel and a hard flush of need swept over his cheekbones.

'So yours,' he rasped with such love in that dear gaze of his that she moaned in sheer awe. 'So ready to let the wide world know I love my wife, will always love her and have loved her for far too long in silence to ever be quiet about it again. Now I have my ring on your finger and you in my bed for the rest of our natural lives, I shall never be able to pretend I'm not fathoms deep in love with you. We won't be walking in Virginia and Virgil's footsteps, my darling. We've got our own road to travel, but I want the world to know we're every bit as besotted with each other as they were and intend to be so for as long as we live. Polite society will just have to accustom itself to that fact or keep away, wherever we are.'

'It sounds wondrous,' she told him with a dreamy smile.

'It will be,' he promised as solemnly as he had the day before, when they stood in front of the altar and made their vows before God.

'Well, that's all right then,' Lady Farenze informed her enthralled lord, then blinked and eyed him a little doubtfully. 'Are you sure the servants won't come in until we ring the bell?' she asked, as all sorts of possibilities suddenly suggested themselves when he gently shifted her over his prone body and she wriggled delightedly at all the wildly sensual ideas he was putting into her head with such promise in his wolfish gaze.

'Come now, love, this is one of Mantaigne's friend's households we're staying in whilst he's up in London, getting ready to be fashionably bored for the Season. Please be serious, wife,' he scoffed.

'Rakes, the lot of you,' she condemned.

'Not rakes, my love, wolves. A rake is a care-for-nobody seducer of any woman who presents him with an intriguing enough challenge. We lone wolves mate for life, which makes us all the more dangerous to unwary ladies like you.'

'Ah, but I'm not unwary any more,' she said with all sorts of untried promises in her violet eyes. 'Can we really?' she added as he splayed her legs over his narrow hipbones and she felt the full force of his arousal against her over-heated feminine core once again.

'I don't know, can we?' he whispered with a plea in his dear eyes to say how very much he wanted to, and a promise behind it that they would not if she felt too new at being a wife to ride to paradise in his arms like this.

'Yes…' she breathed as she solved his dilemma in the best way she could think of. 'Ooh, yes,' she gasped raggedly as she rose eagerly, then sank down on to the rigid and impressive length of his manhood and felt the fire and sweetness of mutual possession roar through her once again. 'I knew I needed to wake up with you, my lord, but until today I didn't know *exactly* why,' she told him as she held his fire and thunder-shot grey eyes with hers, saw the same flash of burning colour on his lean cheeks as she felt on her own.

'Ah, but you see, I did,' he managed to say and thrust up into her wet silken depths at the same moment as she bore down.

Chloe felt her breath hitch even more, her heart thunder in her breast and her core tighten on him as they strove together towards ecstasy and this time she knew what was coming and yearned for it, even as she knew a lick of sadness that, with that lovely, trackless completion, their congress would end, for now. But it ended so gloriously; so passionately, as she bowed back and moaned in extremity and he bucked and shouted his ultimate fulfilment as he shot his seed so high up inside her that spasms of their loving still rocked them when she sank down on to his heaving torso, feeling even more boneless and full up with wonder than last time.

As she lay splayed across him where their last flex of bliss beached her, she spared a brief thought for the sad, bereft Chloe of ten years ago who longed so desperately for love she had even fantasised over her mistress's stony hearted great-nephew.

'As well for me that I *didn't* know,' she observed as she used the light of the strengthening spring sun to peer down into her lover's tender, love-shot gaze. 'I might have humiliated myself and crept into your bed, whether you wanted me there or not, if I'd known this lay in wait for me there.'

'As well for both of us you didn't, then, because I had to learn to love before it could be like that. It never was so with anyone else,' he promised with such earnest need for her to believe him in his eyes that she nodded to admit he was probably right.

'I hate the fact that there ever was anyone else, Luke. I can't help but begrudge this to every other woman who ever faced you in bed of a morning and rode herself to heaven on your lordship's most potent weapon,' she said with a wicked glance at his even now half-alert member that seemed to have a life of its own. He looked half-disgusted and half-resigned about it as he managed a sheepish smile for his new and very demanding wife.

'It's been more of a curse than a blessing to me until now,' he confessed and how could she not love the sheer mannish appeal of him as he lay there all gruff and undefended?

'Has it really?' she said with a dubious gaze that somehow had to linger in fascination on the difference of him, the intriguing drama and details of his sex.

'Yes, when I met and married Pamela need and fury drove me nearly as hard as it did her, we were noxious together, Chloe. Even you would not like the man we made of me between us back then. When she left I was more relieved than angry; she took the tortured need to satisfy her, to somehow please her when the only thing that truly delighted her was to have me force her in some way, and that went against all I wanted to be as her husband. I had a mistress after she went; I admit that to you frankly and can't bring myself to be sorry for it. She showed me that a woman doesn't have to be begged or coerced to let me into her bed, proved

I was physically desirable in ways Pamela never tired of telling me I wasn't.'

'I swear I could tear the vicious little cat to shreds for hurting you so deeply, or at least I could if she was still alive.'

'I doubt it; you don't have enough malice in you to go about avenging yourself on my past lovers.'

'If any of them ever tried to hurt you, your Eve or my Verity, you might find yourself mistaken in that very flattering opinion of my character, Lord Farenze.'

'Maybe so, but luckily I'm not fool enough to look at another woman while I have a wife ready and willing to satisfy me quite royally in bed, and perhaps even out of it?' he suggested with a hint of ever more wicked possibilities in his deliberately melodramatic leer.

'Perhaps,' she echoed, her wild Thessaly imagination feeding her reasons to look forward to exploring them very urgently some time soon.

'What an idiot I was not to snap you up ten years ago,' he murmured as he kissed her tenderly and settled her head against his shoulder, so he could try not to dwell on those tempting scenarios while she was still a very new bride.

'What idiots we both were,' she said dreamily as she lay back against his powerful torso and simply enjoyed the warmth and reality of him after so many long, long nights fooling herself she could live without him.

'Hmm, and now we have a whole decade of loving to catch up on spread before us like a Lord Mayor's Banquet,' he murmured and it was a fit promise for the first part of Lady Virginia Winterley's expected year of wonders.

'Well, we won't have time for lying in bed when we get to Caraway Court; it sounds as if there's far too much to do for that,' Chloe said, wondering if they should have aped his last bride trip and risked the Lakes in springtime, instead of her childhood home that he'd bought for her, despite its ramshackle state.

No, she didn't want any part of her marriage to echo Luke's first one and shivered at the very thought. He mistook it for her being cold and cuddled the bedclothes even more securely round them, then held her close until she dismissed the idea as nonsense. She and Luke loved each other wildly and completely and his first wife had only ever loved herself. It was a truth Virginia had pointed out when Chloe was still pretending not to care one way or the other about the current Lord Farenze. Now something restless and uncertain in her settled as she realised she might be his second viscountess, but she was also his first love.

'Think of the fun you'll have getting the place back to how it was in your however many times grandparents' time; it's a housekeeper's dream come true,' he teased her.

'Or her wildest nightmare,' she replied as she contemplated the mammoth task of restoring her childhood home to anything like its former glory, after so many years of shocking neglect. 'I hope you didn't pay much for it. After what my brothers did to Daphne they don't deserve a penny piece from either of us.'

'Little enough, and it was worth it for their promise to take themselves off to the Continent with the proceeds and never come back. Crowdale House and the London properties will have to be sold to pay off their creditors, but this seemed a good way of getting them out of our lives with as little embarrassment to you and Revereux as could be managed.'

'The Scottish estates will go as well, then,' Chloe said with a suspicion that was poetic justice.

'Revereux said he might bid for those.'

'I hope not, my sister would rather see him happy than living in the past. She must have loved him very deeply to keep him a secret even from me. Verity is Daphne's best memorial and Adam Revereux should be content with her.'

'Aye, we husbands must all learn to be realists,' he teased and Chloe decided she liked his diversionary tactics and snuggled back into his arms to dream of the future as the spring sun shone in and a symphony of birdsong sounded in the ancient gardens below their window.

'Do you really not mind if I'm like Virginia and can't give you a child, Luke?' she asked, as the sounds of a new season and all the life and hope that came with it reminded her this was a time for new births as well as new beginnings.

'I already have one and so do you. Any more will be a bonus. James can spawn a procession of young Winterleys in his image and I'm not sure if I pity the world or James most for that repellent notion.'

'Wouldn't that make you dislike him all the more?'

'No, and I don't dislike him. In a way I pity him for having to carry the weight of his mother's frustrated hopes and dreams all these years.'

'You're a good man, Luke.'

'No, I'm a lucky man, Chloe, and the fact I've finally realised it is Virginia's finest legacy to me. Or should I count my wife as one of those as well?'

'Willed to you as her last bequest? I'm not sure I like the sound of that.'

'Not the fact of you, but the idea of you, perhaps? I think I learnt to hope the day I met your eyes across a cold expanse of January air and you couldn't bring yourself to look away and pretend I wasn't there for once. I was so sad and empty coming back to Farenze Lodge with Virginia dead and it seemed such a waste to know you so little and want you so badly. Oh, I haven't the right words to say it, but that day I knew we would be different. That there was a chance for us, a future that might be opening up in front of us and it looked more wonderful than I dared to dream I deserved.'

'I like your words, Luke. They're so much better than your grim northern silences,' she teased him a little, because it was tempting to give in to the tears stinging her eyes at the thought of him so lonely and grieving that day and this wasn't a time for sorrow. 'I love you, immoderately and passionately, and since ten years of enduring Lord Farenze's gruff rebuffs couldn't stop me doing it, I'm clearly going to suffer the affliction for life. I love you, Luke; today and tomorrow and every day after it that we spend on this good earth together.'

'I'm so glad you love me back and echo every word in my stony and tongue-tied Winterley heart, even if I'm currently hungry as a hunter and in severe need of my breakfast.'

'Oh, dear, that really is sadly unpoetic of you, my lord.'

'I know, my lady, but I'm a mundane man and, as such, could be a sad burden to you for many years to come.'

'I'll still take you, my love; I'm a workaday woman and quite hungry myself.'

'It's been a busy sort of a day and night, getting ourselves wedded and bedded at long last. I'll go and fetch us some breakfast,' he said and jumped out of bed as if about to tear off downstairs stark naked, then get back to her before the bed was cold.

'Luke, put some clothes on, you'll terrify the maids,' she exclaimed, trying to pretend the sight of his magnificent body, gilded by brilliant spring sunshine as the sun crept up the sky, hadn't put all thought of food out of her head.

'Very well, my lady, but don't you go anywhere while I'm gone, will you?' he said with a grin that made her knees knock too much to even think about getting out of bed quite yet.

'As if I would, but I do love you,' she told him with a besotted smile and how could she ever have thought his grey eyes were cold as he stared back at her, as if those words put every other thought out of his head but her.

'I love you too, Chloe, so very much,' he murmured and because he was a practical man he rang the bell instead of astonishing the servants, before leaping back into bed and rejoining his wife. 'Far too much to go anywhere for even that long today,' he murmured and kissed her so passionately and recklessly that they shocked them anyway.

* * * * *

MILLS & BOON®

Why shop at millsandboon.co.uk?

Each year, thousands of romance readers find their perfect read at millsandboon.co.uk. That's because we're passionate about bringing you the very best romantic fiction. Here are some of the advantages of shopping at www.millsandboon.co.uk:

* **Get new books first**—you'll be able to buy your favourite books one month before they hit the shops

* **Get exclusive discounts**—you'll also be able to buy our specially created monthly collections, with up to 50% off the RRP

* **Find your favourite authors**—latest news, interviews and new releases for all your favourite authors and series on our website, plus ideas for what to try next

* **Join in**—once you've bought your favourite books, don't forget to register with us to rate, review and join in the discussions

Visit **www.millsandboon.co.uk**
for all this and more today!